PRINT EDITION
Ascent: Unreachable Skies Vol. 3 © 2020 by Mirror World
Publishing and Karen McCreedy
Edited by: Robert Dowsett
Cover Design by: Justine Dowsett

Published by Mirror World Publishing in September 2020

Mirror World Publishing
Windsor, Ontario, Canada
www.mirrorworldpublishing.com
info@mirrorworldpublishing.com

ISBN: 978-1-987976-73-1

For Jenny, Nicky, and Alec. Love you lots, love you always.

ASCENT
Unreachable Skies
Vol. 3

By Karen McCreedy

mirror world
publishing

One

"**B**lood and betrayal." Dru's eyes rolled, his white mane stood on end. "Death!"

Tumbling from his seat at the end of the council table, he fell at the feet of Kalon, the Prime-in-exile, who jerked back on his throne-stool, reeking of surprise. I'd been seated next to Dru, and leaped to my feet, scraping my tail against the rough-hewn log that served as a stool. All around the table, heads turned, noses sniffed the air. The smell of shock overwhelmed the cramped space, hanging in the air like smoke from the log-built dwelling's single torch. Elver, Kalon's nest-mate, hissed and bared her teeth, adjusting her throne-stool to twist her body away from Dru, while their half-grown youngling, Urxov, seated to the left of his sire, partly-extended his wings and growled. On the other side of the table, Varel, Jotto, and Hynka mirrored Kalon's reaction – upright ears, swishing tails, an audible intake of breath.

The council had gathered to finalise arrangements for my journey back to the Expanse; back to the territory where Kalon's shell-brother Kalis, and his adviser Fazak, held sway, territory from which the wingless and their dams had been exiled almost ten moons ago – and territory which had to be seized by Kalon and those of us with him in the north. Only then could Dru's destiny – to defeat our traditional enemies, the Koth – come about. I had Seen it.

Though I'd not Seen that I would be the one Kalon would send to sniff round the Expanse and determine the current situation there. I'd had moons to get used to the idea of going back, to discover how well – or how badly – the drax on the Expanse were faring, but I knew I would be risking my wings and possibly my life when I went, and Dru's Vision of death and betrayal did not make me feel any better about it.

As for the rest of the council, the initial smell of shock at Dru's jerks and cries gave way to various degrees of surprise and agitation. Everyone there had expected to finalise flight-plans, discuss the duration of my stay, and agree who should accompany me on a mission that was likely to be difficult as well as dangerous.

It was not the best moment for Dru to reveal his talent for Seeing.

Opposite me, Jotto's brown fur was on end. Next to him, his nest-mate Manel looked equally stunned, though her mottled grey fur bore a faint whiff of scepticism. Varel, Kalon's adviser, spiralled a paw across the front of his purple tunic, while his nest-mate Hynka had dropped the leaf on which she'd been scratching a record of the meeting. She made no move to retrieve it – her attention was riveted on Dru, her ears upright with alarm.

The only drax besides me who was unsurprised was Shaya, the hunter who had been on the *Spirax* council when Dru's talent had first been reported. That was almost a cycle ago, but she had kept his secret safe, even from those who had travelled with us into exile.

Dru lay panting in the pool of light supplied by the dwelling's new see-shell. Recently pried from a dead floater by the hunters, and pushed into place between reshaped logs, it made the Prime's dwelling much brighter and more welcoming than when I had first set foot in it. But, as Dru repeated his Vision of death, the light around him dimmed. I knew it was no more than a passing cloud covering the sun outside, but its effect chilled me and my fur stood on end.

"He has the Sight." Varel's whiskers twitched with excitement as he breathed the words. "Such a rare gift. Rarer still for one of high status. I don't think there has been a Lordling with the Sight since…"

"Gazad the Great," I supplied. "I had to ask the fable-spinners." I almost added, 'before we left the Expanse,' but realised there was no need. No fable-spinners had made the journey to exile with the wingless, and Kalon had had none with him when his shell-brother Kalis crippled him and left him for dead in the Copper Hills.

Elver seemed to think that Dru was spinning a tale right in front of us. "Nonsense. He's pretending. He isn't even a half-grown yet." As Dru's Vision left him and he looked around, bewildered to find himself on the beaten-earth floor, she leaned down and, without warning, bit him firmly on the snout. "That's for seeking attention," she said. "I suppose this ridiculous display is because we'd just confirmed that Urxov should go with Zarda to the Expanse?"

Urxov's snuffle of suppressed laughter stilled as I stepped across to help Dru to his feet and said: "He's not pretending, Elver. He has the Sight, and he's had it for some time."

Kalon grunted and rubbed his snout with a paw in a gesture I had come to recognise as signalling confusion or puzzlement. "It will be over a moon before Dru is a half-grown," he said, ignoring the youngling and addressing me. "How is it that this gift is already apparent?"

"I took him to the Dream-cave with me, Lord," I explained, squeezing Dru's shoulder as he stood up and opened his mouth to speak for himself. "I hoped that his presence there would make my own Vision of his future clearer. Instead, the Dream-smoke opened his own mind, and released his gift much earlier than would normally be expected."

"It was reported to the Council at the time, Lord," Shaya said, and I saw her ears flick nervously as she realised she had reminded Kalon of the drax who served his shell-brother.

Kalon ignored her remark and answered me instead. "Yet neither of you Saw your exile coming," he said, "or knew of my survival."

I let go of Dru and spread my paws. "I can't control what I See, Lord," I said, remembering how often I had had to explain the same thing to others, and to Kalis in particular. "Nor can Dru. I believe that Vizan had attained a degree of control over his Visions, but he died before he could teach me how to master the skill. In any case, I believe he needed access to the Dream-cave to achieve the little control he had – and I do not have that any more."

Kalon grunted, and turned his attention to Dru. "So apparently you had a Vision," he said, voice and scent indicating he was still sceptical. "What did you See?"

Dru took a breath, blinking as he composed himself and marshalled his thoughts. "It wasn't clear," he said, rubbing his sore snout. "I couldn't See who…" He moved one of his wingless shoulders in a shrug, his ears flicking with uncertainty. "Just…there was blood. Drax blood. And a sense of betrayal." He turned his head to sweep his gaze over the adults around the table, turned briefly toward Urxov, who bared his teeth at him, and finally looked at me. "You mustn't go back to the Expanse," he said, his ears angled to emphasise his words. "It's too dangerous."

Jotto had been leaning forward, paws on the table as he looked across at Dru. Now he stood, drew himself up to his full height, his ears almost touching the sloping reed roof, and said: "It's been, what, four or five moons since Zarda first suggested a return to the Expanse. Why have you not Seen this before?"

Before either Dru or I could reply, Elver cut in. "Dru is only included in these meetings as a courtesy to Zarda. The understanding was that he would listen and say nothing. Yet here we are, taking his babbling seriously."

"It isn't—" Dru began.

Kalon silenced him with a wave of his paw. "Zarda, have you Seen this too?"

I shook my head. "No, Lord. But if Dru—"

"Dru is an untrained youngling," said Kalon, flicking a dismissive ear. "If you, a Fate-seer, have not Seen this, then why should we believe it?" He stepped away from his throne-stool and paced from one straight-sided wall to its opposite, ears twitching with thought, while everyone else fell silent, waiting. "I see no reason to change our plan," he declared at last, strutting to the end of the table where Dru's overturned stool lay. He ran a paw through his grey mane, extended his one remaining wing, and went on: "As agreed before we were interrupted…" A fierce glance at Dru dissuaded any further dissent. "Zarda, Jotto, Shaya, and Urxov will form the scouting party. They will be accompanied along Death River by nine other flyers—"

"May I request, Lord, that the other two half-growns who are nearing maturity be allowed to fly with the escort?" Jotto lowered his head and set his ears to full apology as he dared a further interruption. Before Kalon could object, he plunged on: "My own pup, Tonil, and Myxot's Yaver would consider it an honour to accompany Urxov on his Proving Flight."

The rumble in Kalon's throat might have been a growl, but Jotto's clever reminder that this would be Urxov's Proving Flight at least prevented him from biting anyone. "Yes," he said, tugging on his beard, his voice gruff, "yes, that is an excellent idea, Jotto. Though Urxov, of course, will have the more dangerous flight, as part of the main scouting party. They will have to live on the Expanse for a whole moon, discover what they can of conditions there, and fly back here as quickly as possible with their report. The other flyers will stage along the route in threes till they reach Falls Camp, so that messages can be relayed if needed. They will all leave at dawn tomorrow, while the Spiral still shines overhead. May its sacred lights watch over them and return them safely to us. So it has always been."

Everyone murmured "May it so remain," and, as Kalon folded his wing and the meeting broke up, I returned my attention to Dru, who was still rubbing his nose.

"Come along, I'll put something on that for you." Outside, clouds drifted on a warm westerly, and I paused to sniff the breeze that drifted over the lake and the island where Kalon had made his home. Avalox and kerzh-grass, both sprouting well in the centre of the island. Chalkmoss, camylvines, and a hint of kestox, their various aromas carrying distinct but faint from the lake's western shore. The shoots and seeds we had planted there moons ago were surely almost ready to harvest. How good it would be to have kerzh-fruits again, to have camyl leaves available for balms and medicines. From the top of the hill where we stood, I looked out across the water to the islands that surrounded ours, and followed the flight-path of nine purple-clad females as they made their way from Rump Island to skim low across the water. Every few beats, clawed toes dipped below the surface and emerged with a wriggling fish. "That's this evening's meals supplied," I said, my mind already running ahead to a bowl of baked white flesh basted in Rewsa's herb sauce. Tomorrow it would be the turn of the drax on Doorway Island to provide our meals, and by then, perhaps, there would be fresh chalkmoss to add to the pots. We had no groxen meat, no zaxel, no hoxberries, but we had sufficient food to fill our stomachs, and enough variety to keep our palettes interested.

More importantly, we were safe. Though how long we would stay that way with battles and enemies to overcome, only the Spiral knew. I moved my gaze to the western shore, and nodded approval as I noticed the nines of younglings climbing the steep-sided bluff of black rock that towered beyond our crops. We would need their climbing skills soon, if my expedition to the Expanse went as planned.

Though Dru's Vision suggested…

I shook myself. What he had Seen might mean any number of things, surely? Besides, in the Vision that my teacher, Vizan, and I had had for Dru's future, I had been beside Dru when he defeated the Koth. If death waited on the Expanse, it could not be for me.

Could it?

Jotto and Shaya emerged from Kalon's dwelling and walked past us, their heads together, the words I overheard indicating that they were still discussing tactics for scouting the Expanse. As they headed down the spiralling pathway toward the log-built dwellings further down the hill, I looked past them to the place I had made my home. Blue fields of kerzh-grass at the bottom of the slope reminded me of the first time I had seen the island, the day we had lost so many drax to the rapids upstream. Two drax – Jotto and Manel I'd later discovered – had been sowing seeds as they walked to and fro along clawed ruts of earth. Enough for the two nines of adults and half-growns who occupied Kalon's Isle at the time. Now, where that flat central section of Kalon's Island had been cultivated, nines of females and younglings with baskets were already busy cutting leaves, gathering fruit, and batting away the flisks and mites that buzzed round them.

"Zarda?" Dru had taken several steps along the path before he'd realised I was not following, and he stood, hopping from foot to foot.

"Sorry, Dru. I was remembering." We followed the path down to my dwelling, which was the next highest on the hill, and I took the time to light a torch and shut the door behind us before I spoke again: "Well, now that Kalon and his council know you have the Sight, it won't be long before everyone else knows." I pulled a jar of dried sweetleaf from the shelf and set a pot of water on the fire to boil, then indicated the logs by the hearth that I used in place of stools. "You might want to tell Cavel and your other friends yourself before they hear it from someone else. Sit down."

Dru was still rubbing his nose. "Elver doesn't believe me," he said, as he lowered himself onto one of the stools near the hearth and edged it away from the heat. "And Kalon doesn't think I See clearly."

I pulled up a stool next to him, and considered his statement. "I think perhaps they won't allow themselves to believe you," I said, "which is not quite the same thing. The Sight is a rare gift, Dru, rarer still in one so close to the throne-stool, and your gift is more powerful than mine." The pot was beginning to steam, so I threw the sweetleaf into it and leaned over to sniff the sweet aroma for a moment. "You must remember that I was not Vizan's first apprentice, Dru, nor even his second. I was a poor third, taken under his wings only because the first two died of the Sickness."

"But you learned. Vizan taught you."

"Yes. But he was *still* teaching me when he went to his last nest. There was much he did not teach me, and much I still don't know. One of the things I don't know is how to control what I See, to sharpen the focus, heighten the smell." I sighed, and brushed a paw across my black Fate-seer's tunic, wishing I felt more worthy of it.

13

"You wish I had Seen who betrays you? Who will die?" Dru's ears drooped and his whiskers twitched with disappointment.

"I think that it may be as well that you did not," I said. "What if the name you had shouted had been Urxov's? Do you think Elver would have contented herself with nipping your nose?"

Elver had growled herself hoarse when I had taken Dru under my wings and into my dwelling after the deaths of his dam and his half-sibling. She had barked and snarled her opposition to Dru sitting in on the council meetings. I had no doubts she would literally fight tooth and claw to deflect any threat to her own pup. For now she was alone in her enmity, but that could – would – change in a heartbeat if Kalon heard some terrible fate predicted for Urxov. A fate which Dru had already foreseen. *'He'll die because he doesn't listen'.* Was that Vision caught up with the one he had had today?

The pot had simmered long enough, and I lifted it from the fire to let it stand for a while. "I worry that I can't help you control your Visions, Dru, because, without control, you may endanger yourself."

"Then so might you." He gave me a steady, appraising gaze, then shook his head. "I don't think that the danger comes from any of us." Tilting his head a little as he tried to remember, he added, "But I'm not sure. It's just a...a..."

"Feeling? An impression?"

He nodded.

"Well," I said, giving the pot another sniff and stirring it with a claw, "I already knew that this mission would be dangerous. We'll all have to try to take extra care, that's all. Now, I think this is ready." I drained the pot, crushed the leaves, and stood up to gently dab his nose with the pulp. "Better?"

"Much. Thank you, Zarda."

If only, I thought, all our problems were so easily fixed.

Two

It felt strange to be flying south, our course guided by the river that had cost us so much. Death River, Varel had called it, and Death River it remained, though its waters fed the lake we now lived on and replenished the fish we took from it.

Ahead of me, Shaya, Azmit, and Marga cut the air with turbulent wingbeats that told me they also remembered what the river had taken, and as we approached the spot where Varna, Doran, and so many others had drowned I noticed some of the other flyers spiralling paws across their tunics. In addition to the hunters, we flew with Jotto, his nest-mate Manel, Winan, Hariz and a couple of gatherers, Lifra and Hexal. All had been selected for their ability to hunt, gather, and wait for days quietly and patiently. The two half-growns Jotto had championed, Yaver and Tonil, flew at the back of our rough V formation, pride in their every wing-flap, but behind me Urxov was already grumbling about the early start and the headwind that brought cooler air from the south. This might have been his Proving Flight, but at that point it seemed to be my temper that was being tested.

I'd not been near the rapids since the day so many moons before when we had plunged through them, and I was surprised by how quickly we reached them. Above us, the Great Spiral was still fading and the sun was barely risen when we flew over the end of the gorge.

How short was the flight between death and safety.

Spiralling a paw across the front of my carry-pouch, I howled a brief but heartfelt prayer for those who had not survived to reach Kalon's Lake. Answering calls and howls from ahead and behind indicated that everyone had responded correctly, but after a few moments I heard Jotto call:

"Urxov, show some respect. Answer the Fate-seer's howls."

"But I didn't know any of those drax."

It was just as well for Urxov that we were airborne. If we had been on the ground, he would likely have been bitten and clawed by everyone within earshot. Jotto waited for the roars of disapproval to die down before barking, "They were Drax, good Drax. That is all you need to know. In future, if a Fate-seer howls a prayer, you answer it."

"So it has always been." Winan, somewhere behind me to my right.

"May it so remain."

The dutiful refrain was barked as we flew over the twisting gorge that the rapids cut through. The high cliffs, diagonally striped with different coloured rocks, were carved with whorls and spirals from top to bottom, end to end. The carvings were ancient. They might even have been made by Koth. Koth, who I had only ever known as the vicious brutes who raided Drax territory, and wounded or killed those who tried to stop them carrying off our crops.

"It's beautiful from up here, isn't it?" Shaya's voice broke in on my thoughts. I glanced around to see her ears dipped in sorrow. "If only I'd realised..."

"It wasn't your fault, Shaya," I called. "It was no-one's fault." Though that had not stopped me blaming myself for not Seeing what would happen.

Below us, the gorge was a shadowed line that split the Forest in two. Crimson tanglevines crept almost to the edges of the cliff tops, while, at the base of the ravine, the river writhed and twisted in ribbons of grey, blue, ochre, and white. Here and there, tumbles of stones and pebbles formed tiny beaches, small refuges we might have used if we had known that the racing river led to the rock-strewn rapids. But then, how would we have got out of the gorge? The younglings would have been able to climb, but the winds swirling between the cliffs would have made flying dangerous for their dams. Still, better to have risked being dashed against the rocks than drowning in the rapids.

I fought back another howl and turned my attention instead to Winan's next words: "If Kalon intends for everyone to travel back to the Expanse, how will those who can't fly get through the gorge?"

"Let's take a closer look at those clifftops." With that, Shaya tilted her wings, felt for a favourable air current, and led the way down.

As we skimmed over the scraggy vinetops, she called, "There are gaps in the canopy. And those vines near the cliff edge look a bit scrawny. They'll be too thin for creepers or vineserpents to nest in. I think the grounders could make their way along the cliff top, so long as they're careful."

Jotto, from behind my left wing, flapped ahead a little, pointing as he barked, "And there's a way back down to the river here."

As the cliffs fell away, the ground on both sides of the water sloped steeply down to meet the riverbank, where the vines immediately closed in.

"We'll need to get those vines cut back," Shaya called. "Make enough room for everyone to camp."

"But the current is strong just here," Hariz, one of our healers, spoke up. "I remember how we got swept into that gorge before we even had time to think about it."

"We were too excited about those carvings to think about stopping, until it was too late." By the time I had called for a halt to look at the carvings more clearly, it had been impossible to stop.

"We couldn't have moored the floats here anyway," Azmit pointed out. "Not with those vines growing right along the bank."

"We need to circle here for a few beats." Shaya suited the action to her words, and the rest of us followed suit. She looked across at Winan, the big russet-furred female who had once been a tunic-maker, but who had done more than her share of cutting down vines over the past twelve moons. "How practical would it be, Winan? Could we cut back enough of these vines to make room for everyone?"

Winan flicked an acknowledging ear. "Yes. But if we're going to use the vinetrunks to make floats, it would be better if we moved up river to the next bend where the current is slower."

"I don't like the idea of our wingless and grounded walking all that way under the vines," said Azmit. "I know it's not far compared to how far we walked on our journey through the Forest, but a lot can happen in a short distance."

Manel spoke up, and I strained to listen over the flap of wingbeats and the rustle of leaves. "What about cutting a path along the shore from the cliffs to the next bend? The vines can be used to make new floats, or pushed into the water, so the river carries them away."

"And cutting them shouldn't be too hard," added Jotto. "Not with those seatach-tooth saws you brought with you."

"Good, then that's settled." Shaya angled her wings and flapped to climb above the vines, circling till we'd all levelled out. "Fate-seer?"

"What? Oh…"

It was my turn to lead the formation and, as Shaya tucked in behind my right wing and Jotto flew up on my left, I watched the river coil beneath us, a twist of blue amid the susserating crimson of the forest canopy.

"How far to those Koth ruins, do you think?" Winan called from beyond Jotto's left wing.

"Half-a-day's flight, perhaps," called Shaya. She looked around, called over to Urxov on her right. "That'll be far enough for our half-growns for one day. We'll rest there overnight and fly on in the morning."

"I can fly as far as you can." Urxov's bark was accompanied by an ear-flick of irritation. I added ingratitude to my list of his failings, reminded myself that he still had some growing and some learning to do.

"I very much doubt that." There was a note of scorn in Shaya's voice that surely even Urxov would take notice of. "In any case, the Koth Ruins are a good place to camp."

They were. The steep, vine-free bank had been the last place we'd camped on our journey north before we'd hit the rapids. It was where I had picked up one of the tumbled stones on its upper slopes, and Seen that they were once Koth dwellings, built in a spiral just as our own clusters were. They had grown avalox in broad, sunlit fields – avalox that had long since gone to the wild, swallowed by the vines that had engulfed the settlement and grown through its ruins.

It had been the last place I'd spoken with my friend Doran.

The last place I'd seen her alive.

It was a good place to camp. But how poignant a night it would be.

"I don't see why I should hunt gumalix. When I'm Prime I'll have hunters to do that for me. It's not as if they're a challenge, they don't even have teeth." Urxov leaned against a mite-mound as he spoke, his stance casual, his tone petulant.

It was only our second night out from the Lake, and already I was simmering with resentment that Elver had persuaded Kalon that their half-grown should accompany us. The previous night Urxov had done little except complain about the feebleness of the fire, the unyielding nature of the ground we slept on, and the taste of the stew. He had contributed a single twig to the fire, and that was only because he had found it beneath his tail when he sat down.

"Perhaps a stray arrow?" I heard Tonil mutter to Yaver as the half-growns moved past me, unstrapping their bows from their carry-pouches.

Yaver's snuffle of laughter was almost lost beneath the rustle of leaves under their feet. "Tempting, but I wouldn't want to be the one to tell Kalon."

19

Jotto, who had already killed a fat gumalix and was hauling it past the mounds to clear ground beyond, called: "Your sire was never too proud to join a hunt for food, Urxov. Especially after such a short flight." The mite-mounds were barely a quarter-day's flight from the Koth Ruins, and there had been some debate that morning as to whether we should bother to stop there; but the consensus was that we would revisit the campsites we'd used as we travelled downriver, since we knew where they were and we knew they were safe. As Jotto dropped his burden and pulled his knife from his belt to begin the butchering, he added, "When I flew with Kalon, his rule was that if you wanted to take from the pot, you had to contribute to the meal."

Somewhere in the vines behind me, a thunk and grunt indicated that Shaya had also felled a gumalix. "If you don't want to hunt," she called, "you can gather firewood with Lifra, Hexal, and Zarda. That will be useful too."

"In any case," Azmit added, as she stalked past, "you need to stop leaning on that mite-mound – otherwise you'll be covered in the things. And they bite."

Too late. Urxov began to wriggle and hop, scratching frantically as he cursed and yowled. "Sweetleaf," he barked, his voice carrying a note of authority even through his discomfort. "Zarda, Hariz, I need sweetleaf."

"There isn't any. Not that you'd want to use." Lifra's nose twitched as she sniffed the air for the distinctive sweet smell of the bush. There were some spindly twigs growing at the edge of the vine-line, but they looked half dead. "I think that's gumalix waste on those bushes over there."

"The river, Urxov. Get in the water." Shaya picked up a fallen branch and used it to push Urxov in the right direction. As he splashed into the shallows, she added, "Get under the surface. Make sure you're wet through – the mites don't like it."

Wet and bedraggled from ears to tail, Urxov slopped out of the river, glaring around as though daring anyone to laugh. I felt a twinge of sympathy. After all, he was still a half-grown, and had not left the familiarity of his lake home until a couple of days ago. My sympathy vanished as he glared at me and snarled, "I hope you've got some salve with you, Fate-seer."

I had a single pot in my carry pouch. I would need most of it for Urxov, and we had barely started our journey.

"I have some." Perhaps Hariz had smelled my annoyance, as she flicked me a sympathetic ear and muttered to me: "It won't be as good as yours, Zarda, but I'm sure it will serve."

Handing me the sticks she'd gathered, she moved across to her carry-pouch, calling to Urxov to join her, while I returned my attention to gathering fuel for our fire. We would need to get it started quickly now to help Urxov dry his wet fur. Taking the sticks I had already gathered to the open ground where Jotto was busy cutting up the gumalix carcasses, I dropped them in an untidy pile and began to arrange them into the semblance of a decent camp fire.

"He's young," said Jotto, gazing over at the river bank where Urxov was rubbing himself vigorously with a drying cloth. "He'll learn."

"He will – if he's prepared to listen." I thought about the nineties of younglings we had taken through the Forest, and of the harsh lessons they had had to learn. Beware of sucker ferns. Don't step in anything swampy. Watch and listen for serpents, spiny slugs, mouldworms and other predators. Don't touch anything, don't lick anything, and don't eat anything unless you have been told it is safe. We had lost drax – too many drax – on our journey, but how many more would we have lost if they had not listened to advice?

Jotto waved his bloodied knife, dismissing my concerns. "Another few moons and he'll be an adult," he said. "He's just testing his wings."

The sticks I had carefully spiralled around the kindling collapsed in a heap and I picked them apart to start again. There was no point in antagonising Jotto by pointing out that Urxov was testing my patience as well as his wings. And no point either in upsetting him by mentioning the Vision that Dru had had moons ago after their first hunt together: '*he'll die because he won't listen*'.

I hadn't asked Dru for details. It was likely he had none to tell. But, as I watched Urxov fluff his fur and strut away from Hariz' ministrations, I couldn't help but wonder whether he would be returning from our journey.

21

"From here on, we should make camp by day and fly at night." Shaya's words came out of the evening shadows as I bent to refill my flask from the river. She had made no sound on the sandy soil as she approached, and I almost dropped my flask in the water as I started with surprise. "Apologies, Fate-seer, I didn't mean to startle you." Shaya settled beside me on the low bank, and looked up at the lights of the Great Spiral, which were beginning to shine overhead. As usual, she looked sleek and well-groomed, and I licked my whiskers and rubbed a paw over my snout, aware that I likely still had blobs of gumalix grease adhering to me.

"I shouldn't have been surprised." I waved a paw at the opposite bank, where the vines hung thick over the water, then indicated the vines that encircled our camp. I was used to the smells now, and the twilight calls of the gumalix, vinecreepers, and glumps were all too familiar. But... "We're in the Forest. I should have been listening for danger, not dropping my guard while I got a drink."

Shaya acknowledged the truth of my statement with a flick of her right ear. "True enough, but it is peaceful here, and we've grown used to the absence of danger. You were never trained to the hunt as I was."

"All the same, it was as well for me that it wasn't a serpent sneaking up on me. That is...I didn't mean that you were sneaking, just..." Shaya looked more amused than offended, so I retrieved what dignity I could, stoppered my flask, and turned the subject back to her initial suggestion. "Anyway, I think you're right about flying at night. On the wing, it shouldn't take us long to get back to the edge of Kalis's territory. The last thing we need is to be spotted by some patrol."

We had left Marga, Lifra, and Yaver behind at the mite-mounds, two days' flight from our current camp. Behind us, twigs snapped and crackled as our campfire burned. The voices of our companions were murmurs on the breeze, and the aroma of gumalix stew almost masked the rotten smell of the Forest. Screeches and squeals in the distance told of predators finding an evening meal, reminding me again of our previous journey along this river, and of the drax – the friends – who had not survived it. I spiralled a paw across my tunic, and looked up, wondering which of the lights was Doran's, hoping that our death-howls had been enough for her to join her light to the rest. The Spiral knew where her last nest was. I prayed that that would be enough.

"I miss them too," said Shaya, moving her own paw in the age-old gesture of prayer and respect. She sighed. "I wonder if there were things I could have done differently. Ways I might have saved them."

"As do I. But Shaya, we are not to blame. None of us are." I gazed up at the Spiral again, seeking strength and comfort. "We have to believe that everything happened for a reason. And we have to believe that the Spiral will continue to light our path. If Dru's destiny is to be fulfilled, we must fly where the Visions lead."

Shaya dipped an ear in acknowledgement, though the scent of her sorrow and regret was still palpable. For a moment, there was no sound but the gurgle of the river and the croak of a glump in the shallows. There was a shift in Shaya's scent to resolve and determination, and she glanced back at the others as she said, "Tonil, Hariz, and Manel will stay here. The rest of us will fly on, and Azmit will stay at the Falls with Hexal and Winan. Jotto and I will fly to Drax territory with you and Urxov, as planned."

I sighed. "I suppose there is no way of making him stay with Azmit, is there?"

The merest twitch of her whiskers betrayed Shaya's amusement. "And have to explain to Kalon that his pup's first adventure was spent camping by a waterfall? I don't think Azmit would appreciate it either, even if Urxov didn't have his heart set on seeing the Expanse."

I thought back to Dru's Vision in Kalon's dwelling. "It would to be safer for him to stay out of harm's way. Dru—"

"Dru said his Vision was unclear. We have no way of knowing what it meant, or who it referred to." Shaya glanced upward. "If the Spiral sent the Vision, then nothing we can do will change it. You of all drax should know that, Fate-seer."

I did. And I could only hope that the betrayal and death that Dru had foreseen were meant for Kalis or Fazak or Murgo.

Because if any of us were discovered, then surely Kalon and the drax with him would be doomed.

Three

Uxov's wing-tip brushed my leg and almost destabilised my flight as I kicked out at him. "Not so close, Urxov! The sky is clear, the Spiral lights our way, the streams below us reflect it, and show the flightpath toward the Ambit. Is it that you are worried about floaters that you keep flying so close?"

His voice was indignant, and I didn't need to look around to know that his white mane was bristling. "Of course not. Floaters don't worry me. I'm not frightened of anything! I just don't see why we have to fly the rest of the way at night."

"Well you should be frightened." I steadied my wings and glided to drop back behind him. "Floater stings kill as surely as a spear or an arrow, if you fly high enough to get caught in them. The Forest harbours terrible creatures that can strike faster than a beating wing, and plants that will kill you slowly and painfully. And if none of that scares you, you should be afraid of what we are about to do, because if we are caught, the best we can hope for is to have our wings removed and be returned to exile. More likely, we'll be dropped into the Forest, wingless and weaponless, to face whichever creatures find us first. Think about that, Urxov, before you tell me you are not scared of anything. Because the idea frightens me to whimpering." I waited a wingbeat or two in hope that the message would sink in this time, then answered his other point. "As for flying at night – it's not likely that anyone will see us this far from the edge of Drax territory. But it is *possible*. Varna knew of Death River because she had flown over it as a curious youngling, and hunters venture further over the Forest than other drax. We're almost at the Ambit now, so it's quite possible someone might see us if we fly by day."

Hearing the snap of Shaya's wings to my right, I glanced over at her and shook my head. Urxov had been told all of this repeatedly, yet still he questioned it, and he flew erratically, as though to make the journey more difficult than necessary for everyone else.

We had stayed for two days at Falls Camp, waiting out a storm that would have blown us back to the lake had we tried to take off. We had left Azmit, Hexal, and Winan hauling a drowned kervhel from the pool at the foot of the waterfall. "I don't think it'll be edible," Azmit had said, looking at the bloated body bobbing on the water, "but we can use the fur and the horns."

Jotto, flying ahead of our remaining group, called over his shoulder: "Look to the south-east – in the distance. The edge of the Forest."

Beneath us, the Forest was a rustling threat of blackness, threaded with random glimpses of silver, but ahead, away to our left, the blackness had a ragged edge, where the vines gave way to the glint of water and, beyond the Ambit river, the deep greys of the Deadlands were distinct and familiar.

How many ninedays, how many deaths, had it taken us to find our way through the Forest to Camp Falls? Yet it had taken a single night on the wing to find our way back.

We were almost home.

Now all we had to do was hope that no-one there recognised us.

A sliver of grey lined the eastern horizon as we stood on the tongue of land from where our little band of refugees had moved into the Forest over half-a-cycle ago. Around us, there were still charred patches where our fires had been lit, and I stumbled over a broken bowl as I folded my wings and stepped over the moss to join Shaya and Jotto where they stood, gazing south. They were looking across the Ambit towards the Deadlands, though I suspected that their thoughts, like mine, had flown further – beyond the Manybend to the Expanse, and east from there to the *Spirax*, which sat like the horn of a great beast at the edge of a plateau on the territory's eastern peninsula. I thought of how much had happened since we had last seen those places: the drax we had lost, the ones we had found, and all we had learned of the Forest. From the spot where we now stood, I had watched the Elite Guard shoot the hunter Milat and the females with her out of the sky. At the bottom of the slope, the vinetrunk the wingless had walked across still hung over the water between the riverbank and the island we called the Eye.

"What's that disgusting smell?" Urxov, brushing himself off from a clumsy landing, raised his snout and sniffed the southerly breeze.

"The Deadlands." I breathed deeply, savouring the familiarity of the stench, foul though it was. "Where we take drax to their last nest." *If they've not been swallowed by the Forest, or drowned in...*

I was saved from further morbidity by Shaya, who added, "It's also where we'd better look for shelter for the day. We're too exposed here, if anyone flies this way – and I'm not going to spend the day under the Forest vines when I don't have to."

I remembered the copse on the hill where Doran and I had once spent an uncomfortable night as foolish younglings. "There's a grove of wild orenvines upriver from the Eye," I said, "on the southern side."

Shaya dipped an ear. "I know it. It's used by hunters sometimes when we're – they're – on a vinecreeper hunt, so we'll need to be careful on approach. Watch for campfires and smoke, follow my lead if we see anything stirring."

"Is it far?" Urxov's wings were slumped, his ears drooping, and I realised he was genuinely tired.

27

"Just over that islet there, and a few wingbeats west," said Shaya.

She pointed and, as Urxov followed the direction of her finger, he nodded. "Oh yes. I see."

Which was odd, because she had been pointing downriver, not south-west across the Eye.

Lowering her arm, she touched Urxov gently on the shoulder. "But you don't see, do you, Urxov?" she said, and everything fell into place: his erratic night-flying, his complaints, his unwillingness to venture under the canopy to find sticks for the fire. He had got himself lost under the vines on a serpent-hunt moons before. Now I understood why.

He pulled away from Shaya, and stalked off a pace or two. "You tricked me, Shaya! You cheated! You...you...how dare you!"

"Urxov." I stepped after him, but made sure I was not within snapping distance of his teeth. With the mood he was in, I didn't care to test whether he would lash out or not. "You've flown all this way in the dark? Why did you not say that you have no night-vision?"

For a few beats, he didn't speak, but I waited while he lowered his head and breathed hard. "It is a weakness," he growled, his voice strangled, "and a Prime cannot be weak. Just as he cannot be..."

"Wingless?" I supplied. I judged that he would not bite me now, and moved a little closer. "Urxov, you have flown for three nights without being able to see where you are going. That is far more remarkable than if you had seen every span we flew over."

"I don't think my sire will see it that way."

"I see no reason for Kalon to know," I said. "Do you, Shaya?"

"No reason for Kalon to know what?" she said, her ears waggling.

"Jotto?"

"I'm sorry," he said, "I was contemplating the beauty of the sunrise. I quite failed to hear what you were saying."

"It truly is not far now," I said to Urxov. "There is the river to cross, and a few mounds of bramblevine to fly over." I looked across at Shaya.

"If we see no campfires or smoke, we'll land," she said. "The copse is at the top of a rise that looks west towards the old Prime brambletrap. That only gets used once a cycle, when the Prime pays his respects to his ancestors."

"And he does that in the melt," I said, nodding. "Urxov?"

He lifted his head and straightened. "I can go a little further," he said. "I can see the river now the sun's coming up. It's the land I have difficulty with. That's why I have to fly close, so I can hear how your wingbeats change, and do the same thing."

"As I said – a remarkable piece of flying," I repeated. Turning, I spread my wings to catch the breeze from the river. "Stay close then, Urxov. After this, you'll just have one more night of flying for some time – I hope."

"There!" Shaya began to circle, pointing her spear downward to indicate the copse of wild orenvine on the hill below, their leaves purple in the dawn light. Memories of my juvenile adventure with Doran washed through my mind, and I could almost hear her voice calling, *"We'll have vinecreeper for breakfast."* My whiskers twitched with amusement at the thought, yet at the same time I swallowed a whimper of sorrow. Dear Doran. What a hole in the sky she had left when the Spiral took her.

"Wait." Jotto flapped past me and swooped low to glide over the copse, then caught an updraught to climb higher to circle it. Like Shaya, he was sniffing the breeze, and his head swung from side to side as he checked the land for spans around us. "There's no-one there," he said, angling his wings to lead the way down. "It's safe."

Shaya's ears were set back and half-flattened with annoyance. "I already checked that," she barked, but Jotto showed no sign of having heard her.

I landed in kerzh-grass on a shallow slope and followed Jotto up the hillside toward the stand of bushy orenvines. I was still several spans from them when the sweet, heady scent hit me and I stopped, closed my eyes, and breathed deep. Orenvines. The smell that marked every cluster on the Expanse. The smell of the plantation where Doran had made her nest with Miyak, the vlydh-keeper. The smell of safety. Of home.

"Zarda, come on – we have to get under the canopy." The urgency in Shaya's voice reminded me that we were a long way from being safe, and I hurried to catch up with the others – though I noticed that while they waited for me they all raised their snouts to savour the sweet air.

At Jotto's wingtip, Urxov sniffed long and deep, and I realised with a start that he had never encountered an orenvine before. "Elver-muz told me how good the orenvines smell," he said, "but she couldn't really describe it. Now I know why."

"Come on." Shaya peered at the dense foliage, searching for a way through that would not scratch too badly. Lifting a branch with the tip of her spear, she added, "This way – under here."

"Don't you think we should check right the way round? There might be better access from the other side of the hill." Jotto took a few steps along the edge of the vineline as he spoke, but Shaya's snarl halted him in his tracks.

"There isn't time! The sun's above the horizon, the Spiral's fading. We need to get out of sight *now*." She glared at me as though I'd been the one arguing with her. "Zarda, get under here. Urxov, stay at her wingtip so we don't lose you – it'll be dark under the canopy. And take care where you are stepping, the roots will break the surface in places."

After so many moons of travelling through the Forest, and living within a wingbeat of its dangers, it felt strange to move into a stand of vines without a weapon or a torch in my paw. My fur stood on end, despite my knowing that the orenvines held no predators. The only danger came from the sharp spines on the vineleaves, and our packs and tunics kept us from being too badly scratched as we pushed our way into the middle of the copse, where the vines thinned.

Dropping my pouch, I pulled out a blanket and looked about for a good spot to settle for the day, while Urxov peered into his own pouch and sniffed, muttering that he needed something to eat.

"I'll find you something, Urxov." Jotto made a show of pulling leaves from his fur, and licked a scratch on his paw – though his silent protest at being forced to use Shaya's route into the copse was wasted on the hunter, who had turned her back on him. With a loud sigh and a grunt, Jotto dropped his carry-pouch, huffing as he pulled a couple of patties from its depths. "Would you like one, Zarda?"

Who to offend, Shaya or Jotto?

"We'll all have one." Shaya's brisk response spared me the choice. "Thank you, Jotto. Most kind."

Jotto grumbled as he rummaged in his pouch, and he made no move to take the pattie across the few spans of clear ground to Shaya, but the set of his ears indicated that he knew she had been right to get us under the vines as quickly as possible. "I don't have many of these left, you know," he said, as Shaya took hers and picked her way back to the blanket she had spread between two large roots.

"Good thing most of you will be pretending to be traders then, isn't it?" Shaya chewed another bite and sat down before she went on: "You can exchange Zarda's lovely spirelles for food and supplies for the flight back to the lake."

"Assuming there's food to spare," I said. Kneeling, I pushed my blanket under an overhanging branch, silently congratulating myself that I managed to do so without snagging my fur or my tunic. "Remember how difficult it was for me to find supplies for you all, before the journey began?" Turning to accept the pattie from Jotto's extended paw, I snagged one of my ears on a leaf-spike and yelped with pain.

"Perhaps we should have brought a healer," said Jotto, his whiskers twitching, "instead of just one of their tunics."

"I'll be fine." I rubbed the offending ear and found it sticky. "Just needs a smear of salve."

Shaya popped the last bite of her pattie into her mouth and flipped open her carry-pouch. "I'd better do it, then," she said, as she searched through the jars and twists of herb she'd been given. "Practice, for when I'm wearing that black-and-green tunic. Jotto, I'll take a look at that scratch on your paw too."

While Shaya stood over me, pulling at my wounded ear, I looked across at Urxov, who had spread his blanket to my left, where a small patch of sunlight filtered through the branches. "Can you see us at all, Urxov?"

He reeked of reluctance to answer truthfully, but after a few beats he admitted: "Not very well. It's better now the sun's a bit higher."

Jotto had made himself comfortable in the lee of a fallen vinelog, on a bed of moss and leaves. "Well, we'll leave as soon after sunset as we dare," he said, "while there's still some light behind the mountains. Perhaps that will help."

Urxov's mutter sounded doubtful, but his reservations were drowned by Shaya who, for once, reinforced Jotto's words: "And you only have to fly straight and level. Just follow Zarda's slipstream as you've been doing for the past three night-flights. Once you reach the Expanse, the torches inside the dwellings will help you find your way."

"And then we can fly by day?"

I realised he couldn't see my ear-flick, and hoped he couldn't smell my irritation that he needed confirmation of a plan we had already discussed repeatedly. "We can fly by day," I said, "just as soon as we get to a suitable place on the Expanse to fly from. We can't be seen flying from the Deadlands. Not without the Guardflight."

"Strange, isn't it?" Shaya had finished smearing salve on Jotto's paw, and had made her way back to her own blanket, which she pulled round her shoulders. "We are in Drax territory. We're 'home'. Yet we are in more danger here than if we had stayed on the lake."

"Yes." I lay down and pulled my blanket around me, grateful that the weather had turned dry and warm. "We'll be in danger every wingbeat of the way while we're on the Expanse. Even dyed fur and different tunics may not be enough if we fly into someone who knows us well." I remembered how Taral, the Guardflight Chief, had seen through my own disguise when he had been sent by Kalis to find his missing Fate-seer. Though Taral had said nothing, even sending his guardflight troops to search in a different direction, I doubted his actions would be typical of everyone on the Expanse. Kalis had offered a reward to the exiles for finding me; I didn't doubt that a better offer had been made to the drax who remained on the Expanse.

"We've known that since before we left Kalon's Lake," said Jotto, and I knew he was thinking back to Dru's Vision of betrayal and death.

I pulled the edges of the blanket around me, and raised my head to look up through the leaves at the Spiral. I had still not had so much as a glimpse of what Dru had Seen, and I sent up a brief prayer to the fading lights that I might be granted a Vision to help us. "You made me a Fate-seer," I whispered, "yet my gift is so weak. Help me to See where the danger lies, I beseech you!"

When I slept, I dreamed of nothing but orenvines and vlydh – yet, when I woke, I felt that the answer was hovering just beyond my reach. Like Urxov with his faulty night-vision, I knew that something – someone – lay in our way; I could guess who that might be, but I couldn't See how the danger would manifest itself.

I could but pray to the Spiral that it would bless me with the knowledge I needed before Dru's Seeing came true.

"What is this stuff?" said Urxov, wrinkling his snout as he leaned over the bowl of kestox leaves. "It smells disgusting."

"Kestox," I said. I used a broken twig to poke at the sludge in the bowl. "We managed to grow some from the seeds and cuttings we had with us when we got to the lake. You've seen it on the western shore – the vines with the orange leaves."

"It won't smell nearly as bad once it's dried," said Jotto, who stood under the gap in the canopy where Urxov had slept, watching the sky. "But those of us who used to live on the *Spirax* plateau, or on the Expanse, need to use it to disguise our scent, and to darken our fur so that no-one will recognise us."

Shaya stood at my wingtip, ready with a bowl of water to douse our fire's low flames the moment I pulled the kestox from the heat. "Zarda's already disguised herself once," she said, "and very successfully. She didn't just fool the other females into believing she was someone else, she fooled the guardflight. She even fooled me!"

I inclined my head a little and dipped an ear in Shaya's direction, acknowledging the compliment and basking in the rare praise. Then I almost burned my paw as I noticed the kestox begin to curdle, and snatched it from the fire. "It's ready. It just needs to cool."

The hot stones that had guarded our fire hissed as the water from Shaya's bowl extinguished the flames, leaving a few wisps of smoke and the odour of ashes in the still air.

"Couldn't we have kept it going for a little while longer? It's been days since we had any hot food. You wouldn't even let us have a fire by the Falls, not even after that storm."

"Sorry, Urxov, but we're taking a risk lighting a fire at all." Shaya turned to put her back to the embers and flapped her wings to disperse the smoke. "We can't keep it going any longer than we absolutely have to." Setting her empty bowl on the ground, she knelt to tip water into it from her flask. "Put the hot bowl inside this one, Zarda, it will cool more quickly. And use a cloth this time, don't burn your fingers again."

"That's clever," I said, easing the hot bowl inside the cooler one. "Why have I never thought of that?"

"It's a hunter trick. We've not needed to share it before."

I stirred the leaves and gave them a sniff. "They're ready, and I think they're cool enough now."

Urxov watched as I pulled one of the leaves from the mixture and began to wipe it over my fur. "I'm glad I don't need to do it. Yuck!"

He turned away, wandered over to his carry-pouch, and pulled out the tunic he would be wearing for the next moon – a pale-blue Trader's tunic with the white collar that indicated a Junior status. We had had none with us at the lake, but there were plenty of females who had worn Trader blue, and it had been simple enough to attach a new collar to one of their old tunics. I hoped that the off-white colour of the trim would not be noticeable, though I had an explanation ready if anyone remarked on it.

Jotto had also acquired an old pale-blue tunic, while I still had one of my own – though I should have followed Shaya's example and taken it out of my pouch earlier in the day. It was horribly creased, and I had to pick a squashed flisk from the hem, but it fitted me, and it would serve. Once we adults had finished dying our fur, I opened my bag of precious spirelles and tipped a nine of the tiny shells into Jotto's extended paw. "These are incredibly rare, Urxov," I said, as the half-grown leaned in for a closer look. "I found this bag in the Fate-seer's dwelling, just before the wingless and their dams were sent into exile. The Spiral alone knows how many cycles and how many Fate-seers it took to collect them all."

"And drax will trade food and shelter for these?" Urxov sniffed at them, doubtfully, his scent sceptical. "Why? You can't eat them!"

"But they bring good fortune," said Jotto. "Do you see the way they spiral, and glisten in the sunlight?"

"They're a gift from the Great Spiral itself," I said, moving a paw over my tunic, "and because they're rare, they're much sought after. Hopefully a few of these will get us our first meal, and enough other items to take on to the next cluster for more trade. We'll need to be careful not to use too many spirelles, or their value will decrease."

"Not to mention that drax will get suspicious," Shaya added. "So don't go scattering them all over the Expanse." She glared at each of us in turn, ignoring Urxov's bristling mane and Jotto's growl. I just dipped an ear – I knew better than to argue with the hunter. Especially when she was right.

"You'll be very close to the *Spirax* when you fly to the estuary clusters," I said, as Jotto tucked the shells away in his tunic pocket. "Be careful, Jotto."

"I will keep my ears pricked, my wings tucked and my mouth guarded," he said. "There's no reason why anyone should see me as anything other than a trader."

I grunted. Even after the Sickness, there were many traders left on the Expanse; a few more should in theory not be noticed. There might be some difficulty if another trader happened to be in the same cluster at the same time, but it was a small risk and one we would have to take.

Wrapping the remaining spirelles and our usual tunics in serpentskin to keep them dry, we buried them between the roots of the vine where Shaya had made her sleeping-place the night before. It was already near sunset, and we needed to start on our way soon if we were to arrive at our designated clusters by sunrise.

"We will meet here in one moon," I said, as we left the shelter of the orenvines and looked up at the rising full moon and the lights of the Spiral that were beginning to appear in the darkening sky. I made the familiar gesture across the front of my tunic, and as the others did likewise I added: "With the Spiral's blessing."

Shaya nodded, her ears set to signal determination, and I smelled excitement and anticipation as she turned into the wind and spread her wings. "Let's see what we can find, shall we? See you in a moon's time, Spiral willing." She glanced up toward the Spiral, and I guessed she was asking for its guidance and help. Then she spread her wings, ran along the hillside to meet the breeze, and took off.

"Where do we go now?" Urxov tugged self-consciously at his tunic and peered into his carry-pouch for the ninetieth time, as though he was not already familiar enough with its contents.

"As far away from the *Spirax* as possible," I said. I raised my head to watch Jotto a moment longer as he levelled out over the marsh and began to fly south-east. Then I turned where I stood and pointed across the Deadlands. "The Copper Hills are south and slightly west of here. We can be there well before dawn, if you can stay in my slipstream."

"I'll stay with you." His voice snapped with impatience, though his scent betrayed his apprehension. "You just concentrate on avoiding the patrols."

I doubted we would need to worry about the guardflight. Their numbers had been much reduced by the Sickness, and I knew that Taral had been forced to cut back on night patrols and concentrate his efforts on trying to prevent the Koth raiding by day. Still, it was possible that things had changed over the past half-cycle or so. The Elite Guard...

I shuddered at the thought of Murgo and his ruthless Elite taking responsibility for guarding the entire Expanse. Bad enough that they had clawed their way onto the *Spirax* plateau. I spiralled a paw over my tunic as I remembered the casual way they had shot down six of our females on the day we had crossed the Ambit. Had Kalis been shocked by their actions? Or had he been the one who sanctioned it? Had they been punished for such unprecedented brutality? Or rewarded?

Well, we would find out soon enough.

Urxov closed his carry-pouch, adjusted the straps about his shoulders and gave his wings a stretch. "Are you sure you're not going to be recognised? You were Fate-seer, everyone on the Expanse would have seen you at least once, even if it was only at a distance."

I acknowledged the truth of that with a dip of my ears. "Yes – I was seen by everyone on the Night of the Two Moons. And before that I'd visited most clusters, either as Vizan's apprentice or as Fate-seer. But the last time I changed my tunic and dyed my fur, my best friend didn't recognise me, so I'm sure we don't have to worry about anyone on the Expanse realising who I really am."

"Well," said Urxov, "we've come all this way. I suppose there wasn't much point doing that if we don't take a risk or two now."

I nodded, secured my own pouch, and led the way to the top of the rise to catch the breeze.

Four

"Traders!" I called, as we circled over the Weavers' cluster near Paw Lake.

We had rested for much of the day in the Copper Hills, and then, as the after-zenith shadows lengthened, flown south to the hills surrounding Paw Lake. We had seen no guardflight, smelled no danger, and we'd turned east, approaching the weavers' cluster from a direction that might have been from a nearby zaxel farm.

The sun was setting in a blaze of crimson, and the smell of boiled zaxel cobs rising on the smoke from the chimneys made my stomachs rumble. "Traders coming in! We have spirelles, very rare, very precious!"

I broke off from my calls to point out more details of the cluster to Urxov, who had never seen one before. "See how each dwelling is built of stones spiralling upward to the apex? The chimneys are always set into the first stones, where the spiral begins."

"And ninety-nine dwellings make a cluster. And the whole cluster makes a spiral. And all the clusters together make one giant spiral across the Expanse to reflect the Great Spiral above." He sounded bored. "I know. Kalon-fa and Elver-muz told me all about it. They scratched pictures."

"But now you're able to see for yourself," I said. "Don't you find the symmetry beautiful?"

"Not especially. Some of those dwellings are covered in weeds, and the whole cluster smells of damp. Can we land now?"

Shaking my head at his detachment and utter lack of curiosity, I gave one last call as we headed for the ground: "Traders!"

As we landed, I had to admit that Urxov's observations were right: the cluster in front of us had an air of tired neglect. Hacklebrush grew over several dwellings, smoke issued from fewer than half the chimneys, and the landing path was pocked with muddy hollows where the mud-burrowers' foraging had gone unrepaired. Urxov's nose sniffed busily, his ears twitching with doubt, and I murmured to him to make more effort. "Set your ears straight, Urxov. We'll get shelter and a hot meal at least. And do stop sniffing – the Welcomer's coming."

The drax coming toward us looked thin, her grey fur dull, though neatly brushed. The tunic she was wearing looked threadbare, and I noticed it was patched at one corner. As she drew nearer, I caught the scent of despondency, noticed the droop of her ears, and wondered what had happened here to reduce an important member of the cluster to such a state.

"By the Spiral's light you are welcome," she said, though the tone of her voice gave the lie to her words. "I am Sajix, nest-mate of Galio, the cluster-cryer."

I spiralled a paw across my tunic and let it rest against my chest. "I am Razad," I said, "And this is my junior, Urxov."

Sajix wrinkled her snout as if we smelled bad, though I was fairly sure the dye had dried sufficiently for its pungency to be unnoticable. "Come," she said, turning to lead the way, "There's hoxberry juice and tea in the Welcome Place, but we have little to trade for your shells."

As we followed her around the spiralling path to the centre of the cluster, I was conscious of drax staring out from the doorways of their dwellings. They all looked as thin and hungry as Sajix, and the few younglings we saw looked sad and tired – though all of them appeared to have wings. They sat in the dust between the dwellings, or leaned against their parents' legs, following our progress with wide eyes and quivering whiskers. So many of the dwellings were empty, their chimneys smokeless, a smell of dust and damp emanating from their open doorways and unswept entrance-stones. Was this cluster typical of the way the drax were living now? If so, things were even worse than we had anticipated.

"I suppose you are finding trade bad everywhere?" said Sajix, standing aside to allow us to proceed into the Welcome Place ahead of her. She followed us in, and bade us sit on the stools by the fire. "The tea's a bit watery, I'm afraid. We've brewed the leaves too many times, but the hoxberry is good." She indicated the jugs and beakers in the middle of the table that lay beneath the building's see-shell.

"Hoxberry then," I said, "for both of us. I thank you, it has been a long journey. I'd hoped to arrive earlier in the day, but we'll be happy to rest here tonight and trade in the morning."

Sajix dipped an ear as she poured three beakers of juice and, once we'd taken ours, she pulled up a stool beside me, sipping at her drink while I savoured my first mouthful of hoxberry for almost a cycle.

"This is good!" Urxov, who had never tasted the sharp-sweet flavour before, had guzzled his drink in a mere breath or two, and stood up to bang his beaker down on the table with a satisfied sigh. "Is there more?"

"Urxov! Where are your manners?" Having barked at him, I turned my attention back to Sajix. "I must apologise for my junior. His sire was so happy he hatched with wings, he rather over-indulged him. I nip his nose regularly, but so far I've not seen much improvement in his behaviour."

Sajix's ears indicated she had not taken offence, and told Urxov to help himself to the juice that remained in the jug. "It's good to see my hoxberry going down so well. Galio says it's not nearly so good as his nest-sibling Galyn used to make – she was our Healer, before…" She stopped, licked her lips, and rubbed her whiskers, then resumed, carefully: "She was our Healer. Lovely hoxberry she made. She gave me her recipe, but I know I don't make it quite the same. Drink up, young trader, I'm glad you enjoy it."

Galyn. The name went through me like a shock from a floater, and I had to make an effort to keep my ears set at a neutral angle. I had known Galyn, eaten her stews, appreciated her calmness and practicality. Mourned her, when she had been taken in the Forest by a serpent. My fur was bristling with anger and distress, and I turned on Urxov as I brushed the hairs flat. "Be grateful our hostess is forgiving," I snapped. "You're not a youngling now, you are almost grown. You should know better than to demand more than you have been offered."

Urxov glared at me, but stayed his tongue as Sajix got to her feet. "There's cob stew in the pot when you're ready," she said, pointing at the blackened cauldron on the hearth, "and the nests were freshened this morning. If you'll excuse me, I need to get back to my own dwelling now. I left a stew bubbling, and Galio has almost finished packing today's fish quota. I'm sure he'll be along later, after the baskets have been collected."

Rubbing her paws together, she dipped a swift bow and hurried out.

Urxov helped himself to more hoxberry juice, but this time he sipped it thoughtfully. "What is a fish quota?" he said.

I shook my head, and stood up to move the battered cooking-pot from the hearth to the hook over the fire. I gave the contents a sniff and a stir: zaxel cobs and a little chalkmoss by the smell of it. Thin stuff, worse than the stews we had eaten on our journey to exile – at least those had been leavened by the dried meat we'd been able to carry, and whatever we had killed – or butchered – on the way. Yet this cluster was close to Paw Lake, why did they not have enough fish to put in their pots? Why were weavers worrying about a 'fish quota'? And who was about to 'collect the baskets'? It was all very strange and extremely disturbing. "I don't know, Urxov," I said, "but I don't like the sound of it, whatever it is."

We'd eaten the stew – supplemented with a few herbs of my own – and I was setting a pot of my own supply of avalox over the fire when we heard the cries overhead: "Elite Guard coming in! Have your quotas ready!"

"What, by the lights...?" I opened the door and looked out. The pathway was lit by the glow of fires and lamps through the see-shells of the occupied dwellings, and supplemented by torches carried by younglings who trailed along the pathway in the wake of the adult drax. It looked like almost the entire cluster was moving around the spiralling path toward the landing ground and, with a quick gesture to Urxov to come with me, I stepped out into a cool, still night, and followed.

At the edge of the cluster, the torches' flickering lights illuminated a half-circle of drax from the cluster, and three – no four, there was another in the shadows – drax in the maroon-and-blue tunics of the Elite Guard. The guards all carried spears and had bows slung across their tunics. The guard in the shadows stepped into the light, and I gave a start as I recognised him from his bi-coloured ears: Ordek. The half-grown who had once been rebuked by the Traders' welcomer for insulting the Fate-seer, the bully who had flown with his friends to terrify young Cavel near Paw Lake, was clearly in charge of this armed pack. When he opened his mouth to bark, "You have filled the entire quota?" I could see that he had sharpened his teeth, and he bared them as he glared around the crowd.

A drax in an orange tunic stepped forward, and I knew from the shape of his snout and his auburn fur that he must be Galyn's nest-sibling.

"That's Galio, the cluster-crier," I murmured to Urxov. "He will speak for everyone."

Galio was cringing, head down, ears set low, and wringing his paws, as his nest-mate had done earlier. "We have the fish, Ordek." There was shuffling and murmuring amid the crowd, then a series of dull thuds, as three drax scurried forward to place large baskets on the ground. Galio was backing away from the guards, his voice pitched so low that I had to twist both ears forward to catch his next words. "We have arrow-pouches too, but not the whole quota. Our numbers are low, and we've had to divert resources to catching the fish. We—"

"I don't want excuses." Ordek stamped across to snap his teeth together a whisker from Galio's snout. "The Elite Guard need arrow-pouches now, not in a cycle's time." He gestured at the baskets on the ground with his spear, and the three Elite with him ran to pick them up. "We'll check the workmanship on the ones you've done, and any which fall short of the required standard will be returned, and added to the quota for next time."

"But—"

The smell of terror was palpable, and in the torchlight I saw flattened ears and swishing tails. I heard whimpering and not, I think, only from the younglings.

"I hope you are not about to say that you will not be able to fill your next quota?" Ordek gestured into the shadows behind him. "We don't bring vlydh with us for the fun of it. They've got empty baskets on their backs that need filling."

I heard Urxov's intake of breath, scented astonishment, and a whiff of trepidation, as a torch flared and he caught his first sight of the pack-creature. "That's a vlydh? It's massive! And those mandibles – are you sure it's harmless?"

"They eat nothing but orenvine leaves," I murmured. "The only danger here is from those Elite Guards."

Ordek was still growling. "Full baskets when we return, Galio, yes?" His ears were raised, wings half-extended, and his sharpened teeth looked fearsome. I saw the cluster-cryer take another step back, ears set to full supplication.

"We will do our utmost, of course," he said.

"See that you do." With a swish of his tail, Ordek turned and stalked into the shadows, wings extended in readiness for take-off. I watched him beat his wings as he ran into the shadows, saw another Elite Guard step out of his way, and knew instantly that I had seen the other young male somewhere before. But where? Who…?

"Culdo!" Ordek's bark was accompanied by a snap of wings as he hovered overhead. "Get the vlydh loaded and come along. We've other clusters to visit before moon-zenith."

Culdo. Culdo, Culdo? Yes! I had seen him before, once, in the *Spirax's* nesting-chamber immediately after Dru's hatching. Back then, he'd been wearing the red-and-white stripes of a guardflight apprentice. He'd brought news of a Koth attack near Far-river farm, but had passed the message to Fazak, Kalon's cunning adviser, before he had told the Prime. Had he perhaps made other mistakes too? Been snapped at once too often by Taral? Whatever the reason, he had clearly abandoned the Guardflight and cast in his lot with the Elite Guard. By the Spiral, things were dark indeed if the Guardflight were defecting to the Elite.

The guards took off in a clatter of wingbeats, and I turned away as they followed Ordek into the night. I had seen quite enough.

"Well," I said, as I drew Urxov back toward the warmth and comparative safety of the Welcome Place at the centre of the cluster, "now we know what the fish quota is – and I know who is behind it."

"Kalis," said Urxov. "The drax who cut my sire's wing."

"Ultimately, the decision must rest with him, yes," I said. We reached the Welcome Place and ducked inside, to be greeted by an angry bubbling from the pot of avalox, and clouds of steam. I rescued the pot, blistering my fingers in the process, and poured the tea into a couple of scratched beakers I found on the shelf. There was no nut-syrup in the Welcome Place to sweeten it, but at least it would be stronger than the over-stewed leaves Sajix had offered. If we'd known to bring more avalox, we could have traded...

Well, I'd not Seen any such need, so it was no use regretting what we didn't have. Our spirelles would have to serve.

Pulling my stool up next to the table, I handed Urxov his tea. "As I was saying – yes, Kalis would have approved the order for these 'quotas', and authorised this new Elite Guard, but the responsibility lies elsewhere." I sipped my tea, sniffed it, and swallowed it down. "Too bitter," I said.

Perhaps it would have tasted better if I had not also had to swallow the knowledge that Fazak was still running the *Spirax* – and the entire Expanse.

Five

"Raiders on the lake! Everyone! Bring your weapons!"
The cry went up before dawn, and I dragged myself out of my overnight nest with some reluctance – soft and warm, it was by far the most hospitable part of our stay at the Weavers' cluster. But if Koth were raiding the lake, the cluster would need all the help they could get, even from such poor fighters as I, so I roused Urxov, strapped on my tunic, and pulled my knife from my belt.

"Urxov, do not go back to sleep!" He had muttered a mild curse at me and shifted about in his nest, then closed his eyes again. "There are Koth raiders on the lake. It will go better for us if we help drive them off."

I lit a torch so he could see, then had to wait, hopping from foot to foot with impatience while he crawled from his nest – how had he managed to make such a mess of it while he was asleep? – and pulled on his tunic. "Bring your knife," I said, "and the torch – it's not yet light outside." I led the way out of the door and around the path through the cluster. Other drax were spilling from doorways, some armed with knives, others brandishing makeshift spears, all with a determined set to their ears and a smell of anger.

It was not till we had taken off that I realised the raiders were not Koth. As we circled upwards towards the unshrouded lights of the Spiral, I looked towards the lake, and all I saw were Drax. "Where are the Koth?" I called, seeing Galio just below me, flapping toward the water with a swiftness that left me breathless. "Where are the raiders?"

He used the spear he was carrying to point. "They're not Koth. They've flown over here from the next cluster to steal their quota from our lake!"

Before I could point out that Paw Lake had always provided fish for anyone to take, not just one cluster, he had intensified his efforts and flown further ahead of me.

Over the clatter of wingbeats, the sounds of yells and cries carried over the water, but I dared not fly too fast for fear of leaving Urxov behind. His torch flared bright in my night vision, but I doubted he'd be able to see much beyond its tiny circle of light; I needed to make sure he could at least see my tail and feet. "Follow me down, Urxov," I called. "We'll land at the lake edge. I want no part of this quarrel."

Besides, I had no idea which artisans belonged to the Paw Lake cluster, and which were the interlopers.

Landing on the soft moss at the water's edge, I looked out across the water. Even with my night vision it was hard to make out what was going on – the twisting, swooping, crowded mass of drax almost seemed to be one as they dived and yelled. I counted fifty breaths before three drax – barely half-grown to judge by their size – broke away from the main mass of bodies and flew away, keeping low across the water. Their flight was greeted with cheers, and a few beats later Galio landed beside me.

"We have driven them off," he said, then shook his head and looked down at his feet. "It shames me that we should have to do that, but the quotas take so many. We barely have enough fish to add to our own stews – as you'll have realised when we couldn't provide a proper meal for you last evening."

Sajix fluttered down beside him, in time to hear his last comment. "We don't blame anyone," she said, quickly, giving Galio's wing a tug. "Galio is just stating the facts. We don't want any tales carried about disloyalty."

"We don't carry tales," I said, pressing a paw to my chest and setting my ears upright. "Only the few poor goods we have to trade for our food and shelter." I glanced east, where the clouds were beginning to pale in the dawn light. "Once the sun's up, we'll set out our wares."

"Then I'll bring you some more stew," said Sajix. "I expect you'll be flying on to the next cluster once we've traded." With a dip of her ears, she turned into the breeze and ran along the shore to take off.

Galio watched her go, then stretched his own wings. "I'll make sure everyone knows you'll be trading soon," he said, and followed his nest-mate into the sky.

"Well, that was a flight to nowhere," said Urxov. The eastern sky was glowing now, the first rays of the sun creeping over the horizon, and he threw his torch into the lake where it floated and hissed, smoke curling from the end of the bobbing vinewood.

"And that was a waste of a perfectly good torch," I said, as I watched it float away in the direction of the Manybend river. "Why did you do that?"

Urxov shrugged a wing. "It was no use to me. I couldn't see much with it, and I don't need it now the sun's coming up."

"But we could have simply extinguished it and returned it to the Welcome Place. It was not intended for your personal use, Urxov. Now the cluster will have to make another torch for their visitors." He rubbed his whiskers and looked away over the lake; the set of his ears was unchanged, and I realised he did not especially care about making difficulties, however minor, for our hosts. "As for it being a flight to nowhere," I went on, "it was no such thing. We have some idea now how bad the situation is here. Drax are being driven to steal, or to defend with force what they see as theirs. Clusters are being frightened into giving the Elite Guard whatever they demand—" I roared with frustration, not caring who heard me. "These are Artisans – weavers. They make carry-pouches, tunics, nets…they shouldn't be fishing in the lake for anything except their own suppers, and they shouldn't even need to do that unless the weather is too poor for the traders to bring the Fishers' catch from the sea."

There was a clatter of wings overhead as more weavers flew back to their cluster and I sighed at the state of their tunics and fur. "They'll want a spirelle to bring luck to their cluster," I said, "but we'll not take food in exchange. They've little enough as it is." Spreading my wings, I felt for the breeze, and looked around at Urxov. "Are you sure you can see well enough to fly back? We have some trading to do."

I had hoped that the weavers' cluster was an isolated example, that they had somehow suffered more than others under Kalis and Fazak's new regime.

The reality was worse than I had feared.

At every cluster we visited, we found hungry younglings and despairing full-growns, empty dwellings where the weakest had died, and much demand for the few spirelles we carried, which they blessed as good omens and good luck, even while they scraped around for adequate goods to exchange for them.

"We'll go as far south as we can, to the Gatherers' cluster by Far-River," I said to Urxov as we took off into a sky of broken cloud. It was four ninedays since we had left the relative safety of the orenvine grove in the Deadlands; four ninedays since we had had more than a morsel of meat; four ninedays since I had heard anyone speak of hope, or scented contentment. It would be two ninedays more before we could return to the grove to rendezvous with Shaya and Jotto, and I was beginning to wish that we had set a shorter timescale for our reconnaissance. Urxov's constant complaints didn't help: *I'm wet – I'm hot – My wings ache – I'm hungry – This stew smells bad.* Still, he had proved to be adept at trading, perhaps because his constant aim was to make sure he got the best of any bargain. We had canox in our pouches to carry back to Kalon's Island, hoxberry seeds, powdered zenox, nut-syrup, and even a little zaxel, if it could be coaxed to grow by the lake.

"How much further is it?" Urxov called, a whine in his voice. "I'm tired. That thin soup we got at the last cluster wouldn't keep a glump alive."

"Drax are giving us what they can," I barked, reminding myself as much as Urxov. "They don't have much to spare, we have to be grateful to get anything at all." A momentary glimpse of sunlight brought a sparkle to the view ahead and I raised a paw to point. "You can see the river now. The Gatherers' cluster is tucked into a bend where it curves south." Smoke was visible now, in the distance, curling skyward above the familiar white stones of the dwellings and the patchwork colours of chalkmoss, orenvines, and kestox. "This will be the last Outer cluster we visit. Tomorrow we'll start north again and call at some of the Inner clusters. They have to rely on ponds and streams and rain for their water supplies, so they've always traded for their fish and meat. With the Elite taking so much, those clusters must be even worse off than the ones we've already seen. In fact, I don't see how they can survive, but some of them must have." I dipped a wing to circle, noting the wisps of smoke drifting from the clusters on the plain around Guardflight Rock. Everything looked so peaceful from the air, so normal, and I felt a pang of loss for hearth and home – not solely for my own dwelling and warm nest, but for everything and everyone who had once been part of that world. How had I not Seen these changes coming?

Urxov's bark interrupted my thoughts. "Floaters, Zarda – we need to fly lower."

Sure enough, the clouds ahead held a tell-tale purple glow, and I flicked an ear to acknowledge his warning, gliding down till we were skimming over the tops of the kestox vines that were planted around each cluster. I spotted Swalo the fable-spinner sitting at the edge of the cluster below, a clutch of younglings around him, all no doubt listening raptly to whichever tale he was telling. I almost called out to him as we flew overhead, till I remembered that he would not know me as a russet-furred female in a worn trader's tunic. What story was he telling? The legend of Tomax the Bold? The story of One-Wing?

Or perhaps the cautionary tale of the wingless, their dams, and how they were banished by Kalis.

Sending them into exile was supposed to appease the Great Spiral, to bring renewed prosperity to the Expanse, and ensure a bright future for all drax. So far, the only drax I'd seen who appeared to be prospering were the Elite Guard.

"The system worked the way it was."

I hadn't realised I'd barked the words aloud until Urxov replied: "I know. Elver-muz explained it – the exchange of goods within and between the clusters, making sure there were enough hatchlings to replace the drax who died, moving younglings to apprentice in the clusters where they were most needed, with the excess food and goods going to the *Spirax*. Why has it changed?"

"Because one drax was not content with the way things were," I called, "and I don't mean Kalis."

"Fazak? The Record-keeper?"

"Record-keeper no longer, I suspect," I said. "I suppose there have been drax before him who were just as ambitious, but Fazak had the advantage of being Kalis' friend *and* being able to take advantage of the results of the Sickness. There were fewer drax to oppose him, the council was mainly filled by inexperienced drax like me, and with the Koth raids increasing he was able to fill Kalis' head with his own ideas."

"But surely Kalis can see that the ideas aren't working?"

"Kalis won't see anything Fazak doesn't wish him to. The Prime rarely ventures beyond the *Spirax*. I'm sure Fazak is reporting all sorts of successes to him, and who will say to him otherwise? Especially now that the Elite Guard has spread its wings beyond the peninsula."

Urxov said nothing for a couple of wingbeats, then he looked across at me and said: "This is good, isn't it? For us, I mean?"

I was about to snap at him for being so selfish, but clamped my jaw shut when I realised he was right. The hopes of Kalon and the exiles rested on discontent and disarray among the drax on the Expanse, and that was exactly what we had found. I flicked an ear to acknowledge the truth of Urxov's observation. "But," I added, "that doesn't make it any easier to see."

Six

"Is it like this in your cluster?" Dabri, an elderly female in a patched brown tunic, shuffled toward the hearth, where a fire glowed beneath a dangling pot. She scratched at her fur, which was thin and tangled, and I recognised the early signs of fur-clump. Would it be thought odd if I traded the herbs she would need to treat it? No Trader would have offered such things directly to the sick a cycle ago – the Healers would have been shocked and offended – but times had changed. Clusters lacked healers, nest-nurses, cluster-cryers, and welcomers. Dabri had taken us under her own roof because there was no-one else in the cluster when we arrived. "All off gathering," she'd explained, as she'd ushered us into her dwelling. "Even the nestlings. It's the only way we can gather enough for the tithes, and have enough to spare for ourselves. You're lucky I'm here – I've not been feeling well, so they've left me behind for the past few days."

Her paws were steady enough as she ladelled stew into bowls, and I smelled boiled roots and fungus. I glanced at Urxov, reading by the set of his ears that he was disappointed to find yet another cluster where meat and fish appeared to be non-existent.

"It has been like this at every cluster we've visited," I said, sidestepping the question. "We've met many drax who are unhappy about…" I broke off, not knowing how far it was safe to confide discontent. The drax we had traded with had been reluctant to complain too openly, no doubt worried that any criticism would somehow reach the *Spirax*. "About – you know – things."

"The new system, you mean?" Dabri snorted, her greying ears flattened to indicate disgust. "It's alright, you can speak your mind in here. Sit – sit and be comfortable." As we pulled stools up to the table, she ladelled stew into a bowl for herself and sat down between us. Near-empty baskets stood in the centre of the table, and I knew they were supposed to be filled with berries, roots, nuts, and leaves. Dabri poked at them, pulled out a solitary kerzh-fruit, and said, "Daft, I calls it, this new way. Fewer drax after all that Sickness, and half the flock being sent off into exile with their younglings, yet everyone is expected to send more to the *Spirax*. It isn't just zaxel or fruit either."

"The fish." I nodded, remembering that dawn fight over Paw Lake.

She gave another snort, and pulled a face as she spooned up another mouthful of stew. "Fish," she said. "*And* roots. *And* nuts. *And* meat. The Spiral provides, but the *Spirax* taketh away."

"Dabri," a new voice spoke from the doorway behind me. "You should not speak to strangers in that way. They might believe that we are disloyal."

"Hazul!" She pushed herself to her feet, and shambled over to put the pot of stew back on the hearth to warm. "You're early."

The male flattened his ears as he looked us over, his dark fur and mane standing on end. "If you keep gossiping to strangers, Dabri, then one day I may be too late."

She waved a paw at him and bade him sit. "These are traders, Hazul – Razad, and her junior, Urxov. They tell me that there is discontent in other clusters too – all the way to the coast, in fact! Is that not so?"

We had told her no such thing, but we each nodded and dipped affirming ears, and Hazul grunted, his mane settling as he relaxed

– though a quick sniff told me he was still worried. "Even so," he said, dropping a half-full basket of berries near the hearth, "my nest-mate talks too much."

"Well, I'm not the only one to complain." Dabri filled another bowl with the thin stew and placed it in front of him as he sat down at the table. "The fish are scarce and the fishers want more in exchange for them. We have to find more nuts and berries to trade *and* more again for these new tithes. Why in the name of the Spiral do they need so much food up at the *Spirax*, that's what I want to know. They never used to ask for so much."

"They never used to have the Elite Guard," said Hazul. He sniffed at the bowl, grunted, and spooned down a couple of mouthfuls before he spoke again. "They all have to eat."

"*We* have to eat," said Dabri, seating herself again and waving her spoon at him. "The artisans, the fishers, the makers and dyers, the farmers – the drax who actually produce things, *we* have to eat! Fazak and his trained lackeys just flap about all day and…"

"Enough, Dabri!" Hazul's voice was a growl, and Dabri subsided.

Urxov buried his snout in his bowl and concentrated on licking it clean. I decided to take a different flight-path. "We saw Swalo at the neighbouring cluster as we flew here," I said. "We've not heard news from a fable-spinner for a couple of ninedays – have you heard anything fresh?"

"Nothing." Hazul answered too quickly, and I didn't miss his warning glance at Dabri.

"Nonsense." Dabri put down her spoon, scratched at the fur on her arm and set her ears forward. "If Swalo can repeat it, I don't see why we should not." Even so, she leaned towards me as she spoke, and pitched her voice low: "They say that Kalis has picked out a new Nest-mate. Morla, Fazak's eldest. She's hatched a proving-egg with Miyak, they say, and she'll move to the *Spirax* in the melt."

Miyak. The vlydh-keeper who had been Cavel's sire and Doran's nest-mate. So, he had a new youngling now, one that presumably had wings. For moons, he had tried to accept Cavel, had even invented the harness that allowed the wingless youngling to ride a vlydh, but when the scheming and pleading and insinuations had done their work, he had voted with Fazak and condemned the wingless – and their dams – to exile. How would he feel, I wondered, if he knew that Doran was dead?

How would he feel if he knew that Cavel still lived?

Dabri was still talking: "…and Kalis will have an heir. One with wings this time."

The correct response to such news was '*May the Spiral be praised*', but I couldn't bring myself to choke the words, managing merely to spiral a paw across my tunic. Kalis already had an heir – an heir who would defeat the Koth. I had Seen it, Vizan had Seen it. Even Dru himself had Seen it. Yet Kalon should be Prime, and Urxov after him. And if Kalis had another hatchling…

I turned my gaze toward the dwelling's rather grubby see-shell, gazing out and upward in the direction of the Great Spiral, silently praying for guidance, an answer to help me See how Dru would ever wear the white tunic.

Nothing.

I sniffed again at the stew, scooped up a generous spoonful—

Blood. Teeth. Arrows. Elite Guards. Death.

I was on the floor, my bowl beside me, the remains of my stew spattered across the front of my tunic.

"By the Spiral!" Dabri righted the stool I'd fallen off, handed my empty bowl to an alarmed Urxov, and offered a paw to help me up. "You have the Sight!"

Hazul spiralled a paw across his tunic, and Urxov had the sense to copy the gesture. They were both on their feet, manes and ears raised in shock, though their scents were subtly different – one astonished; the other merely startled.

I could hardly deny Dabri's observation. But what to say, to prevent it being reported to the *Spirax*? I waited while she fetched a cloth, took it gratefully, and dabbed at the stains on my tunic. I didn't have another – and that would seem strange too, unless… "Lights, this is the second tunic I've dirtied this nineday. I'll have to fly home for a clean one." Returning the cloth to Dabri, I looked from her to Hazul as I said: "My Sight is weak, a feeble talent that assails me only once or twice in a cycle. Vizan himself tested me as a possible apprentice, but I was deemed too poor a prospect for him to teach."

"But we have no Fate-seer at all now, since Zarda vanished." Dabri seized my paws in hers, warm with excitement, tail swishing. "Any talent is better than none, surely?"

My ears were quivering with alarm, and I eased my fingers from Dabri's and spiralled a paw across my tunic. "I'd...not thought of it in that way," I said. "But the idea of living on the plateau, of speaking with Kalis..."

"You'll need time to think on it." Urxov, surprising me with a helpful suggestion, ran a paw over his mane to flatten it, and flicked his ears to signal caution.

"Yes. Yes, of course." I sank onto the stool, and pressed a paw to my tunic as my stomachs grumbled. "Might I trouble you for a drink, Dabri? All this excitement has given me a thirst."

As I picked up the beaker of weak hoxberry juice she pressed into my paw, I realised I was shaking. I had begged the Spiral for a Vision, prayed daily that I would See something of what lay ahead. Now I was sorry that my prayer had been answered. The danger of discovery – of betrayal – was suddenly much greater.

And I had learned nothing.

Seven

The remainder of the moon passed in an agony of trepidation. Every beat of every day I waited for word of my 'feeble talent' to reach the ears of the Elite Guard, though I had begged Dabri and Hazul to say nothing. "I need a few days to come to terms with the idea," I'd said as we'd left, taking care to stand upwind of them so they would not smell the lie, "then I'll get word to Kalis myself."

Each morning, as we left one cluster for another, I looked skyward for Elite tunics, and each evening I imagined Dabri and Hazul remarking to each other that they had still not heard news of a new Fate-seer.

My anxiety made me edgy and impatient, barking without cause and snapping at Urxov for the slightest fault. "I'm glad we're starting for home in the morning," he said, after I snapped at him for taking the nest nearest the hearth in the last Welcome Place we would stay in. "You've done nothing but moan and bark since you had that Vision at the Gatherers' cluster. And you smell…" He sniffed, paused, sniffed again. "You smell sad, I think, as well as nervous."

I settled into the other nest, reminding myself that it was warmer, softer, and more comfortable than many a place I had slept on my journey with the exiles, and smelled better than the nest I'd made on Kalon's Island, being threaded through with zaxel stems and marsh-reeds. Pulling a blanket over my feet, I set my ears to full apology. "I seem to spend each evening apologising to you, Urxov. I am sorry, truly. As I've told you before—"

"You're worried about the Elite Guard finding you. I understand that. I worry about it too – after all, what would happen to me if they discovered who you are?"

Ah. So his concern had not been for me at all. Disappointing. But not, I suppose, surprising.

"What I don't understand," Urxov went on, fidgeting in his nest as he made himself comfortable, "is why you're so miserable. After all, this was your home. You and the others, you've always spoken of it with such…such affection."

I looked around the spiralling walls of the Welcome Place, smelled the damp and dust that should not have been there, noted the absence of zaxel stems on the floor, the solitary torch we'd been reminded to extinguish before we slept. "From the air, it all looks so familiar," I said. "The clusters, the dwellings, the blue of the kerzh-grass, the orenvines near each landing-path for the vlydh to eat, the orange leaves of the kestox marking the boundaries, the chalkmoss underfoot. I want to howl for what's been lost – and I don't just mean the drax who have died, or the crops that have withered because there aren't enough farmers to tend them." I waved a paw toward the door. "Every drax out there is afraid, Urxov. And they're not fretting about when the next Koth raid might come, or whether there'll be a decent amount of zaxel to go round this cycle. They're afraid of *other drax*. I can't check the Records, of course, but I can't think of any tales or even legends that speak of such a thing. It's a terrible thing to witness – though it does mean that your sire is likely to find plenty of eager followers if he returns."

"*When* he returns." Urxov perked up at the mention of his sire's prospective assault on the *Spirax*. Ears up, the tip of his tail twitching where it hung over the edge of the nest, he reeked of excitement. "I can't wait to tell him what we've found here. He'll be over the clouds."

"I expect he will, yes." Though I hoped that Kalon's elation would be tempered with pity for the drax who were ill with hunger, for the clusters who were struggling to maintain viability even while they were forced to increase their tithes, and for all those who had lost nest-mates or younglings to the Sickness or exile.

We'd forgotten to extinguish the torch. There was no point asking Urxov to do it, he'd never find his way back to his nest. With a sigh, and the silent reflection that Vizan would never have had to do this for himself, I pushed back my blanket and heaved myself out of my nest to put out the flame.

We set off as soon as it was light enough for Urxov to see his way, flying first to Paw Lake, and then north along the western section of the Manybend river towards the Copper Hills. "We'll rest here and have a cud-chew till sunset," I said, while Urxov sniffed around the striated rocks and tumbled stones, searching for the patch of leaves and moss we had rested on a moon ago. "We'll have to finish the journey to the grove after dark."

It was not a night for full dark, though. The sky was clear, the Great Spiral and the full moon lit the way so well that even Urxov could almost see where he was going. "It's murky," he called, as he flapped along in my slipstream, "but if I stay slightly below you, I know where you are because you're darker than the sky."

"Don't go too much lower," I said. "I'm flying near the ground as it is, so any flyers in Kalis' territory won't see us between the Expanse and the mountains. The last thing we need is to be silhouetted against the Spiral."

We flew in silence for some time, while my mind churned over everything we had seen, smelled, and heard. The moon and Spiral were bright overhead, but the shadows beneath us were dark, and when we reached the Deadlands they stank of decay and death. I took a last glance over my shoulder at the lights from the dwellings on the Expanse, and the flames from the beacon on Guardflight Rock. I was their Fate-seer, and I was leaving them behind. Again. Perhaps if I...

But no. Kalis would no more listen to me now than he had when I was on his council. There were other drax depending on me now and – Spiral willing – we would be able to help those on the Expanse as well before too much longer. For now, we had to be content that we had gathered the information we needed, and had managed to do so without getting caught.

"We are close to the orenvine grove now, Urxov," I called, seeing the curve of the hill as a paler shade of grey in the distance. "I'll take us down to the bottom of the slope, and we can wait there for a while if Shaya and Jotto haven't already arrived."

We did not have to wait long. I had scarcely had time to set down my carry-pouch and find a cold pattie in its depths before I heard wingbeats approaching.

"You shouldn't have waited for us out here in the open," Shaya chided as she folded her wings.

Jotto glided down beside her. "We could have been anyone," he said, "and we could see you quite clearly against the moss as we flew in."

I dipped a contrite ear. "We've not been here long, and it's difficult for Urxov to see his way even out here. I didn't want to move under the orenvines unless we had to."

"As I said," Jotto repeated, unstrapping his carry pouch and dropping it to the ground beside an old vinelog, "we could have been anyone."

"Well you weren't." Urxov sounded sullen, and I smelled his irritation at being told off. "We're all here now, and if we hear any other flyers, we can go and hide. So can we stay out here for now? I can't see much, but it's better than being under the vines."

Shaya's ears twitched, and twisted toward the orenvine grove at the top of the hill. "Did you hear that?" She raised her snout and sniffed, suspiciously. "I can't smell anything odd, but the wind's in the wrong direction." Keeping her ears turned toward the vines, she turned her head to look at each of us in turn. "None of you heard anything?"

"Just the wind through the branches," I said, listening now for whatever it was that Shaya had heard.

She grunted, and turned her attention away from the vines. "It must have been a hammer beetle – though they're not usually active after dark."

"It's a bright night," said Jotto, "and the day was warm. It's not impossible that there'll be a few of them about."

Urxov had pulled a blanket from his carry-pouch and held it loosely in his paws as he looked around. "So are we staying here?"

Shaya gave a last sniff, flicked her ears, and said: "For the moment, yes. But we'll move under the vines before dawn."

Settling himself down, Urxov burrowed through his carry-pouch and pulled out a paw-sized slab of dried meat. He must have carried it all over the Expanse – we'd certainly not traded for it, nor even seen a piece of meat that size since we left Falls Camp. "I'll be glad when we can have a decent meal," he said, downing it in two bites without offering anyone else so much as a nibble. "We didn't get one on the Expanse, that's for sure."

"The drax we saw shared what they had, Urxov." I spread my own blanket next to his, while Jotto and Shaya brushed debris from the old vinelog and sat down, facing us. I sighed. "Though the Spiral knows they had little enough."

Jotto nodded. "In the clusters I visited there was a lot of unhappiness about the new system and the increase in tithes," he said. "I saw some Elite Guard at one of the clusters – nothing but a bunch of jumped-up half-growns who've been given too much power and enjoy using it." He bared his teeth in a growl. "I'd have liked to shake a few of them lightly by the throat. Lucky for them I had to keep up the pretence of being a trader."

"We found the same thing," I said. "The drax we met were too afraid even to admit they were afraid. Clusters are skirmishing with each other over who fishes where – and the Elite Guard strut about, snarling threats."

Shaya plucked a stray leaf from her fur and released it on the breeze. "Did you know that Taral and the guardflight have been made subordinate to Murgo and the Elite?" She bristled as she spoke, her tone and ears reinforcing her indignation.

Shocked, I sat upright, tail twitching, ears set back. "But that's ridiculous! Are you sure?"

"Oh yes." Shaya leaned forward, paws on knees, her ears drooping a little as she confirmed her news. "I went to Guardflight Rock—"

"You *what*?" Jotto jumped to his feet as he roared at her. "We agreed that none of us would go anywhere we might be recognised! That we'd keep away from danger!"

Shaya held up a paw, appealing for calm. "Guardflight Rock has no healer," she said, "and I was asked to attend to one of their flyers. It would have been more dangerous for me to have refused to go than to fly there and do what I could."

"I hope it wasn't too serious?" I said, "That it was something you knew how to treat?"

Shaya gestured for Jotto to sit down again, waited till he'd grudgingly lowered himself back onto the log. "A couple of the guards had fur-clump," she said, "and the Spiral knows I've seen more cases of fur-clump this past moon that I'd ever seen in my life before. Was it always so rife, Zarda? Was I not aware of it because I was out hunting?"

I shook my head. "You'd not have seen or heard of many cases because it was fairly rare. No more than a nine or so cases a cycle, I would say."

"Well, I've seen nines of cases just in this past moon." Shaya tilted her ears in sorrow and disgust. "Just as well you taught me how to mix that salve. Anyway, as I said, I went to Guardflight Rock. And Taral was there."

My stomachs felt as though I'd swallowed a glittermoth – I must have been hungrier than I thought – and my tail twitched. "You saw Taral?"

"Did he recognise you?" Jotto's worried question overlapped mine, and Shaya addressed her answer to him.

"Not at first. But—"

Jotto was on his feet again. "Shaya! You didn't—!"

"Tell him who I was? I did – and before you get your tail in a knot, I didn't mention any of you. So far as Taral's aware, I came here alone. Oh, do sit down, Jotto." Turning her attention to me, she went on: "When he came to see how the guard was, I smelled his anger, his exhaustion, his…his misery, and it was obvious from the set of his ears that it wasn't a case of fur-clump that was causing any of it. So I took a chance." An ear-flick in my direction, a twitch of her whiskers. "He asked about you, Zarda – said he'd recognised you with the exiles when the guardflight came looking for you."

I flicked an ear and rubbed my snout. "He recognised my carry-pouch, I think," I muttered. "But when he sent his guards away, and said they would look elsewhere, I was sure he would say nothing to Kalis about finding me."

Shaya and Jotto glanced at each other, then at me, as though they shared some private joke that I was excluded from. "You spent a lot of time together after Vizan died," said the hunter, "I suppose it was natural that you'd have grown close."

Urxov snuffled, and my tail twitched again. "We didn't grow 'close'." I remembered Doran's remarks about Taral and I liking the smell of each other, and how I'd protested that she was mistaken. She had been mistaken. Just as Shaya was. "We were Fate-seer and Guardflight Chief," I said, determined to respond in as dignified a way as possible. "Of course we spent time together – just as Taral would have done with Vizan, if the Spiral hadn't taken him."

Shaya dismissed my protests with a flick of her ear and a wave of her paw. "It doesn't matter," she said. "Even if Taral wanted to report me – or us – to Kalis, he has no access to the Prime these days, except with Fazak's permission."

Silence settled as the import of her words sank in. A glump croaked somewhere to my left, and another answered from further away. A gust of cool southerly wind toyed with the edge of my blanket. The shadows seemed to close in around us, and I looked up to remind myself that the Spiral's lights still shone down on us.

"But..." Jotto rubbed at his fur as if he felt cold. "What about the council meetings? The Guardflight Chief has to attend those."

"There are no council meetings." Shaya's voice was flat, though her ears were not. "Kalis dismissed them all, moons ago." She rubbed her snout, obviously perplexed and upset. "I've never seen Taral so despondent." Her ears flicked in hope. "But it did cheer him to hear our news, and learn of Kalon's survival."

"Will he help us, then?" said Jotto, "When we come back?"

Shaya nodded, slowly. "He said he will do what he can," she said.

"Thank you!"

The voice was that of a male, but it was not Urxov who spoke, nor Jotto. It came from the orenvine grove, just where Shaya had thought she'd heard a noise, and a moment later its owner stepped out of the vines, glaring down the mossy slope to where we sat.

The drax was large and imposing, bared teeth backed up by his readied bow, and a nocked arrow aimed right at us. Under the lights of the Spiral it was easy to see that the uniform he wore was the maroon-and-blue of an Elite Guard.

"Murgo."

Fazak's pup. The ruthless young male who had led the Elite when they had shot six of our exiles out of the sky, and tipped Varna and the log she stood on into the Ambit. He was full-grown now, with a wispy beard he had combed into a point in the manner of his sire, and held his snout up as though to avoid an unpleasant smell beneath it.

"You recognise me, Zarda? I'm flattered." With a flourish, Murgo waved a paw, and a brace of guards crashed out of the vines to stand on either side of him, their bows nocked with arrows, wings half-extended to emphasise the threat. "Stand up, all of you."

We did as we were bid, moving closer together as we did so till we were standing in a line with our backs to the fallen log, Jotto and I at either end. Urxov was rocking on his feet next to me, and I smelled rebellion, determination. "Steady, Urxov. Don't get yourself killed." It was clear that there was no point trying to even take off, let alone try to reach safety, and I put a restraining paw on his shoulder to emphasise the point.

"My sire will be delighted when I bring our errant Fate-seer back," said Murgo, "and I'm sure he will advise Kalis to send a small force north to find Kalon and his sorry group of exiles." He smoothed his beard, reminding me of how irritating I had always found that gesture, then strolled closer, to examine each of our faces in turn. "Zarda," he said, when he reached me, "Kalis should have taken your wings when that groundling freak hatched out of the egg. Still, at least that is one mistake he can rectify now."

He stepped back, spiralling a hand across the front of his tunic, and I prayed that the Spiral would recognise the gesture for the empty parody it was and strike him down that instant. But nothing happened, save that the guards raised their bows in our direction. One of them was Culdo, the Elite Guard I had seen in Galio's cluster, the drax who had once been Guardflight, who had flown with Taral. The other was Ordek, the bully with the sharpened teeth. I remembered Dru's vision of betrayal and death, and for a heartbeat I thought we were going to be executed out of hand. But if ours were to be the deaths he foresaw, then who had betrayed us?

I set my wings and ears in a gesture of defiance. "How did you know we were here?"

Murgo made a noise in his throat that I realised was a chuckle, then raised his voice and called, "You can come out now – Dabri."

Dabri! I flattened my ears and lowered my head as the kindly female who had fed us, confided in us, and witnessed my Vision stepped from the shadows of the vines. "That's the one," she cried, pointing at me. "That's the one who had the Vision. She said she'd report it to you. I kept waiting for an announcement, for news that we had a new Fate-seer, but a nineday went by and—"

"And so you reported it yourself. Yes, yes, yes. Don't worry, you'll get the extra food and salves, as promised." Murgo silenced her with a wave of his paw and turned to stand in front of me. "I've had you watched for days," he said. "A female drax with the Sight, clumsy, untidy, carries her tail a little low when she flies."

Was I? Did I?

"Surely there could not be two drax with the Sight who matched that description? My sire agreed. Such a female had to be Zarda. And if Zarda had returned, why had she done so? And who else might be with her?" He was preening now, and I wrinkled my snout against the scent of triumph as he sneered: "When I got word that you'd flown to the Copper Hills, I sent Elite Guards to wait along the Ambit in case you flew straight to the river. I guessed you'd be flying back to your friends in the Forest. How are they, by the way?" He moved away from me, strutting past Urxov as he continued: "Not all slug-fodder yet, to judge from your conversation?"

He howled and stepped back as Shaya snapped her head around and, without warning, bit him hard on the nose. "*Fwerkian* mud-crawler," she hissed. "You were scrambled in the egg, Murgo, you—"

"Enough, Shaya." Jotto stepped between them and drew Shaya back into line. "He's not worth it."

Murgo snarled, snapping his own teeth within a whisker of Shaya's snout. "Do that again, and I'll have you shot." All the same, he retreated a few paces before signalling for his guards to come closer. "Ordek and Culdo are going to escort you back to the *Spirax*," he said, delight edging his voice, "while I fly on ahead to report to my sire and Kalis. I trust you will not attempt to escape during our flight? I picked these two for their shooting skills, and the arrows have been tipped with rotberry juice, so even if you are merely grazed you will not survive the experience."

I looked across at the others, saw Shaya twitch her ears and snout to indicate that, for now, we should go along with this. I could see no way out of it anyway – we were unarmed, unprepared, and threatened by trained archers with poisoned arrows. The slightest wrong move would likely get us all killed.

Shaya was right. We had to go with the Elite. We had no choice.

Eight

All I could scent from my companions was alarm, distress, bewilderment. Were we about to take our final flight? Would there be an opportunity to escape, to do something…? Perhaps, though I couldn't think how. My wing-struts itched as I remembered Varna's howls of agony when her wings had been removed, and I tried not to think about what would happen when we got to the *Spirax*.

I dipped my ears and put a paw on Urxov's shoulder. "We'll come," I said, "but let the half-grown go. He—"

I broke off, hearing a clatter of wingbeats, loud and sudden, coming from beyond the hilltop. I assumed that a larger escort had been arranged to accompany us, till I realised the guards ahead of us were not reacting as though they were expecting reinforcements. Instead, they raised their ears, then their snouts, sniffing the wind for the location of the flyers.

Murgo turned and rushed back up the slope, yelling orders at his guards and pointing skyward, wings extended and flapping hard to achieve take-off.

He never got off the ground.

The first arrow speared him in the shoulder, another sliced into his side; a third hit his chest as he faltered, and the breeze caught his suddenly-still wings and tilted him backwards.

I looked up, seeing a blur of wings as three large drax swirled and dipped in the air currents overhead. I couldn't see the colour of their tunics against the brightness of the Great Spiral, but they had to be Guardflight – they had been the only drax on the Expanse trained to use bows and arrows, until Murgo's Elite Guard was formed. And they were assuredly not Elite. Ordek turned as if to run back beneath the vinetrees, but he had taken no more than a couple of paces before he fell to the ground with arrows through his side, while Dabri's howls of terror were silenced by a shaft through the throat.

Urxov's fur was standing on end, and I shook myself as I realised my own was doing the same. Though my heart thudded in my chest, I tried to calm myself with deep, steady breaths and, as the wingbeats above slowed for descent, I went to examine the drax on the ground. I needed to do no more than give them a cursory sniff and rest a paw on their chests to confirm what I already knew.

"Are they…?"

I stood, slowly, wrinkling my snout in a vain attempt to rid myself of the smell of spilled blood. "Yes, Urxov. They're dead."

"It's regrettable, but I could see no other way." It was Taral, ears flattened, grey fur and black mane on end. The smell of his distress was palpable, and his paws shook as he fumbled to restrap his bow across his chest.

With a clatter of wings, Veret landed beside him, the scar on his snout distinguishing him from Jisco, whose torn ear signalled his own alarm and anguish as he glided down next to his shell-brother.

Taral set his ears upright and hurried past me, striding up the slope to clasp paws with the one remaining Elite Guard. "Culdo. Thank you for the message, we came as quickly as we could."

Culdo, the one-time Guardflight apprentice I had seen at the weavers' cluster. Not a traitor to Taral after all, then – though perhaps I should not have felt relief when I had just witnessed Drax kill Drax and thanked the Spiral for it. Lights help me, I looked up at the Great Spiral and breathed gratitude for my life and my wings, spiralling a paw across my tunic, even as Murgo's blood congealed at my feet.

Taral mirrored my action, before turning to look down the slope, his tail betraying his continued distress, though his ears and scent signalled anger and determination. "Ordek was a fool," he said, "and Murgo an ambitious show-off. But we couldn't let you be taken, any of you. I'm sorry about Dabri, but we could hardly let her fly back to the *Spirax*, telling more tales." He stared down at the bodies for a few beats, stilled his tail, and shook himself to smooth his fur. "For all my training, I have never killed another Drax."

Jotto bent to pull the arrows from Ordek's body. "They'd poisoned their own arrows, did you know?" he said, his tone matter-of-fact. He wiped the business end of an arrow on the dead guard's fur and set it on the ground to dry, reaching for another.

"And we watched them shoot unarmed females out of the sky." Shaya's voice shook with rage, tail waving with sorrow and anger as she remembered those who had flown to their deaths on the day we'd crossed the Ambit. She grasped the front of Murgo's tunic and shook him, banging his head on the ground repeatedly. "Unarmed. Females," she repeated, then let him go, stepping away from the body with a growl.

"'*Betrayal and death*'," I said. "Dru Saw it – though his vision was unclear. This was meant to be, Taral. And I for one thank you for saving our wings – and our lives."

Taral straightened as I spoke, and dipped a respectful ear. "Zarda. You've dyed your fur again."

I brushed an arm with a paw, suddenly conscious that my pale blue tunic was spattered with mud, and still bore stubborn stains where I'd spilled stew over it. "So you did recognise me then, that day on the dunes. I can't tell you how panicked I was when I realised I was holding the carry-pouch with the blood-stains on it."

Taral's whiskers twitched in that way he had when he was amused. "I recognised the pouch first," he said, "but once I looked beyond your dyed fur, I was sure you were the one holding it."

"And yet you said nothing – you sent your guards away." My tail was twitching of its own accord again, and I made a conscious effort to still it. "That was good of you, Taral. That was brave."

He waved a paw, dismissing my praise. "I would never have taken you back to Kalis. It was bad enough seeing Varna without her wings. I couldn't be responsible for having our Fate-seer suffer the same fate. As for tonight—" Taral looked around, and gestured at the guard in the maroon tunic. "You can thank Culdo for saving you. If he had not risked his own wings to get a message to me, you would all be on your way to the *Spirax* by now, and Fazak would be howling with glee."

"Fazak." I looked across at Murgo's still form and could not repress a shudder. "For all his faults, he loved Murgo. He was so proud of him. When he finds out what happened…"

"He won't." Taral stepped across to the body and leaned down to retrieve his arrows. One of them was stuck fast and I saw Taral's nose wrinkle with distaste before he pulled the knife from his belt and cut it free.

Urxov spoke up. "Can we share the hearts?" He must have smelled my disgust or caught my look of disapproval, for he shrugged and went on: "I told you, I'm hungry, and in any case, it's tradition, isn't it?"

"It is tradition to share the heart of a respected elder or a friend," I said. "These drax were feared, not respected – and they were most assuredly not our friends." I edged closer to where Taral and Shaya stood looking down at Murgo's body, and tried not to gag on the smell of congealed blood. "What shall we do with them?"

Shaya's fur was still on end and her paws were clenched, but her voice was matter-of-fact: "We're at the edge of the Deadlands," she said. "I say we drop them in the nearest unassigned brambletrap. They'll not be found."

Taral raised his snout to sniff the wind and gaze up at the Great Spiral. "We may not have time," he said. "It'll be getting light soon, and we don't want to be seen by any of those Elite Guards that Murgo posted along the Ambit."

"I agree." Jotto handed the arrows he'd collected to Culdo, and walked down the slope toward us. "Better to roll them into the marsh, let the worms and sludge take them."

Taral dipped a respectful ear at the approach of the older drax. "Jotto," he said, inclining his head slightly. "My sire spoke highly of you at the Ceremony for the Dead, when you were thought to have been slain with Kalon."

"And I remember you as an eager youngling shooting training arrows at anything that moved." Jotto clasped paws with Taral, then indicated the bodies on the ground. "I'm very glad you practiced so long, and learned so well."

Taral spiralled a paw across his tunic. "I trained to kill Koth, not fellow Drax." He still smelled remorseful, though his ears now had a more determined set. "At least I won't have to answer to a jumped-up hatchling any more."

"And Fazak?" I was still concerned about what would happen when Murgo failed to return to the *Spirax*. "And Kalis? What will you tell them?"

"Nothing." Taral practically spat the word. "What Murgo and the Elite Guard do is none of my concern. If they've taken it into their heads to fly to the furthest edge of the Deadlands, that's their prerogative. Kalis can't expect me to know where they might have disappeared to." He shook his head. "There have been so many Koth raids this cycle – I'm sure they sense that we are more vulnerable than ever. It won't be difficult to suggest that Murgo shouldn't have ventured too close to the foothills."

"You'll need to get airborne soon, if you're going to get back to Guardflight Rock before dawn," said Shaya. "If you're seen over the Deadlands…"

"We weren't seen coming here, and we won't be seen heading back." Taral glanced around at his wingflyers, signalling for them to ready for take-off. "But Culdo will have to fly north with you. He can't return to the *Spirax* alone – Fazak would have his wings."

Culdo had been talking with Jisco and Veret a few spans away. Hearing his name, he came across and stood over Murgo, opposite me. "I'll be happy to tell you everything I know about the Elite Guard, and what's been happening at the *Spirax*."

"You'll be welcome, Culdo," said Jotto. "I think a feast in your honour will be the least we can do. We owe you our lives."

The young guard reeked of pride and embarrassment, scuffing the moss with his claws while he mumbled something about 'duty' and 'doing what was right'.

"You risked your wings," said Shaya, dipping her ears in respectful salute. "Duty or not, that was incredibly brave."

Over the river to the north, a vinecreeper screeched, an early herald of the coming dawn, and Jotto turned to Taral. "You must go – now, and quickly before the sun comes up."

Taral nodded to each of us in turn. His scent told me he was still upset about what he had had to do, but the odour was overlaid with a whiff of determination, and his ears had settled to a less agitated angle. "We will see you again, and soon, Spiral willing. We have hope now." He dipped a bow and an ear in Urxov's direction. "Your sire has my loyalty, Lord. As do you."

Urxov preened, but the rest of us had no time for anything but our farewells, which were brief, but no less heartfelt for their haste. It pained me to watch Taral and his wingflyers take off over the malodourous Deadlands mud, but I comforted myself with the knowledge that the betrayal Dru had foreseen had been balanced by the friendships – the alliances – we had made.

As the sound of guardflight wingbeats faded into the shadows, Jotto pulled his knife from his belt and began to cut the wings from the bodies. "We'll need to be under the orenvines before sunrise. Let's get these bodies in the marsh."

Nine

"**S**hould we attack now? They are clearly weak, vulnerable." Kalon sat on his throne-stool in the centre of his log-built dwelling, Elver on his right and Urxov on his left. The rest of the party who had returned from the Expanse was ranged around the table, beakers of hoxberry juice in front of us – brewed from the pawsful of berries Jotto had managed to trade for – and our leaf-scratched reports in an untidy pile at one end. I had wanted Dru there too, but this time Kalon had refused. No matter: I could tell him all about the meeting when I returned to my own dwelling.

For the moment, I considered the question at paw. "If Kalis and Fazak continue to enforce their Spiral-high tithes, the freeze will weaken the drax there even further – so I would argue that that is a good reason for moving now, to spare more drax from hunger, cold and death."

"Your compassion does you credit, Zarda," said Kalon, "but I am more concerned with the practicalities. Are we ready to attack now? We will have one chance, we mustn't waste it."

Jotto nodded. "Much as I would like to spare other drax from further suffering, I believe we must wait till the next melt. The wingless are barely half-growns, and they're still learning how to use their weapons – as are most of the females. With practice, and more practice, they may be ready for a battle by the melt, but not until then."

Culdo spoke up. "If I may, my Lord? I agree with Jotto. From what I saw of the practice session yesterday, there are still a lot of arrows flying wide of their targets, and those with spears were a little timid with their thrusts."

The targets in question were sawn logs, tipped on their rough bark sides to show the marks that spiralled from the centre of the trunks. They had been cut from the vines at the top of the vertical cliffs on the western shore, and set out there along the vineline. Culdo, Jotto, Shaya, and a pawful of others were able to hit the centre of the trunks with ease, even from the air. The best of our half-growns, Dru included, could get close to it. Most could put their arrows on the target some of the time.

Culdo was right. Everyone needed more practice.

Kalon flicked an ear in acknowledgement. "And what of this Elite Guard you were involved with, Culdo? How well trained are they?"

"Most are not much better than the worst of your half-growns, Lord, but they are all adults. Right now, they would have the advantage of height, weight, and stamina. Some of the guardflight might side with them too – Taral is careful about who he trusts – and *they* are extremely well trained and well practised."

Kalon turned to his left. "Urxov?"

"The weaker they are, the better." Urxov held his chin up and sat very straight, obviously conscious of his own importance. "Another seven or eight moons will make more of them sick and reduce their numbers." He snorted. "They're already fighting among themselves over who fishes where. They were pathetic – cringing and begging when the Elite Guard arrived."

"They're not used to threats," I said. "There was never any need for them. The traditional system worked well, until someone got greedy and ruined it."

"Enough, Zarda. Urxov is not your trading apprentice any more." Kalon's half-growl was accompanied by a brief wing-flare, so I dipped an ear in apology and buried my snout in my beaker. Urxov had played his role well while we had been in Drax territory, and had been grateful for my help – and my silence – regarding his lack of night vision. But as I looked across at him over the rim of my beaker, I saw that he had returned to playing the role he liked best: heir to the true Prime. Had he, I wondered, learned anything at all from our mission? It seemed to me that if he had hatched on the Expanse he would have been more likely to join the Elite Guard than work against it. Certainly he would not make a good Prime…but perhaps he would not get the chance. Dru had Seen that Urxov's arrogance would be the death of him.

The question was, how much damage might he do to the Drax before Dru's Vision came true?

"What do you think, Zarda?"

Dru stood beside me on the western bank of Kalon's Island, his friends Chiva and Cavel a little behind us, all anxious to hear my verdict on the float that Oztin was guiding past us.

"I think it's astonishing."

Oztin, whose dam had been shot from the sky along with Milat, was now an inquisitive, shaggy-maned half-grown. When he wasn't doing chores, or throwing spears at targets, he would usually be found with Milat's pup, Nixel, climbing rocks or paddling a float hard and fast around the lake. Today, however, he was not paddling his float, nor pushing it along with a pole, yet it was cutting through the water fast enough to leave a wake of white water behind it. In the middle of the float, a sturdy post held a frame of thin vinewood, and a blanket that bellied in the breeze. At the back of the float, Oztin, his grey mane wind-blown, brown ears upright with pride and delight, used a flat board to manoeuvre the little craft as it bobbed past us and headed for the mooring place at the southern edge of the island. "How did you think of doing such a thing?" A cycle ago, we had not known how to make a float – had not known such things were possible, since we had never needed to travel on the water – but we had created and we had learned. Kalon and his people, who had had longer to experiment with such craft, had shown us how to shape them and paddle them, but Dru, Cavel, and their wingless friends had already thought of a way to improve them further, and I could but admire their inventiveness and initiative.

"Chiva noticed how the tunics and blankets caught the wind when they were hanging between the dwellings to dry," said Dru, "and she thought about how those of you with wings sometimes spread them to catch the breeze when you're in the floats."

Chiva and Cavel were already bounding away along the mossy shore to meet the float, and I indicated with a half-turn and a dip of an ear that Dru and I should follow. "So you cut up a perfectly good blanket to make a wind-catcher for the float?" I had to spread my wings in a gliding assist to keep up with the half-growns, and my question was punctuated with a couple of gasping breaths. Truly, the pace the wingless could move across the ground was astonishing.

"It was an old blanket," Cavel called over his shoulder, a defensive note in his voice.

"And we asked Winan-muz first," Chiva added, her words nearly lost beneath the rattle of pebbles underfoot and the slop of water against the shore.

I waggled my ears to indicate I had been teasing, though they were too far ahead of me now to notice. Truth be told, the blankets we had brought with us were wearing a bit thin. Without any furred animals in the vicinity to provide fleece and hair to produce more, the weavers were experimenting with plant fibres, but the results so far had been disappointing. It was probably just as well that the freeze here was not so bad as it was in Drax territory. "Why is the pole set in the middle of the float, and not at the front?"

"We tried it at the front," said Dru. We crested the rise to the west of the inlet, and the half-growns slowed their pace as we made our way down the slope to meet the float. "But it didn't work very well, and we couldn't steer the float properly."

I wasn't sure it could be steered properly now – not against the wind. As Oztin had turned for the inlet, the little craft swayed from side to side and veered right and left. Still, it was heading more or less in the right direction, and I didn't want to dampen their enthusiasm by pointing out the flaws in their invention, so instead I said: "Your steer-board works well, Dru – how did you think of that? Did you See how it might work?"

He shook his head. "I just watched how drax fly," he said, simply. "You all use your tails to help change course. Then I thought about how the fish have tails too, and how they move them from side to side to travel through the water and steer where they're going."

"So you used, what, strips of hide to attach it to the float?"

It was Cavel who answered, his russet fur and the line of his snout as he turned his head reminding me of his dam. "We used some of the seatach-gut bindings that the weavers made. Winan said we could."

There was a rattle of stones and a startled cry, as Oztin grounded the float on the shingle beach near the mooring place in the inlet.

Dru sighed. "We haven't found a way of stopping properly yet," he said. "If we try to turn the float so the wind-catcher doesn't work, the current takes us, or the wind blows us anyway, and we end up on the beach."

"Or in the water," provided Chiva, giving a little shake, as though drying her fur. With its russet hue, she might have been Cavel's sibling, rather than the foster-siblings they had become when Winan took him in.

I dipped an ear to acknowledge her remark, and hurried down the slight slope to help Oztin from the float. "Are you hurt?"

He shook his head, and ran a paw through his mane. "It's always doing that. Can you help get the wind-catcher down, Zarda? If we leave it on the float the whole thing will blow over."

I climbed into the float, which wobbled precariously as I stepped over to the centre pole. As I reached up to release the strap that held the wind-catcher's frame to the post, a gust of wind caught it and I almost fell as the whole thing pitched sideways. I clutched the post and held on, grunting as the edge of the frame hit the ground, dislodging my grip and jolting me onto the stones…

…unyielding black rock underfoot, a broken spear in my paw. Wings clatter. The air is thick with yells, cries, the smells of spilled blood and overwhelming fear. I look up. A drax in a maroon-and-blue tunic looms over me, spear poised to strike…

I jerked back to reality and dropped the piece of broken vinewood I'd been clutching, as the three half-growns fussed round me, brushing my arms and my tunic, asking if I was hurt. "Just bruised," I said, as I climbed to my feet and flexed my wings to check they weren't damaged.

"What did you See?" Dru bent to pick up the shard I'd dropped, and I held out my paw, underside up, noting the scratches and feeling for splinters in my fingers.

I shook my head. "Conflict. A battle, a skirmish? I'm not sure."

"Who was fighting? The Koth?" Chiva held out a rather grubby cloth in the direction of my paw, and I shook my head.

"No thank you, Chiva, it just needs a lick. I'll put some salve on in a little while." I took a moment to lick a bleeding finger, then addressed her question. "It wasn't the Koth. I Saw an Elite Guard with a spear."

I decided not to mention that it had rather looked as though the Guard would be the death of me, and instead deflected their attention back to the remains of the wind-catcher. The corner was broken where it had hit the ground, and half a span of dirty blanket flapped in the sand. A pity. It had all looked so graceful on the water, so simple. I scratched my snout, and brushed again at my tunic. "There must be an easier way."

"Zarda, I would have thought you had better things to do than stand here watching blankets dry."

Shaya had ducked out of her dwelling and stepped across to me as she spoke. I was standing on Rump Island, between her dwelling and Rewsa's, and had been so intent on my study of the way the wind caught the washing that I had not noticed the time passing.

"The blankets catch the breeze well, though they are only held in place at the top," I said, gesturing with a paw in the direction of the line. "I wonder if perhaps the wind-catcher on the float would work better if we took the side-lathes off?"

"Well, if you're going to try it, don't let Elver see you," said Shaya, looking around to make sure there was no-one nearby, and lowering her voice to a whisper. "I heard her yesterday, muttering about the wingless wasting their time on the water when they ought to be tending the crops, or learning a skill, or doing their target practice."

I sighed. "Perhaps I should not have reported my Vision."

When I had told the council of my brief glimpse of future conflict, Kalon had taken it as a sign that our attack would succeed; Elver had read it the opposite way, and decided that we were doomed to failure unless everyone worked harder, practiced more, and doubled every effort.

Urxov, ever eager to impress, had volunteered to make sure everyone spent at least a quarter-day firing arrows and spears at the targets, but fortunately Jotto had pointed out that until his Maturity ceremony Urxov was still officially a half-grown, and was in no position to give instructions to adult drax. "I'll decide who practices what, and when," he'd said, and Urxov had tucked in his wings and growled his way into a sulk.

Shaya unclipped the blanket from the line and rolled it up. "You're a Fate-seer, Zarda. If you have a Vision you know it must be important. Of course you had to report it."

"True enough," I said. "In any case, Kalon would have found out about it sooner or later from one of the half-growns. They—"

A howl of terror and pain drove further debate from my mind. Shaya dropped the blanket where she stood and, as one, we spread our wings and ran to take off.

"It's coming from the top of the cliffs," Shaya called, pointing west toward the high ground where the targets for shooting practice had been set up. We had already flapped high enough to see the knot of half-growns gathered near one of the targets in the middle of the line. Others, who had been at the furthest ends of the practice area, were hurrying toward the stricken half-grown who lay howling on the well-trodden ground. I recognised Cavel and Chiva amid the milling youngsters. Nixel and Oztin were running to join them, still clutching their spears. There was Dugaz, his grey mane and beard contrasting with the darker fur he'd inherited from his dam, Galyn. I spotted Dru's white mane, thanked the Spiral that he'd not been hurt, and heard a huff of relief from Shaya as Ravar bounded up to stand beside Dugaz.

Ahead of us, Hariz glided down to land, a carry-pouch clutched in her paws, and I thanked the Spiral that the healer's dwelling was on West Island, closer to the training area than we had been.

Hearing wingbeats behind us, I glanced back to see nines of anxious females all heading for the source of that fur-raising noise, and as we circled to land I identified the source of the howling: it was Ellet, Rewsa's half-grown, who lay writhing on her back, with several nines of other half-growns standing around her. Hariz the healer was already kneeling beside her with a paw on her shoulder.

I smelled the blood as we landed, but it wasn't until the knot of half-growns parted to let me through that I saw what the problem was. An arrow was embedded in her leg, just above the knee.

"It wasn't my fault." Urxov spoke even before I had folded my wings.

"I told you to wait!" Dru stepped from the group, his voice hostile, hackles raised and ears upright. If he'd had wings, they'd surely have been raised in a challenge.

"She was spans from the target!"

"And you are a terrible shot!"

"I am not! I shot that serpent, didn't I?"

"You fell and the arrow loosed. The serpent just got in the way! You never allow for the wind, Urxov. I told you to wait, why did you shoot?"

"Urxov does not like being told what to do," I said, keeping my voice calm as Hariz stood and, with a respectful flick of her ear, stepped back to give me room to kneel beside Ellet. I'd barely glanced at the wound before a flurry of fur and a familiar howl drew my attention:

"All that blood! Ellet! She'll die!"

"No, Rewsa, she won't." Hariz' voice was soothing, and I left her to calm Rewsa while I returned my attention to Ellet. The arrow-point was embedded firmly in the fleshy part of her thigh, and her fur was sticky with blood, but it looked to have missed the bone, thank the Spiral. It would heal readily enough with a little camyl-balm and rest. I glanced up at Urxov and the half-growns surrounding him. "None of you like being told what to do, even by adults who know what they are talking about. We'll have to organise your training better in future, to make sure there are enough trained adults here to supervise what you're doing."

I flattened my ears against the protests, the mumbling and grumbling. Ellet had stopped howling, but she whimpered with pain, and I thanked the Spiral I had brought supplies of both zenox and canox from the Expanse. Both would be needed if I was to cut out the arrow-point without Ellet – or Rewsa – deafening me with howls. Hariz had already bitten through the shaft of the arrow, leaving only a short length embedded in the flesh, and sprinkled the wound with canox powder to stem the bleeding.

"Shaya, fetch a carry-net, please. We'll take Ellet back to my dwelling, I can tend to her better there." As Shaya spread her wings and took off into the breeze, I stood up and looked around. The winged adults had each moved to stand with their offspring, or the orphaned pups they had taken under their wings, and there was a good deal of murmuring and pointing which, I guessed, amounted to blame-shifting and excuses. "Quiet!" I had no clear idea of what I was going to say, but surely something had to be done to concentrate minds, and spell out acceptable behaviour. As Fate-seer, they would – I hoped – listen to me and perhaps pay some attention to my words. "This is not a game," I said, looking from one half-grown to the next, smelling guilt and a trace of fear on each of them. "You have been told not to practice your arrows or spears without an adult. That is not just because there are a good many of us full-growns who also need the practice! It is to keep you from accidents such as this." I looked down at Ellet. She had stopped whimpering, and I knew that the canox was taking effect. Still, she would need to be tended to properly before the sun dipped another width. I looked around again, my gaze settling on Dru. "I thought you were coming to the western shore to practice your climbing?"

"We climbed," he said, gesturing to the almost-vertical drop behind us. There was a note of petulance in his voice that was typical for a half-grown, but which I had not heard from Dru before. "We've been climbing the bluffs here since we got to the Lake. They're easy." He glanced at Urxov, then shrugged. "When we got up here, Urxov was shooting at the targets over there on his own. The other targets weren't being used, and the arrows…"

I could guess what that glance was about. Urxov was almost a cycle older than the wingless, and would not have enjoyed watching the younger half-growns scamper up the rocks as quickly as vinecreepers bounded through branches. Doubtless there had been some taunting and daring and scornful remarks from the older drax before the wingless youngsters took up his challenge. But, if no-one was going to start flinging accusations, I would not stir the pot.

"So you were bored with your climbing and decided to practice with your bows instead. I see. What was Ellet doing so close to the targets?"

"Picking up the stray arrows from the first shots." Urxov spoke up, though he kept his head down and avoided my gaze. He twisted the bow he held, and kept glancing across at Ellet's prone form. "I thought she was far enough away. I'm sorry."

I grunted. The Spiral knew we had all done foolish things when we were young – indeed, if Varna had not been fool enough to fly over the Forest as a half-grown, we would not have known the river that led north existed, and would not even be here – but in the normal course of things, we were not given blades or arrows at that age. Even the Guardflight's hatchlings practiced with blunted arrows till they were issued with real ones at their Maturity ceremony. Yet here we were, putting sharpened weapons in the paws of half-growns and expecting them to use them wisely. "Learn from this," I said, raising my voice to make sure all of them could hear me. "Learn when to listen, when to wait. Learn the difference between doing something for fun and doing it in earnest. Above all – learn to shoot where you are aiming!"

There were a few nervous snuffles, but the fearful miasma disappeared. As Shaya returned, to land with a clatter of wings near the cliff edge, I took the net from her and spread it on the ground beside Ellet. "Urxov, come and help."

The group broke up into small knots of half-growns and females, and I closed my ears to the murmur of excuses and lectures and threats.

"She will be alright, won't she?" Urxov's voice was threaded with anxiety as he helped me lift Ellet onto the net. "She's gone awfully quiet."

"It's the canox powder," I said. All the same, I put a paw on Ellet's chest just to double-check that her heart was beating well. "It's eased the pain and she's gone to sleep. I think you should help me carry her back though, Urxov, don't you?"

He nodded, his ears drooping a little in contrition. "I'll help."

"Good. Because Ellet will need to be tended for a while, helped about, that sort of thing," I added, "and Rewsa won't have time to do it all herself."

Urxov sighed, his ears drooping further. He said nothing, but I hoped that this time the lesson had gone home.

I really should have known better.

Ten

While Ellet healed, and Urxov's patience wore thin with her demands and requests, I returned my attention to the wind-catchers for the floats. It took almost two moons of testing and experimentation – as well as several overturned floats and wet half-growns – but eventually we hit on a method that worked.

"You see," I explained to Kalon and Elver late one evening, "there is a horizontal pole near the top of the vertical one, but the bottom corners of the wind-catcher are held by the ropes, and they can be adjusted to help steer the float. The half-growns have even worked out how to zig-zag the float against the breeze."

We were standing at the end of the mooring-planks at the southern end of Kalon's Island, while Dru and Chiva raced past in a couple of floats fitted with the new style of wind-catcher.

Kalon grunted. I wasn't sure whether he was unimpressed, or annoyed that Urxov had had no part in this invention. "I can see that it's clever," he said, "but what use is it? There is nowhere to go, other than around the lake, and the paddles serve well enough for that."

I suppressed a sigh. "The wind-catcher craft can move as fast as a vlydh," I said. "Faster, perhaps, if the wind and current are both running in the same direction. They will be of enormous help when we need to move everyone upriver in the melt."

"And how will we get them through the rapids?" said Elver, shading her eyes as the last rays of the setting sun caught the water, glistening in the wake of the racing floats.

I dipped an ear to acknowledge her point. "Floats will have to be constructed on the other side of the rapids," I said. "We identified a suitable spot when we flew upriver – it was in our report, Lord, if you remember – though we assumed they would have to be paddled upstream. But if we build them with wind-catchers, they will move much more quickly against the current than they would with paddles alone."

"I do remember," said Kalon, "but it's too early to start making them yet, wind-catchers or no wind-catchers." He stroked his beard, thoughtfully. "Once Urxov's Maturity Ceremony is behind us, I'll have Varel draw up a timetable. Once that's been approved by the council, those with functioning wings can take turns flying beyond the rapids to cut vines for floats and clear enough space for a camp. But right now, these half-growns have spent enough time on these wind-catchers, and so have you. There are other things to tend to if we are to take back my rightful place in the *Spirax*."

"And they are being done, Lord," I said, trying to keep the irritation out of my voice. "I have consulted with Varel on how to slice the days, and the half-growns spend most of their time at their weapons practice, or their lessons. As do I." I indicated the floats, which had reached the southern end of the lake and were turning against the breeze as Dru and Chiva adjusted their wind-catchers. "We have made sure everyone has some unscheduled time each day to do as they please. Dru and his friends chose to use their time to improve the floats."

There was that grunt again, grudging but with a note of acknowledgement in it. "What of their other lessons?" he said. "What do they know of Drax history and tradition? Of reading and leaf-scratching?"

"Of herbs and healing? Planting and making?" Elver put in.

I closed my teeth on my first retort, and concentrated for a few moments on the smell of the water, the chitters and screeches of the creatures in the forest, and the tug of the breeze against my fur. When I was sure I could respond politely, I took a deep, slow breath. "All the half-growns attend their lessons, Elver," I said. "Lifra and Hexal teach about planting and reaping, Shaya has been teaching us all how to hunt since we first entered the Forest, and we have all learned how to build, weave, and gather. It is all in hand, I assure you." I hesitated for a moment, then added, "Urxov does not attend my lessons on salves and tinctures as often as he should."

Elver waved a paw, dismissively. "Urxov? He learned so much from his journey with you, and he will have his Maturity Ceremony in a nineday. If he doesn't wish to attend lessons with half-growns who are a cycle younger than he is, I see no harm. Especially since he can fly, and they cannot."

"True," I said. Elver's pride in her offspring filled my nostrils, along with a faint hint of contempt as she spoke of the wingless. There was something else there too, a scent that tickled my memory and came up with an image of Fazak. There it was again! Yes…ambition! Elver was ambitious for Urxov in a way that she was not for Kalon. Did she, perhaps, think that Urxov should be Prime instead of his crippled sire? I wondered, briefly, how she would react if I told her that Urxov had weaknesses of his own, but put the idea aside. I had given Urxov my word that I would tell no-one of his night-vision blindness, and I would not break it. Instead, I directed my next words to Kalon. "Urxov's aim with an arrow is still not as good as it might be. I wonder, sire, if it might be better to allow him more practice time with the spears? He does well in the paw-to-paw contests."

That was mainly because Urxov was not only bigger than the other half-growns, he was also adept at kicking and biting, but I thought it best not to say so. "He hit the serpent well enough," said Kalon, his wing stirring a little as I smelled his annoyance. "If he is not hitting the targets, it is because he doesn't wish to."

"I expect he finds it a little boring after all those adventures," said Elver.

In front of us, Dru and Chiva had set their floats to head toward the mooring place, furling the wind-catchers as they did so, and using the steer-boards to turn the craft with judgement and skill – qualities that Urxov singularly lacked. "Well done," I called to them, raising a paw in acknowledgement. "You make it look easy." I returned my attention to Kalon. "Some of the other wingless are already clamouring for wind-catcher floats of their own," I said. "Are you content for Dru, Cavel, Oztin, and Chiva to spend time teaching others how to work them properly?"

Several beats passed while Kalon considered the request, then he nodded. "I can see that that would be sensible," he said, "but they are not to interfere with their lessons or their chores."

I dipped an ear and sketched a bow. "Thank you, Lord. And Urxov?"

Kalon's single wing twitched and the set of his ears indicated there would be no point in arguing. "Urxov is a good shot," he said. "He has no need to practice. From here on, I will take him under my own wing, and teach him the strategy and tactics he will need when we take the *Spirax*."

Ignoring Dru and Chiva, who had tied up their floats and were dipping bows as they stood on the roughly-worked boards, Kalon and Elver turned as one and began to make their way back across the island toward their dwelling.

"What Urxov will need," I muttered, "is to be able to shoot, and to be able to see." I looked up. The first faint lights of the Spiral were already showing in the darkening sky and I wound a paw over my tunic. "Great Spiral help him!"

"Help who?" Chiva skipped up, brushing a paw over the edge of my wing in greeting.

"Why, Dru of course," I said, covering the lie by turning to put a paw on Dru's shoulder. "He will have a lot of work to do – as will you, Chiva. Kalon has agreed that you can spend time teaching other half-growns how to steer your floats."

The two of them twisted away from me, bouncing about and snuffling with glee. "We did it!" Dru shouted, punching the air with a clenched paw. "We made the floats fly."

I reached up to ruffle his white mane. He was a head taller than me now, though he lacked the extra bulk and muscular strength that would come with adulthood. "I have told you since you hatched that the Spiral did not *remove* your wings, it *replaced* them," I said. "You can jump high, and climb, and travel on the water. No drax has done those things before."

"And no drax has ever beaten the Koth," said Chiva. "But Dru will, won't he?"

"Dru will." I dipped an ear as I spoke. "I have Seen it, and so has he." I was even beginning to believe that some day it might happen.

But Dru's celebratory mood had passed, and I heard him sigh, smelled the longing that clung to his fur. "I still wish I could fly."

It had been a while since I'd attended a Maturity ceremony. Back on the Expanse, where nines would become full-growns within days of each other, entire clusters would celebrate together – usually with a roasted groxen, or a netful of fish. The odd beaker of berrywine might also be guzzled down, for they were carefree, joyous occasions.

It would certainly not have been a subject thought worthy of discussion by the Prime's council, but with Yaver, Tonil, and Urxov being the first of the exiles' young to reach maturity, no precedent had been set on how to mark the occasion.

"At least there'll be no shortage of berrywine," Varel murmured to me from his seat on my left. "I sent flyers as far as Falls Camp to find enough hoxberries."

At Elver's demand, no doubt. The same Elver who had objected to the half-growns spending their time improving the floats.

Still, that berrywine did smell good. Kalon's dwelling reeked of it, and a bubbling pot set next to the glowing embers in the hearth indicated that there was more brewing. Outside, the day was cool and damp, and I had been grateful for the warmth when I first entered the dwelling, but now I rather regretted taking the seat nearest the hearth. I reached for the water-jug and poured myself a cold drink, dipping an ear to acknowledge Varel's remark.

Jotto's nest-mate, Manel, spoke up from the opposite side of the table. "There are plenty of fish in the lake."

"And we could find some gumalix," Shaya added, leaning in from her seat next to Varel to look down the table toward Kalon. He sat on his throne-stool, Elver and Urxov on either side of him, stroking his beard as he contemplated the suggestions.

"Or there's some pickled serpent-meat, Lord, if you think the gumalix might be too greasy to make a decent feast?" Varel put in.

Urxov made a sound in his throat as though he was going to regurgitate, and Elver raised her snout and her voice: "Urxov doesn't like anything pickled. Besides, I think a Maturity ceremony should have fresh meat, don't you?"

Her query was clearly directed at Kalon, who grunted agreement and got to his feet to pace around the cramped space. For a moment, all I could hear was the scratching of Hynka's claw on a record-leaf and the soft beat of Kalon's feet on the earthen floor. He stopped his pacing to run a paw over the spiral pattern of shells set into the wall opposite the see-shell, then turned where he stood. "What says our Fate-seer? Will fish and gumalix be sufficient, do you think?"

What was the alternative? Vinecreepers? They had left their nests to scavenge through the branches for nuts and seeds in readiness for the Freeze, and would be almost impossible to catch. Another serpent? Spiral forbid! "The Maturity Ceremonies are social occasions," I said. "Celebrations, rather than rituals. Fish have always been part of those celebrations anyway, and we have no groxen, but the Spiral has provided an alternative. It would be ungrateful of us not to make use of what we have."

"Gumalix it is, then," Kalon pronounced. He looked across at Urxov as he went on: "We can make a hunt of it. Urxov will lead it, and the three maturing half-growns will each take down a gumalix."

I smelled surprise around the table, noticed several pairs of startled ears shoot upright, and then Jotto spoke up: "Sire, there has never been a hunt connected to the Maturity ceremony. The groxen and fish are traded—"

"You heard the Fate-seer." Kalon stepped across to loom over Hynka at the end of the table. The record-keeper hunched her shoulders and ducked her head in an attempt to seem smaller, and darted looks at each of us as though beseeching assistance. Kalon however showed no sign of biting anyone, and instead waved a paw as if to swat away Jotto's words. "The ceremony is a celebration, not a ritual. If we wish to have some sport with it, there's no reason not to."

"It'll be fun," Urxov put in. He was listening in on the meeting as a courtesy and shouldn't have been allowed to speak, but Kalon flicked an indulgent ear and indicated he should continue. "Besides, we're always being told to practice our arrow-shooting and spear-throwing." He jumped to his feet, shaking an imaginary spear as he barked, "Let's find something other than targets to aim at."

Elver's pride in her offspring was palpable as she smoothed her tunic with a paw and rose to stand beside him. "I'd like to witness the kill, Jotto, if you'd arrange that?"

To my right, annoyance was pouring from Shaya's every hair, and I heard her breathe deep as she reached for the water-jug. It was Jotto who dared to voice the obvious: "Elver, we'll need to find some gumalix first, and to do that we'll need to identify a suitable clearing."

"And I can't fly."

An audible sigh of relief circled the table, as we stopped wondering who would be brave enough to point out her handicap.

Elver was undaunted, her stance and scent reflecting stubbornness and determination. "Surely it will be easy enough to net me over to the clearing once you've found one?"

If I'd Seen what would happen, we would never have taken to the air. But no Vision came, and there were no more objections or obstacles to carrying out what should have been a straightforward plan.

And the next morning, we set off by wing and by net, scouting the Crimson Forest on the eastern lake shore for a herd of gumalix.

Eleven

Everything went well at first. The mist that hung over the forest canopy filtered the early morning sun and lit the vines with a warm, diffuse glow. It made the Crimson Forest look deceptively beautiful. But snapping twigs below our flapping wings, and warning screeches from the creepers foraging in the vinetrees, provided a reminder of the dangers that lay beneath those damp leaves. A squeal and a hideous sucking noise somewhere beneath us made me shudder and, even though we were several spans above the topmost branches, I brushed a hand over my tunic and fur, to check that nothing clung there that shouldn't.

Shaya, Jotto, and the hunters Azmit and Marga flew on ahead to scout for clearings where the gumalix might gather; Yaver and Tonil followed with slow, steady wingbeats, bows slung across their chests in readiness, while Urxov flapped around them, shouting suggestions to his fellow maturing half-growns that were studiously ignored. I flew behind them, keeping to the left of Elver, who did her best to look dignified as she dangled in a net held by four of our strongest females.

"There!" Jotto pointed with arm and snout, and he and the hunters angled their wings to circle the clearing they'd found, checking for threats with twitching ears and noses.

Spans wide, scattered with a mulch of dead leaves, scrubby sweetleaf bushes, wild avalox, and tussocks of moss, it would have been a good place to make camp, had we still been tramping through the Forest. A dead vine lay across the middle of it, its roots torn from the soil, its rotting branches smashed and scattered. It would have provided so much fuel for our campfires – and Doran would have had that wild avalox brewing in a pot in no time…

Elver's shout interrupted my thoughts. "There aren't any gumalix."

"I can hear them," called Shaya. "They're in the vines, just to the south. Once the sun reaches that dead trunk, the mites will fly and the gumalix will come to feed."

Around us, the vines shook as screaming creepers bounded away, but my straining ears couldn't detect any other creatures, harmless or otherwise. As I followed the half-growns down to the ground, I sniffed about for spiny slugs, mouldworms, vineserpents – but smelled nothing but decay, wild avalox, mosses and damp earth, with a hint of sweetleaf shrub in among the vines.

Elver was lowered to the ground beside me, and stepped clear of the net as the corners were released. "Shouldn't we hide?" she asked, sniffing as she looked around, ears upright and alert. "Surely the gumalix won't come if we're all standing here."

Tonil took a tentative pace toward her and dipped a respectful ear. "So long as we kneel, and we're not too close to that dead log—"

"They won't see us as a threat." Urxov spoke over her, waving a paw to indicate the other half-grown should step back. "We don't smell like any Forest predators they know. So all we have to do is keep still and keep quiet till we're ready to shoot."

Tonil glared at him, then turned away and checked her bowstring. "That's almost word for word what Jotto-fa told us all before we set off," she muttered to Yaver.

The other half-grown flicked a sympathetic ear and pulled an arrow from his pouch. "Well, at least it proves Urxov was listening, for once."

It was warm in the clearing, and restful if you closed your ears to the receding screeches of the creepers and the occasional distant squeal. The half-growns settled down to wait, and Elver knelt beside Urxov at the far end of the line from me. I didn't especially want to talk to her either, so I sat down, picked a few stems of wild avalox, and watched the shadows retreat from the fallen vine. As the mist fled, and the sun crept across its rough, shattered surface, the light caught the clouds of tiny mites taking to the air, and I listened for the sound of hungry gumalix moving toward us.

Tonil, waiting in a half-crouch with an arrow ready to paw, heard them first. "They're coming." Her voice was little more than a whisper, but Urxov and Yaver both tensed and nocked their arrows. All three of them leaned forward a little, heads all turned to the left to look south across the clearing, to where the unmistakeable rumble of gumalix hooves on damp mulch sounded through the vines.

The small herd burst into the clearing with squeals of what might have been delight or anticipation. They lumbered toward the log, spreading out as they moved along its length, their long necks and tongues rising from squat, hairless bodies as they began to feed.

"Now."

At Urxov's call, all three half-growns rose to their feet, arrows nocked, bows drawn. Tonil and Yaver fired almost at the same moment, barking with triumph and excitement as two of the beasts went down.

"Shoot, Urxov! Quickly before the others bolt!" Jotto shouted, as he circled overhead.

That was when it all started to go wrong.

Urxov aimed first at one, then another of the panicking gumalix, the tip of his arrow wavering back and forth as he tried to decide which one to shoot. Shaya and Jotto were hovering above him and shouting advice, Elver was by his side contradicting them – and the gumalix were bolting, back in the direction they'd come from, back to the cover of the vinetrees.

Urxov loosed his arrow at last, hitting one of the creatures in the rump, and he barked with anger and set off after it.

"Urxov, don't go under the vines!" The words tumbled from my mouth as I climbed to my feet and scurried after him. If he pursued the wounded animal under the canopy, he'd not be able to see where he was going…

"Urxov, no – it's wounded."

"The smell of blood will bring predators from spans around."

The calls and cries from Jotto and Shaya went unheeded, and I pushed my legs to a run as I pursued Urxov, still calling to him to stop. Before I reached the vines, Elver darted ahead of me and I switched to night-vision as I plunged under the canopy. Nothing. No-one. Then, a glimpse of Elver's tail flicking as she ran headlong between two tanglevine trunks. Just as I was about to follow her, Urxov crashed out of the sweetleaf bushes on my right. "Elver-muz," he called, swatting angrily at a hooked branch his right arm was tangled in, "I'm here. I couldn't catch the wretched thing. Come—"

If he finished his sentence, I didn't hear the words: they were lost beneath the ear-rending howls of pain that carried through the vines. Howls that rose in volume and pitch for several terrifying heartbeats – and then, abruptly, stopped.

Twelve

I'm struggling to understand."

Kalon was slumped on his throne-stool, tugging at his grey mane with curled fingers. The scent of his distress and anger filled the dwelling, almost masking the smell of Urxov's grief and shame. From where I stood, on Urxov's right, I could see he was shaking, though whether that was due to Elver's death or the fear of Kalon's reaction I couldn't say. Jotto stood behind the half-grown's left wing, his bow still in his right paw, his ears and head dipped to signal his own sorrow and self-reproach for what had happened. The rest of the hunting party had taken little persuasion to wait outside, and I could hear their subdued murmurs beyond the closed door. I rather wished I was with them, but as both Fate-seer and primary witness my place was at Urxov's side. The early mist and sunshine had been smothered with cloud while we flew back to the lake, and the light through the see-shell was subdued, barely illuminating the centre of the space where we stood – but there was no mistaking the gleam of Kalon's teeth as he drew his lips back in a snarl.

"It was a gumalix hunt!" He levered himself to his feet as he roared, pushing his snout within whisker-length of Urxov's, making the half-grown flinch and take a step back. "They are slow, they have no teeth, and if they are threatened, they run. Yet somehow you manage to get your dam killed. How is this possible? How?"

With a snap of his teeth that barely missed the end of Urxov's nose, Kalon turned away from him in disgust and flung himself down onto the throne-stool again.

"It wasn't my fault." Urxov rubbed at his unbitten nose as he spoke, his whimper barely audible. "I just wanted to finish the animal I'd hit."

"By running straight into the Forest with no thought for what might have been lurking under the canopy? Have you learned nothing in the two cycles since you hatched?"

Urxov's ears were flat against his head, his white mane still bristling with shock as he shook his head. "The gumalix were running that way—"

"The gumalix were panicking! Two of them had just been shot, there was blood and squealing and shock. They'd have run over a cliff edge or straight into a mouldworm to get away from you."

Urxov opened his mouth to say more, but Kalon waved him to silence and turned to me: "And what were you doing while my half-grown was falling into a bush and my nest-mate was stepping on a sucker fern?"

"I was barking at Urxov to stay in the clearing, Lord." I bowed my head and shook it. What was there to say that would not sound like a lame excuse? "I ran after him too." If Elver had not been faster than me across the ground, it might have been me who encountered the sucker fern. I shivered at the thought, and spiralled a paw over my tunic before adding, "Elver must have run past him. I suppose she didn't see him fall."

Kalon stared hard at me for several beats, and I flattened my ears and dropped my gaze long before his head turned in Jotto's direction. "And you, Jotto? Where were you while all this was going on?"

Jotto dropped to one knee and bent his head so low his snout almost brushed the dry mud that formed the dwelling's floor. "I'd been circling the area with the other flyers, Lord, looking for serpents and sniffing for mouldworms and slugs. When I saw Urxov pursuing the gumalix into the vines, I flew down to the clearing. But by then…"

By then, the howling had already been choked off.

Kalon sat straight, paws on knees, eyes closed, breathing deep. No-one moved, no-one spoke. The murmuring from outside had ceased – probably stilled when they heard Kalon's roars. I counted eight heartbeats.

Nine.

Kalon opened his eyes and heaved himself to his feet. "Do get up, Jotto, there can be no blame attached to you – or to you, Fate-seer, save that you had no Vision of what would happen." As Jotto stood up and I kept my ears flat in contrition, Kalon moved to stand in front of Urxov. "I had thought you had learned by now not to be so reckless. Time and again you've wandered off from us on Serpent Island, and every time we have told you to be more careful. I'd hoped that that brush with those insects on our last hunt would have taught you the lesson you needed. But still, clearly, you will not listen."

"Kalon-fa, I—"

"Enough." Kalon held up a paw, growled low in his throat. "Tonight, there will be no ceremony other than the death-howls for your dam. Tomorrow, we will have the Maturity feast for Yaver and Tonil. They hunted well today. They have proved themselves worthy. Your own Maturity ceremony will have to wait for another half-cycle. Till then, you are still to be regarded as a half-grown."

"But I'm the same age—"

"Is. That. Clear?"

Urxov smelled angry now, as well as upset, but he lowered his head, flattened his ears and muttered, "Yes, Kalon-fa. I just—"

The door crashed open and Shaya barged in, her bad manners forgotten the moment she spoke: "There are flyers heading for the lake, Lord. Nines of them, coming from the south. We may be under attack."

Thirteen

The dark specks flying toward us in the southern sky kept low over the trees, avoiding any danger that might lurk in the gathering clouds.

"Are they Koth?" Urxov sniffed the wind as he spoke, but it was blowing from the north-west and carried no scent from the oncoming flyers.

We'd all rushed outside at Shaya's announcement, and stood now outside Kalon's dwelling, a knot of shock and fear. Urxov had positioned himself on Kalon's right, where Elver had always stood, but his presumption went unremarked. His question though brought a sharp response from Jotto, who stood behind him: "Not Koth, no. They're not big enough."

Shaya stood beside me, to Kalon's left, and she pulled her gaze from the sky to glance across at Urxov. "Koth have a much bigger wingspan," she said.

"Koth are bigger, full stop," Jotto added.

"Whether they're Koth, or they're Drax from the Expanse makes no difference," Kalon snapped, looking about him as though he could will up another wing, or a vlydh to carry him aloft. "They're heading straight for us. Don't stand here gawping at them – get airborne!" As Jotto and Shaya spread their wings and turned into the breeze, he barked: "Gather everyone who can fly and wield a weapon. Go! Urxov, why are you still on the ground? Fate-seer, you can fly can't you? Get aloft!"

I took that to mean that I was also to join the prospective battle, and dipped an ear in hasty acknowledgement as I spread my wings and felt for the breeze. Kalon roared an oath as I ran and flapped, gaining the air swiftly and banking around to glide up just behind Jotto's left wing. I pulled my knife from my belt, though I had no thought of how useful that might be against flyers who might have better weapons. If they were Elite Guard…

I shuddered, remembering how they had shot unarmed females from the sky on the day we had crossed the Ambit. Had they discovered what had happened to Murgo? Found out where we now lived? Surely Taral would not have betrayed us?

Would he?

Shaya brandished her spear and barked at me to stay behind her. Azmit and Marga, trained hunters both, flew up to guard her wings, bows in hand, and Jotto had already nocked an arrow into the bow he carried. "Urxov," he called, "Yaver, Tonil. Fly to every islet and rally everyone who can fly. If they can flap a wing and carry a weapon, I want them airborne."

Meanwhile, the dark specks were getting nearer, the sound of their wingbeats carrying on the wind, faint but persistent, like a distant fall of pebbles.

"They're not Elite," said Shaya, whose thoughts had clearly been running parallel to mine. "They're wearing lots of different tunic colours."

"Thank the Spiral for that," called Azmit. "With all the practice we've had, we should be able to out-shoot them at least."

"Especially now we outnumber them." Marga's silvery fur rippled as she swooped in a circle, pointing back to the lake we were already leaving behind. I turned on the breeze to see drax scurrying from dwellings as Urxov, Yaver, and Tonil swooped low, barking the alarm. On the ground, howling half-growns waved bows and spears, some of them launching floats, paddling hard toward the river-mouth, or raising wind-catchers to billow in the breeze.

"Better circle for a few beats," said Jotto, matching his actions to his words and dipping his tail to check his momentum. "Let the rest catch up." He turned his head from side to side as he circled, sniffing the wind and keeping his ears twisting, and I realised he was checking to see whether there were any other strangers approaching. If this was an attack, perhaps whoever it was hoped to encircle us, or at least to drive attacks from more than one direction.

But, as more and more of our females got airborne, and those heading towards us drew closer, it became clear that we outnumbered the ninety or so I counted. And, unless my eyes deceived me, each untidy V formation of nine was leading a...

"Vlydh! They've got vlydhs with them." Marga's bark of surprise confirmed my observations, and deepened the mystery.

"Do we go to meet them?" Hariz called, as she levelled out and hovered behind us.

"Not yet." Shaya waved her paws to direct each ascending female to circle or hover. "Remember what happened to Milat and the others."

"We'll die." A cry I'd not heard for a while, though I knew immediately who was bleating it. "We'll all die!"

"No we won't, Rewsa." Azmit was circling and pointing. "They have their paws extended – they're not armed."

"All the same," called Jotto, who had not removed the arrow from his bow, "stay alert. Stay ready."

The newcomers drew nearer and we hovered with weapons in shaking paws. The tension could have been slashed with a claw – until I recognised the lead flyer and caught my breath. With frantic ears and flapping paws I signalled to Jotto that he should put his arrow away. "It's Taral!" I could scarcely believe I was saying it. Taral! Here?

With a whoop, Culdo overtook us, flapping headlong toward the incoming flyers, barking a greeting to his guardflight comrades and, as though carried on a current of relief and delight, the rest of us followed, calling and waving as we recognised old friends. I saw Swalo the fable-spinner, Sajix and Galio, who I had last seen at their weavers' cluster at Paw Lake. Jisco and Veret were there, leading the formations behind Taral's, and there was Peren, Jonel's nest-mate, calling and waving.

Peren.

He had left his dwelling and everything he knew, flown all this way to find his youngling and nest-mate. My stomachs churned as I remembered my last sight of Manda and Jonel, speared by the spiny slug and dissolving in the slime it excreted...

Lights, how would we even begin to tell Peren that he wouldn't find them here?

I pushed the thought aside as our formations converged, swirled and twisted in a flurry of shouts and wingbeats.

"What are you doing here?"

"Have you room for us all?"

"What's in the vldyhs' packs? They look full to bursting."

"Were you followed?"

"It's so good to see you!"

"We'll explain everything when we land."

Below, on the lake, the half-growns were turning their floats to head to Kalon's Island, and I wondered if there would be room on the gathering place at its southern tip for everyone to land.

"Split up," Jotto called. "Shaya, take three nines to Rump Island. Azmit and Marga – three nines each to the East and West islands. The rest to Doorway Island with Manel and Culdo. Zarda and I will take Taral and the guardflight to Kalon."

We landed at the foot of the hill at the northern end of Kalon's Island, just as I had done when I first found the lake. Not till I'd folded my wings did I notice how tired and thin Taral looked. His tunic was patched and dirty, his mane uncombed, and he scratched at an arm that bore the unmistakeable signs of fur-clump.

I put a paw on his arm. "Taral, what's happened?"

"He can tell Kalon." Jotto landed alongside Taral, and set off up the spiralling path. "Come on, Taral – this way."

In front of the dwelling on the summit, Taral and the eight guardflight with him all dropped to one knee in front of Kalon, and I took my place as Fate-seer on the Prime's left, while we waited for Taral to speak.

"The drax I brought with me have been driven from their homes." Taral's head was bowed and he looked… I searched for the right word. *Diminished.* Yes, that summed it up well. It was not just that he looked thinner, though he did, nor that he smelled of defeat and despair, though he did. It was obvious that whatever he had been through in the moons since we'd last seen him had made him feel less than he was, less than he hoped to be, and my heart went out to him.

"Stand," said Kalon, "all of you. If you have come seeking help, you must know that we cannot return to Drax territory until we are much better prepared. We have food – the Spiral has blessed us with a good harvest this cycle – but we have no orenvines for your vlydh."

Taral dipped an ear as he got to his feet. "We have brought supplies with us – such as we had. There was little enough to spare. The packs are mostly full of orenvine leaves for the vlydh, and saplings to plant – Spiral willing they'll grow here. We've come to seek help, yes, and we're grateful for the refuge, but we also intend to help *you* if we can." He bowed and added, "Lord," which had the effect of making Kalon stand a little straighter and stretch his wing in acknowledgement.

Urxov stood next to him, a pale imitation of his sire. "Go on with your story," he said, after a glance at Kalon.

"The Koth attacks worsened through the gathering season," said Taral. "They began to attack whole clusters, rather than isolated farms – it must have been obvious that some of them were already struggling to cope. Some of the clusters on the fringes sent their criers to Kalis to petition him to let them move to spare dwellings in clusters nearer the centre of the Expanse. He refused. Others asked if they might be spared the burden of the tithes, since the Koth had made off with most of what they'd had. Kalis refused that too. The Guardflight…" He sighed, his ears and wings drooping. "There were too few of us to make any difference – and we grew fewer as the Koth grew bolder. The Elite Guard refused to help – Fazak insisted that their role was to protect the *Spirax*, not to…" He halted and I saw his paws clench. When he continued, his whiskers were quivering with rage, his snout set in an expression of utter contempt. "Fazak's exact words were that the Elite Guard were 'not there to look after the lesser lights'."

There were cries of outrage and much murmuring. Kalon's mane and ears flared up and out, Urxov's wings twitched, and the wind bore the musky smell of collective rage.

Kalon drew himself to his full height and extended his wing. "Even One-Wing would not have dismissed hard-working drax in such a way!"

I straightened where I stood, glanced at Kalon to make sure he had finished speaking, and raised my own voice: "The Spiral needs all its lights, if it is to continue to shine on us. Greater lights or lesser lights, they all contribute to the whole. So it must be with the drax – none is unimportant!"

"That is no longer the way of things in Kalis's territory," said Taral. I noticed how rough his fur looked, how quickly his chest rose and fell as he breathed, and I realised he must be exhausted.

"Lord, these drax have flown for many days to find you," I said to Kalon. "They have asked for shelter…"

He grunted. "They shall have it – so long as they are prepared to build their own dwellings." Then, raising his voice so that those on the hillside could hear: "We have a death-howl to carry out this evening. For Elver – my nest-mate and Urxov's dam. But tomorrow there is to be a Maturity Ceremony, and you will be welcome to join the feasting. After that, I will summon a council, and we will hear more of this story." He turned to me and said, quietly, "Look to their welfare, Zarda. See that they all have somewhere to sleep."

I looked at the bedraggled guardflight who had accompanied Taral – at their torn tunics, drooping ears and matted fur – and thought of the clusters that Jotto, Shaya, Urxov, and I had passed through a few moons before. How many of the drax we had spoken with, who had traded for our shells, offered us hospitality, had already died at Koth hands? Or starved because they had to give the little they had to the *Spirax* in tithes? I recognised Jisco's torn ear and Veret's scar as I looked around the group and returned my gaze to Kalon.

"Do you doubt their story, sire?"

"Of course not. But I have learned the hard way that you can never be too careful."

Fourteen

Vinecreepers were netted, fish were clawed from river and lake; flyers were sent upriver to hunt gumalix, and to gather nuts and berries; another serpent was brought to ground and its meat sliced and dried.

"I believe we'll have food enough for all," Varel confided, as the two of us walked along the western shore on a warm afterzenith, looking over the cultivated fields. To our right, kestox was being harvested, its orange leaves falling to the rhythmic cuts of seatach blades, wielded by nines of purple-clad drax. I spotted Galio and Sajix working alongside Myxot and Bidra, and I noted with relief that Galio's ears no longer drooped with the sorrow he had felt when he'd learned of his nest-sibling's death. There had been several nines of the new arrivals who had had to be told that their younglings and nest-mates and siblings had gone to their last nest, and it had fallen to me as their Fate-seer to break the news. What a strange time that had been – the grief and howls had echoed Kalis' anguish for Elver even as the flames from Yaver and Tonil's Maturity Feast died down, and were set against the relief and joy of those who had journeyed safely and found rest, sanctuary – and loved ones. I knew that Galio still mourned – we all did – but it was good to see him out in the sun with Sajix, learning new skills.

Beyond them, Winan straightened up, stretched her wings, and pressed her paws to her back. Chiva, her half-grown, teased that Winan couldn't keep up, and the big female bent to her task again, barking that she would show the youngsters what hard work was.

Further on, pale stubble was all that remained of the chalkmoss, and that would also be collected soon. We would crush the roots to add bulk and flavour to stews, and the remainder would be used by the dyers. We had avalox and kerzh from Kalon's Island, and camyl ripening in the sun. Perhaps, come the melt, we might even have a little zaxel! Zaxel, so difficult to grow on the Expanse, had surprised everyone by producing tentative shoots from the traded roots we had planted on our return from our reconnoitre.

Even now, with the gathering season almost at an end, I found the warmth hard to cope with. My winter fur was beginning to grow in, but if Varel and Kalon were to be believed, there would be no snow, no real freeze for it to cope with.

"It is a nuisance," said Varel, seeing me pluck at the lengthening strands on my arms, "but we have the lake and the rivers. If we get too unbearably warm, we can wade in and cool off." He indicated the half-growns splashing and yipping in the shallow water that lapped the mossy banks of Doorway Island. Winged and wingless together, they were playing some sort of game involving a loosely-woven net and a couple of gumalix skulls, which were being thrown about. Varel sighed. "You'd think that half-growns would be too mature for such games." He gave an indulgent wave in the direction of his own half-grown, Hynel, then sighed and shook his head. "Just so long as they are not neglecting their work."

"I'm neglecting mine, I'm afraid. I should have been at the top of the cliff by now for spear-practice." I glanced up as I spoke, and waved a paw as Jisco and Veret skimmed overhead. "I'm coming," I called. "Tell Taral I'll be a few beats."

I caught a whiff of Varel's envy as he watched the two guardflight glide up and over the cliff, and realised he would never be able to reach the target-practice area. "I'm sorry, Varel. You must find it very frustrating, watching others go to shooting practice when you can't."

He grunted, rubbed at his crippled leg and acknowledged the truth of my words with a dipped ear, then waved them away with a paw. "If it wasn't for this leg, I'd try climbing up there. But then how would I fight, anyway? I can either cling to a vlydh, or wield a bow. I wouldn't dare try both. Kalon won't be able to fight either, not in the vanguard anyway." His ears drooped briefly, then straightened. "But I'm sure we'll find something useful to do – and with luck, there'll still be some skirmishing to do when we land." He glanced up at the cliff again. "At least I know the training has been improved since Taral and his wingflyers arrived."

'Improved', I discovered, was an understatement. As I touched down on top of the cliff, drax were lined up in nines, bows in paws, waiting their turn to shoot at the targets. The targets themselves had been moved further from the cliff edge, along with the vine-line. Spears, bows, and ninety upon ninety of arrows had been cut and shaped from the toppled vines, and a separate space for spear-practice had been marked out at the southern end of the cleared area.

"Ah, Zarda, there you are." Shaya strode across the trampled ground toward me, a spear in each paw. "We thought we might try you with a spear today."

I dipped an ear, accepting that what she actually meant was, 'you can't hit a hillside with an arrow, surely you can't do any worse with a spear'.

Perhaps it helped that I'd carried a spear in my paw for most of our journey to exile, and had already learned a little about the best way to hold and throw. Or maybe it was simply that the targets for spear-throwing were closer than those for the arrows. Either way, I was delighted to land it on the edge of the target three times out of my nine throws, and tried not to be too chagrined that every half-grown practising with me managed to spear the middle of the target every time.

"Well, given that you didn't learn as a youngling, I suppose that's not too bad." I took Shaya's grudging remark for praise and resolved to try harder next time. "Maybe you should try some paw-to-paw." She handed me an untipped stave, while I tried to work out what was different about her appearance today. She looked bulkier somehow, bigger, yet still groomed and elegant. Gesturing to Ravar and Cavel, she added, "The wingless have come up with an interesting technique I've never seen before."

Ravar came at me first, his moves as graceful as his dam's, but more muscular. I parried his first strike successfully, jabbed my blunt spear at him, then flapped my wings in an effort to take off and gain the advantage of height. Ravar, anticipating, dropped to one knee and raised his spear, and would have skewered me right through my middle had the weapons been sharp and the fight in earnest.

"You see?" Shaya's pride carried on the breeze as Ravar got to his feet, and she placed a paw on his shoulder. "The wingless can't go higher – so they drop lower, and take any winged opponent by surprise."

"Impressive." I turned to the half-grown. "You'd better teach me that move, Ravar, I'm going to need all the help I can get, and if surprise gives me any advantage at all, I'll take it."

The other half-growns had been watching, and there was some murmuring and snuffling amid the group – doubtless observations about just how poor my skills were, though I couldn't hear the exact words. The breeze that snatched them also ruffled our fur and I realised why Shaya looked different.

"Your fur," I said. "Your longer fur for the freeze. You've – what? – trimmed it?"

"I cut it shorter, yes. Not sure it helps much, because it's still thicker than it would be in the melt and the warm season, but at least it's easier to cope with this way."

"I'm having mine done next," said Ravar.

"And me." Ellet, fully recovered from her arrow wound, chiming in from the edge of the group.

"Not till after practice," said Shaya, firmly. "Ellet, Cavel, all of you – throw again, and this time I want to see more power from the shoulder. Watch Nixel over there, see how he powers through the whole move?"

106

Nixel, another half-grown who had seen his dam shot from the sky by the Elite Guard, had grown into an imposing, black-maned half-grown, and I watched with admiration as he hurled his spear at a target with a roar of aggression. As he bounded off to retrieve his weapon, he glanced across at the watching group and barked, "Just imagine you're spearing those *fwerkian* Elite."

"You will be, soon enough," called Shaya. "For now, take over from Ravar and help Zarda with her spear-practice. Ravar, Ellet – let's see you throw your spears the way Nixel does. More than once, please."

Repeating the moves I'd been taught was warm, gruelling work. Even at the slower pace Nixel adopted to take me through the basics, there was so much to remember – fold wings so they couldn't be slashed, move the feet, parry, move the feet, thrust, move the feet, dodge, move the feet, drop and thrust. Not necessarily in that order, and never one thing at a time.

"I think you're beginning to get the hang of it." Nixel didn't sound or smell entirely convinced of his own words, but after nine laborious repetitions of the moves he had shown me, I was warm as flame and panting for breath and cool air.

"I'll practice whenever I can," I promised, handing the practice spear back to him. "I know I need to be better than this."

"Do you?" Nixel checked over his shoulder, to make sure Shaya couldn't hear, then took a step closer to me and lowered his voice. "You are our Fate-seer, Zarda, do you actually have to fight?"

I put a paw on Nixel's arm, turning him to look across the training area and sweeping a paw to indicate all the drax there: half-growns lining up to fire arrows at targets that were spans away; females flying low to do the same; a nine of winged and wingless throwing spears. "There are gatherers here, Nixel, weavers, dyers. Any of them could plead that they are not fighters, nor even hunters. But we all learn and train because we wish to – because we believe that Kalis and Fazak and those who support them are wrong and must be fought. If I plead special circumstances, then others might too – and besides, when I think about all that happened on our journey, I feel I have to strike back. However badly I might do it."

"Yes, I see." He dipped a respectful ear. "I expect we'd all be doing something different if we were still on the Expanse."

He sounded wistful, and I wished heartily that life had been kinder to him and to all the wingless young. Here they were, learning to shoot, intending to fight – and likely kill – fellow Drax, when they should have been in apprentice stripes, learning to weave or gather or hunt.

"We'll be back on the Expanse soon enough, Nixel," I said, "and you'll be able to put your spear to good use in the hunt, Spiral willing."

It was a trite reply, patronising even, but it was the best I could do. For a beat or two, we stood watching as a nine of hovering females swooped down to loose their arrows, Rewsa and Hariz surprising me with their accuracy from nines of spans. Then Nixel said, quietly, "I'm not very good at hunting. I can't keep quiet enough. Even the gumalix hear me coming."

"Well," I said, "I'm sure you'll find something to do. You're very good with that spear. Perhaps the Guardflight—?"

"No." Nixel waved a paw in the general direction of the lake, and the Forest beyond. "When we were travelling...it was horrible what happened to Milat-muz and everyone else who died, and it was frightening all the time. But...well, it was interesting too, learning new things, finding things like that seatach that I never would have seen if we'd been back on the Expanse. It makes me wonder what else is out there. What's beyond the Forest, Zarda? What's beyond the mountains?"

"I can tell you what's beyond the Forest," I said, a little taken aback by the extent of his curiosity. "Ocean. Just ocean. I've Seen it. As for the mountains..." I paused, glancing over my shoulder at the peaks that rose toward the clouds in the south and west. "I'd not given it any thought, since we can never get there anyway."

"Yes, but—"

Nixel stopped talking as Shaya stalked towards us, calling for him, and as they both bounded away, I turned to look out across the lake. Beyond the mountains, indeed! What did it matter?

The half-growns who had been helping to harvest the kestox had finished their chore and were cooling off in the shallows or skimming across the water in floats. Chiva, however, was sitting beside Oztin on the lake shore, her russet-furred head and his shaggy grey mane both bent over a carry-net, and I realised they were working on another of Chiva's ideas. *"There must be a way to make it easier to net a vinecreeper or a gumalix,"* she'd told me, in the aftermath of Urxov's disastrous hunt, *"or maybe even tangle up a mouldworm or a spiny slug."* As I watched, the two half-growns finished tying pebbles – or chips of vinewood perhaps, it was impossible to tell from the top of the cliff – to the corners of a carry-net, and Chiva threw it in Oztin's direction. It splayed briefly before enveloping his head and shoulders, and I nodded understanding and silent approval, even as Chiva shook her head and helped Oztin untangle himself.

Raising my head I looked out toward the islands, where logs and reeds were being trimmed and set in place as the work on new dwellings continued. Smoke rose from chimneys and from the makeshift shelters where those whose dwellings were not yet completed still huddled. A couple of Island-hatched half-growns flew low over the water, and I shaded my eyes against the sun to watch their flightpath…

Huge black wings beat slowly as three Koth skim over the lake. They land on Doorway Island, where nines of Koth are gathered round a spit. The severed head of a serpent is being tossed about, as easily as a Drax half-grown might throw a gumalix skull…

"Zarda!"

"Zarda? What did you See?"

I was on the ground, moss beneath my claws, Taral and Shaya standing over me, both reeking of concern and curiosity.

"Give me a moment."

I took Taral's proferred paw and clambered to my feet, brushing my tunic and smoothing my fur. Shaya almost deafened me as she looked over my shoulder and barked, "Go on with what you were doing!" and I realised that everyone on the clifftop was hovering in place, or standing still to look at me.

I waved a paw. "It was just a Vision of the lake and the islands," I called. "I'll report the details to Kalon. Don't be concerned."

Slowly, with a good deal of muttering and murmuring, and a number of paws spiralled over tunics, the groups of drax returned to their training – though some still stared my way, and others sneaked glances when they thought I wouldn't notice.

In front of me, Taral placed his paws behind his back, and Shaya folded her arms. They glanced at each other, then turned their attention to me.

"You know we're close enough to you to smell when you're not telling the truth, don't you?" Shaya, straight to the point.

I sighed, and pushed past them as I moved away from any straining ears and walked nearer the cliff-edge. "I didn't lie," I said, as Taral and Shaya flanked me. "My Vision was about the Lake."

"And...?" Taral, prompting.

I looked again at the scene below us, the dwellings, the floats, the shelters, turned my ears and snout to take in the sounds and smells of the various tasks and activities on the islands and lake. "I Saw Koth. On the islands. They were roasting a serpent."

"Koth? Here?" Taral glanced skyward, one paw reaching for the bow that was slung across his chest.

"We've not had a sight or a sniff of Koth since we left the Expanse," said Shaya, "except those you Saw in the Forest when we found those ruined dwellings."

"Yes." I shook myself, still trying to rid myself of the scare the Vision had given me. "Yes, of course. A Vision of the past. The Koth in those dwellings must have known about the lake. Perhaps they used the islands for special ceremonies."

When I reported my Vision to Kalon, I told him the same thing: a Vision of Koth on the lake, a Vision of how things had once been.

But I wasn't sure that was true.

Had the Spiral shown me what would be? Or given me a glimpse of what *might* be if Dru failed to fulfil the destiny that had been foreseen for him?

Koth on the lake. What did it mean? And what did it say about our own future?

Fifteen

"**L**ights, Zarda, what happened to you?" In the moons since his arrival, Taral had gained weight, though even with his winter fur he still looked thinner than he once had. His long fur was sleek, the smell of defeat and despair had vanished along with the fur-clump, and as he stood in my doorway, his whiskers twitched with amusement as he gazed across the dwelling at me.

"Oh. This." My tail spasmed with embarrassment, and I wiped a paw down each arm in turn in a vain attempt to flatten the tufts of fur that made me look like an unmade nest. "Well, you know it's too warm here for winter fur, and I noticed yesterday that lots of the females have been trimming their fur, like Shaya, and it was such a warm day, so…" I stopped gabbling and sighed. "I should have known better than to do it myself."

He barked with laughter, then immediately dipped an ear in contrition. "I'm sorry, Zarda. I shouldn't laugh. But I haven't had much to laugh about for a long time and…sorry, but you do look funny."

I suppose I should have been insulted, but I knew he was right. I shook my head, snuffled a rueful chuckle. "I know. I'm the Fate-seer, Taral. I'm supposed to be a beacon of dignity and respect. Vizan would have given me a good nipping for being so stupid – and another for looking it. How long do you think it'll take for the fur to grow out?"

"I've no idea. Moons maybe." Taral stepped into the dwelling, nose busy as he looked round, and I felt a wash of relief that for once there were no unwashed tunics, unlicked food bowls, or unemptied waste buckets lying about. I'd known Taral would be coming, so I'd tucked everything neatly behind the woven screen in front of my nest. I would deal with clearing up properly later. Taral's whiskers twitched as I pulled at my fur again. "Maybe if you lick it and brush it? You can't stay here till you moult, we have a ceremony to plan."

"I know, I know. I suppose it's worth a try."

I licked the fur flat as best I could, brushed it all in the same direction, and declared that it would have to do. "Where are we meeting Varel?"

Taral led the way out of the dwelling, onto a dewy hillside that sparkled in the low morning sun. Already there were floats on the lake, propelled by paddle and wind-catcher, while calls and barks carried across the water from the other islands, accompanied by the sound of wingbeats. The usual cries and screams of the forest creatures had become a routine background accompaniment to our activities, and even the screech of a frightened vinecreeper somewhere in the canopy did nothing to disturb the beauty of the morning. "We're going to that lump of rock just off the southern edge of Itch Island. Varel's gone on ahead, I said we'd meet him there."

Good. If we flew straight there and straight back I'd be able to retreat to my dwelling again without too many drax noticing me.

"Strange to think that by this time in the last cycle we'd already been to check how much of the Manybend had frozen," Taral called, as I followed him into the air. "Thank the Spiral the weather is warmer here, or we'd never have got our new dwellings built."

His paws swept from east to west, indicating the scattered islands and the spirals of dwellings that occupied them. The ones that had been constructed by the renegades stood out from the rest, not only because the vinewood was raw and dark, but because they were neatly circular. The builders Taral had brought with him had transformed the design with the simple trick of putting the logs on end and leaning them slightly inward. With a single post in the centre to support a roof of leafy branches, and a space cut near the doorway for a hearth, their dwellings were a much better match for those we had left behind on the Expanse. So much so that others, Kalon among them, had pulled down their previous efforts and replaced them with the new design.

The vines for the new dwellings had been cleared from the western shore, and the orenvine saplings planted in their place, the spiral plantation a small replica of the one where Miyak and Doran had hatched Cavel. It was Cavel who had taken charge of the nine vlydhs the renegades had brought with them, who made sure they were fed till they spun their cold season cocoons, and who tended the spindly orenvines. "They should be alright by the lake," he'd said. "And I'll put lots of waste round the roots, it'll help them grow quicker."

Doran would have been so proud of him.

I pulled my thoughts away from that sad direction by looking ahead to our destination. Itch Island was a mossy, wing-shaped lump near the northern edge of the lake, its hillocks and dips dotted with abandoned, half-built dwellings that were already beginning to rot. At its southern tip, a small cone of black rock poked out of the water. Tumbled rocks between it and the islet indicated that it had perhaps once been attached to its bigger neighbour, but any soil and vegetation that might once have clung to it had long since disappeared. It was nothing now but a hump of bare rock, with – perhaps – just enough room on its rounded upper surface to construct a ritual bonfire for the Night of the Two Moons.

Varel was already limping about, pacing around the rock, then crossing from one side to the other.

"He said he'd have the measurements by the time we get there," Taral called, as Varel paused to scratch something on a leaf. "Varel! We're coming down."

We landed on the rock's highest point, which was a scant few spans above the surface of the water. The shoulder of the rock sloped gently away from us in every direction, and a swift sniff and a scrape of my claw along the surface told me that this was a similar type of rock to the huge black edifice that formed the plateau and the *Spirax* back in Kalis' territory.

"I've walked as far down the slope as I can, without extending my good wing," Varel announced, waving his notes as he limped up the slope to meet us. "And I'm sure there'll be enough room here for—" He stopped, abruptly, several spans away, and looked me up and down. "Zarda, your fur! What…?"

I put my arms behind my back in a belated effort to conceal the shorn tufts. "I thought cutting it shorter would be cooling."

Varel sighed with what smelled like relief. "Thank the Spiral. I thought you'd developed a dreadful case of fur-clump overnight."

I ignored Taral's snuffle of laughter and concentrated my attention on the leaf Varel was clutching. "You have the measurements?" The snap in my voice made Varel start, so I signalled apology, extended a hand to take the leaf, and resisted the urge to try smoothing my fur again.

"We can see all the inhabited islands from here," said Taral, while I bent my snout to look over Varel's scratched calculations. "We'll just have to make sure that there's a suitable gathering place on each islet, so that all those on the ground can see the ceremony and the flames." He turned to Varel. "If you're having to measure the available space, I assume you've not used this place for the ceremony before?"

Varel shook his head, and turned to point back in the direction of Kalon's Island. "There were so few of us, we all had room to gather on that mossy bank at the south end of the island, near the inlet. With no Fate-seer, no kervhel, and so few of us able to fly, we weren't sure the Great Spiral would accept our offering – especially during that first cycle, when we were still recovering from our journey."

"Not exactly traditional," said Taral. "Fazak would not approve."

I glanced up, acknowledging Taral's statement with a dipped ear. "No, he wouldn't, yet the Spiral has not punished the drax here. Kalon and those who came with him have survived for cycles. They've not had the Sickness, they've grown food, built shelters, learned to make floats, hunted and gathered, and—"

"And now we have a Fate-seer, islands full of drax, and the beginnings of a plan to return to the Expanse." Varel rubbed his paws together, clearly as pleased and proud as if he had produced such resources himself. He opened his mouth as if to say more, hesitated, clasped his paws together, and set his ears upright, though his twitching tail and perplexed scent were at odds with his positive stance. "There is just one thing I should mention, Zarda..." He seemed reluctant to go on, and I smelled his uncertainty. A mauve-tinged cloud drifted across the sun, and Varel glanced skyward, fur bristling. "A floater. They stay late in the cycle here, but I've never seen one this close to the Night of the Two Moons."

He fell silent, and I was about to prompt him to go on with what he'd been about to tell me when he turned first to Taral, then to me, and said: "The Night of the Two Moons. Yes. You should know Zarda that when..." His tail swished. Whatever it was he needed to tell us, it clearly caused him great anxiety. He drew a deep breath, spoke rapidly: "Jotto and Manel have carried the torches at the past few ceremonies. As our only adult flyers...well, that doesn't matter. What *does* matter is that neither of them could see the second moon, even though the nights were clear and the Great Spiral lit the sky."

"The second moon was visible from the *Spirax*," I said, scratching an ear. "I saw it."

"As did I." Taral put his paws behind his back, and rocked back and forth as he was inclined to do when deep in thought. "Perhaps Jotto and Manel missed it – it's very small, and they're not trained—"

"Nonsense. Jotto was guardflight, he knows where south is, and he'd seen the second moon before. If he says he couldn't see it, then it wasn't there to see."

The sun emerged from behind the floater-filled cloud, but I'd gone cold. The lights were always with us, they were the lights of our ancestors, our relatives, our friends. They would increase as each of us joined our lights to theirs, but they would surely not disappear! Yet... "The *Spirax* can't be seen from here either," I said, thinking aloud. "We couldn't even see it from the sky over Falls Camp. We'd travelled too far."

Varel snorted. "The *Spirax*, for all it's on the edge of a high plateau, is on the ground. The second moon is in the sky. And the lights in the sky—"

"Are always with us. Yes, I know. But...perhaps the light of the second moon is somehow tied to the *Spirax*. If we can't see one, we can't see the other – maybe?"

"Whatever the reason," Taral said, reaching across Varel to take the leaf from my paw and glancing at it, "how will you know when to make the sacrifice and start the fire if you can't see the Second Moon? I remember Vizan conducting the ceremony, that cycle when it hailed, but how did he know when to complete the ritual? Did he See it?"

"I wasn't his apprentice at the time," I said, brushing the tufts of fur on my left arm and looking from Taral to Varel as I spoke, "but he told me about it later when I asked the same thing." I sighed, glanced skyward, and looked over at Taral. "He guessed. That's what Fate-seers have always done if the lights are obscured, and that's what I'll have to do if I can't see the Second Moon on the horizon." To Varel I said, "That's what Jotto did too, I assume?"

Varel wrung his paws, tail swishing with alarm. "Please – both of you – don't tell anyone else. We don't want the entire settlement worrying that..."

"That I might get it wrong," I finished, as he broke off with an apologetic ear-flick.

We all spiralled our paws over our chests in silent agreement, but Taral hadn't finished with his questions. "Vizan guessed wrong, didn't he, Zarda? And the Sickness came with the melt."

I nodded. On the lake, floats and flyers headed for the eastern shore, where the vines grew thick, and the felling for the ceremonial bonfire would begin. Water slopped against the base of the rock we stood on, and I caught the scent of damp earth and wet leaves on a faint breeze from the south-east. Overhead, the brightest lights of the Great Spiral were fading as the sun rose higher. "Better pray to the Spiral to guide my paws," I said. "Or hope that I'm a better guesser than Vizan was."

Sixteen

Thunder rumbled over the forest to the south, lightning jagged groundward, and a cloud glowing purple with a feeding floater drifted overhead. It was not an auspicious start to the Night of the Two Moons. It had been hard to tell when daylight ended and the night began, but the *spirorn* had been sounded for the beginning of the ceremony, and Urxov and I had stepped out of Kalon's dwelling into a storm of driving rain.

"Oh, perfect," Urxov muttered, as we made our way around the dwelling till we were facing north. The torch in my paw hissed and flickered, then flared again as the sweetleaf oil I'd smothered it with overcame the threat of the water. I had wrapped a spare torch in a piece of seatach skin and pushed it into my belt along with a dry firestick, just in case – though it would not be seen as a good omen if the original flame went out.

Across the lake, on the islands around us, the flightless and wingless were gathering in spirals, guided from the air by Shaya, Jotto, and Manel, who were circling over their heads and calling directions. Young Tonil was already in the air above Kalon's dwelling, no doubt thrilled and terrified in equal measure that she had been entrusted with the job of guiding the Prime and his council into the correct formation.

The rest of the winged drax were hovering in a wet spiral above the ritual bonfire, guided by Taral and his guardflight. As the rain intensified to a deluge, I sent up a brief prayer of thanks to the Spiral that I had doused the vinewood with a bucketful of sweetleaf oil earlier in the day. At least it would catch light.

"Can you see *anything?*" I said, raising my voice over the tumult of rain and wingbeats.

Urxov was tilting his head this way and that, narrowing his eyes as he peered through the darkness and the curtain of rain. His ears twitched nervously, and every few breaths he would wipe at his fur and his whiskers in a futile attempt to keep them free of rain-drips. His white mane was bedraggled and lying flat against his head, his tunic dark with moisture. Not that I looked any better, I was sure, but at least I was able to see what was happening.

Urxov shook his head, and a shower of droplets flew from his fur. "I can see your torch," he said. "That's about it."

"It will be better when the other torches are lit," I said. "Just follow the lights."

Yaver sounded his *spirorn* again, and I lifted my torch to the south, the west, and straight up. "Deliver us, moons. Deliver us, Great Spiral from the darkness and the cold," I roared. My words drowned in the rain, and I had no idea whether they were repeated by the drax around me. I would have to simply continue the ritual and hope for the best.

A clatter of wings announced the arrival of Taral and his guardflight – the sound of the *spirorn* must have carried across the lake, thank the Spiral – and Taral lit his torch from mine. The guardflight lit their torches from his and they all glided off to light the other torches – one per island to the wingless, Taral, Jisco, Veret, and the rest to the winged.

The lights spread, as more and more torches were lit. A boom of thunder muffled the repeated incantation. As Kalon, Veret, Hynka, and the other council members edged around the dwelling to light their torches from mine, Taral flew back to hover in front of us, waving his torch, and I raised my arms to signal the next part of the ritual.

The mass of torches on the islands began to move as the crowds waved them, while the airborne drax moved into the traditional helix formation over and around the pyre. The guardflight called and barked as they circled, making sure everyone was in place, and Taral flew to take his place at the top of the spiral of lights.

"Now, Urxov." I spread my wings to catch the breeze, flapped hard to shake off the water, and launched myself into the night air, flying swift across the lake toward Taral's raised torch, and checking back over my shoulder to make sure Urxov was following. We carefully flew down around the spiralling passageway the torches made, and I held my own torch out to my left as I'd promised Urxov, while I chanted the next stanza of the incantation.

The gumalix that had been tethered to the pyre in place of a ritual kervhel was curled into a ball, allowing the rain to slough off its back, and while Urxov roared the end of the incantation, I gave it a firm poke with the unlit end of my torch. It unrolled with slow reluctance, but barely had time to grunt a protest before Urxov despatched it with a quick slice of the knife, catching the blood in a clay bowl and lifting it above his head.

The crowd cheered, perhaps because the ceremony was as well done as it could be, but mainly I suspected because it meant we could all get out of the rain.

Torches were already hissing as they were thrust into the pyre, but the platform for the sacrifice had provided some shelter for the logs beneath it, and they caught light readily enough. "Well done, Urxov," I called, as we hovered near the bonfire to enjoy its light and warmth for a few moments. "We can go back now. Stay close and I'll guide you back."

But as I flapped my wings and banked around, he barked, "You don't need to treat me like a hatchling, Zarda. I can see well enough now with the torches and the fire." I glanced back, saw with horror that he was already several spans above me, and climbing. "I can see that gap in the clouds too – it's shining over the lake."

"Urxov," I barked, not daring to fly after him, "that's not a gap in the clouds! Don't fly towards it, there's a float—!"

I'll never know whether he heard me and ignored my advice, or whether my warning was lost in the storm.

Seventeen

Kalon's grief was terrifying, his rage terrible. He blamed me, he blamed the ritual, he blamed the wingless, the rain, the Spiral, and the Moons – everyone and everything but Urxov was at fault.

"Now I have no heir but Kalis's wingless abomination," he growled, pacing around his dwelling with his mane and ears raised, and his remaining wing half-spread.

I had prepared a tincture of zenox to try to calm him after Urxov's death-feast, but he knocked the beaker out of my hand, and snarled "leave it!" as I bent to wipe the spillage with a cloth. As he strode about the chamber, his wing clouted the council table, the stools, his new reed screen, and the recently-constructed curving walls, but he seemed oblivious to the pain it must have been causing him.

"I will have to choose another nest-mate," he growled, kicking an overturned stool out of his way, "and hatch another Egg." He clenched a paw and banged it against the wall, hard enough that the logs vibrated. It must have hurt, but I didn't even think of offering to fetch a poultice. Instead, I stood clutching the empty beaker I had picked up from the tea-stained floor, casting about for an excuse to leave before Kalon decided to tear my wings off.

He was still ranting. "I should never have given you shelter, any of you! If I didn't need every warm body that can wield a spear or fire an arrow, I'd tell the lot of you to be off downriver right now, and the darkness take you. I tell you, Zarda, it's only the thought of my shell-brother sitting snug in my place in the *Spirax* that checks me. I need you, I need Taral and his guardflight, I even need the wingless, Spiral help me. But once I'm back in the *Spirax*…"

He left the threat hanging, and I thought it prudent to exit. "I understand, Lord," I said, bowing so low my snout nearly touched the earthen floor. "Shall I send someone to tidy up in here?"

For a heartbeat, I thought he might rip my throat out, and I took a step back nearer the door. Then he sniffed, scratched his beard, and his ears flicked to a slightly more thoughtful angle. I got the impression he was pondering who might have the ability to do more than straighten the furniture. "Yes. Send someone. Send…what's her name? That weaver. Sajix, is it? Served me an excellent gumalix stew at Urxov's death-feast, she can bring me some more when she comes."

I sighed with relief at getting out of the dwelling unscathed, but once outside I had time to think on what Kalon had said. Surely, if the wingless and the renegades helped return him to the *Spirax*, he would not exile them again? Even the thought was painful. And what of Sajix? The winged hatchling she had produced several cycles ago had been taken by the Sickness. Was Kalon considering her as a potential nest-mate? Someone who might produce another egg, another heir for him? Should I mention my suspicions to her? Or to Galio? No, I would look foolish if I had misread Kalon's signals, and I wasn't sure whether Sajix would welcome his attention or scorn it. Best let matters take their own course for the moment.

I shivered. The cold breeze from the south that ruffled my fur smelled of snow, the grey clouds overhead were depressing, and the haunting call of a gumalix carried to my ears from the Forest to the east. Rubbing my paws together for warmth, I flew low over the lake to Sajix and Galio's new dwelling on Rump Island, to deliver my message. "And put this in the stew," I said, pulling a twist of powdered zenox from my carry-pouch. "If your cooking doesn't calm him, this will."

"He's lost his nest-mate and his heir in the space of a few moons," she said, as she fetched a bowl from the ordered shelves and put a pot of water on the hearth to heat. "It's no wonder he's out of temper."

I nodded. "We'd all just better hope his grief doesn't blind him to justice."

The freeze was harsher than it had been since Kalon's group arrived on the lake, Jotto said, though if I heard anyone muttering about ill-luck being brought by the ritual on the Night of the Two Moons, I took pains to point out that Elver's death had preceded it.

"Urxov's own stubbornness caused Elver's death," I said, "and his own stubbornness caused his own. He never listened – you know that."

Upriver, beyond the rapids, the work of cutting vines and shaping floats went on. Though Urxov's Maturity Ceremony had never taken place, the council meeting that followed Elver's death had seen Varel tasked with overseeing the work we'd discussed. Every few ninedays, I flew there myself to see how things were progressing, to admire the workmanship on the floats, and to be ready to add my report to Varel's when Kalon requested it.

But Kalon requested nothing. He kept to his dwelling. He called no councils. He wouldn't even see Jotto. Only Sajix was given access to his chamber, and she reported that Kalon said little and did less.

"He's worn the same tunic for nigh on a moon!" she said, when I found her in her dwelling one morning, washing a very dirty white tunic. "I only coaxed him to change by reminding him that the Prime is expected to set an example." She held the tunic out of the tub, examined it with a critical eye, and plunged it back into the water for another rub. "I left him brushing his mane – he must have been close to getting fur-clump, he was in such a state."

"He's been eating, though," I said, pulling up a stool and sniffing the jug that stood in the middle of the table. Hoxberry juice. Lovely. "Galio says your stewpot is never off the hearth."

She nodded, though her attention was still on the tunic, which she wrung firmly and shook out. "There, that's better. I'll put it by the fire, it's too damp outside." She draped the garment over a stool, moved it closer to the hearth, and stepped across to pour us both a beaker of juice from the jug. "Yes, he likes my stews, does Kalon." She dipped an apologetic ear and added, "I'm sorry I wasn't able to serve you and Urxov something decent when you came to the Expanse."

"You gave us warmth, shelter, and hospitality as best you could," I said. "The Spiral asks no more. The hard part for me was seeing so many empty dwellings, and so many drax who were sick and despondent."

"And afraid?"

I nodded. "That too." I leaned toward her as she sat down next to me, and confided, "What frightens me is the thought that Kalon has lost the will to set things right. Has he said anything to you about returning to the Expanse? Attacking the *Spirax?* Anything at all?"

Sajix cupped a paw around her beaker and gave it a sniff. "He doesn't say much. But I think it's only the thought of pulling Kalis's wings off that's keeping him going."

I sipped my juice and extended my feet a little nearer the fire as I shifted on my stool. "He won't get to pull Kalis' wings off if he doesn't start planning his campaign very soon," I said. "The melt will be here in another moon or so. When does he intend for us to travel upriver? What will we eat while we travel? How are we going to get our floats to the Ambit? And when and how does he wish us to attack?" I put the beaker down and licked my whiskers. "You are the only drax he sees, Sajix." I pointed to the white tunic, from which faint wisps of steam were rising. "He listens to you. Tell him that he needs to call a council meeting – Jotto, Taral, myself, Dru."

"But..!" She put the beaker down and clutched at her tail – a show of nerves I'd only previously noticed from Rewsa. "I can't tell Kalon what to do. He'll roar. He'll bite. He'll—"

"Nothing will happen to you, I'm sure." I placed a paw over both of hers, waited till she'd let go of her tail. "You don't need to *tell* him anything, but you have to find a way to suggest that we all need to know what he wishes to do when the melt arrives, because we need to start planning for it now." I sat back, drained my beaker, set it down. "If he wants Kalis' wings, he can have them. But we have to get to the *Spirax* first. How are we going to do that?"

Eighteen

Another moon passed before the council was summoned. The water level of the lake was nudging upward with early meltwater from the mountains, and young Yaver swore he'd heard vinecreeper mating calls in the Forest. In our new orenvine plantation, where the vlydh were emerging from their cocoons, the vines looked bushier and taller, while to everyone's amazement, the zaxel roots that had been planted on the western shore grew straight and strong. None of the farmers Taral had brought with him had heard of zaxel growing anywhere but on the eastern-facing slopes of the hills near Far-river. Even Swalo the fable-spinner had no stories of it sprouting anywhere else.

"I've plenty of tales of failed crops and gallant tries," he'd said, when we'd flown together over the grey stems, sniffing the air, "but none of success. Not for zaxel." He'd paused to consider it further, then dipped a regretful ear as he'd added, "Perhaps in the Archives...?"

Perhaps indeed, but the Archives lay in the Hollow Crag in the bay to the south of the *Spirax* peninsula. And Fazak – unless he had more important things to do these days – was in charge of them.

Maybe one day I'd have the chance to take a look through them again, but first we had to get back to the Expanse, take the *Spirax* from Kalis, punish Fazak…

As I waited outside Kalon's dwelling for Dru, my thoughts turned over the dangers and opportunities that lay ahead of us. How might nineties of us make our way to the *Spirax* plateau without Kalis being alerted? How many Elite Guard were there now? Who led them? How many of Kalon's drax wished to stay out of any fight? How many of Kalis' drax might wish to join it? And whose side might they take?

Hearing Dru's distinctive footsteps on the pathway below me, I checked to make sure my tunic was straight, and took a moment to admire the moontrap buds that were thrusting a few tentative tendrils out from beneath the logs of the dwelling. Heaped clouds scudded overhead, borne on a warm north-westerly, and broken by shafts of sunlight. No floaters today. If only…

But no. The Spiral had sent the storm and the floater, and Urxov had died so that Dru might be Prime, just as he was in our Vision. It was terrible, regrettable, but assuredly not something I could have prevented.

"The melt's started, hasn't it?" Dru broke in on my thoughts, bounded along the path to stand beside me, and turned right around where he stood to take in the view. "The lakewater's rising, and the river is running faster." He brushed rather self-consciously at his tunic – a cream one, befitting the Prime heir, freshly woven and dyed since Kalon would not allow the use of Urxov's old tunics. He was sprouting a beard, white like his mane, and I was startled to realise how close he was to being full-grown. Another seven or eight moons and he would be an adult. There would be a feast to mark the occasion, as there had been for Urxov. Would it, perhaps, take place in the *Spirax*? Might we begin to dare think of going back there at last?

Kalon's dwelling seemed dim in contrast to the brightness of the daylight, and it took me a moment for my eyes to adjust to the filtered light of the see-shell and the torches. A scattering of

127

sweet-smelling avalox across the floor bore testament to Sajix's touch, torchlight was reflected in the newly-polished throne-stool, and most of the smaller stools for the council were already occupied. Shaya, Jotto, and Manel sat together on one side of the table, with Hynka and Varel opposite. Dru headed for the stool at the far end, nearest the Throne-stool – he knew better than to claim a place next to Kalon – while my eyes were drawn to the nines of paw-wide moontrap leaves that had been stuck together to produce one huge scroll, big enough to cover much of the curving wall opposite the see-shell. Torches burned in sconces at the leaves' upper edges and, as I stood staring in the flickering light, I realised what had been scratched on them: a map, showing the layout of the land all the way from Kalon's Lake to the orenvine copse at the edge of the Deadlands, and onward to the Far-river in the south, and the hills beyond. Death River and the Ambit were marked, Paw Lake was scratched clearly at the head of the Manybend, and tiny spirals marked the clusters. Guardflight Rock, the *Spirax*, and the mountains were marked with small pointed shapes, and labelled.

"Someone's been busy," I said, pulling out a stool opposite Dru and sitting down, while the half-grown took charge of pouring beakers of warm hoxberry juice from the jug on the table.

Jotto nodded. "Kalon. I recognise his scratchings."

Taral knocked on the door and entered, ducking his head as he stepped through the low doorway. He didn't take a stool, but stood with his paws clasped behind his back as he studied the map on the wall. "This is fine work," he said, his snout moving back and forth as he took in the landmarks and carefully-scratched topography. "Very detailed."

"Thank you." Kalon emerged from behind the woven-reed screen that now stretched across the back of the dwelling, and there was a scraping of stools and rustle of avalox stems as we stood and bowed. He waved us back to our stools and went across to stand next to his map, while Taral seated himself on my right and accepted a beaker of hoxberry juice from Dru. "It's been a long time since I saw the land myself," said Kalon. "I hope I've not forgotten anything?"

Kalon's fur was brushed, his mane and beard combed. There was a sprig of fresh sweetleaf blossom pinned to his spotless white tunic, and his ears indicated resolve. Only the faintest smell of grief and anger emanated from him as he looked us over, and I had to admire the way he had mastered his sorrow, and masked any feelings of blame or distaste.

"It's good to see you looking so well, Lord," said Jotto, voicing my thoughts.

I was glad I'd not spoken when Kalon retorted, "Spare me your platitudes, Jotto. My sole interest now is in returning to the *Spirax* and avenging myself on my worthless shell-brother. I suggest we concentrate on discussing the task ahead."

Jotto inclined his head and dipped his ears. "As you wish, Lord. Have you a plan in mind?"

Kalon nodded, and pulled a sharpened stick from his tunic belt, using it to point as he spoke. "I believe we have enough drax and vlydh to split into three groups: one of flyers, one with non-flyers and floats, and one with non-combatants, flyers, non-flyers, and vlydh. But we'll start our journey together." The stick slapped against the scratching that represented the lake and islands, slid along the curve of the river. "We'll all gather at the newly-cleared ground beyond the canyon. From there, we'll split into three groups and travel in stages up Death River to Falls Camp. Varel – work out the logistics and send flyers upstream to fell vines around the existing landing places. Make sure there's enough room at every campsite to take at least a third of our numbers."

Varel opened his mouth as though to remind Kalon that the vine-felling had already begun, then thought better of it and contented himself with dipping an ear. Hynka began to scratch notes on a leaf, while Kalon moved his pointer across the map.

"From Falls Camp, flyers will carry our floats to the head of the Ambit, under cover of darkness. Those of us who are grounded will need a path cut from one river to the other, to give us a rapid journey – and a safe one. Once we're at the Ambit, and the floats are ready, Taral will take the guardflight and ninety armed females to the guardflight training area in the south-east mountains." Kalon stabbed the stick's point at the southern foothills, beyond the Expanse's southern bay and the mouth of Far-river.

"We'll have to fly low at night. I suggest we move first from Falls Camp to the orenvine grove at the edge of the Deadlands." Taral indicated the route on the map as he spoke. "From there, we can fly to the Copper Hills, follow the Manybend south as far as Paw Lake, then fly through the valleys beyond till we reach Far-river, which we can follow east towards the coast. It's a short flight into the mountains from there."

Shaya half-raised a paw as she interjected: "That many drax in flight will make quite a racket. Perhaps you should wait for a rainy night before you fly around the borders of the Expanse?"

A rainy night like the one we had had for the Two Moons ceremony. A couple of beats passed while everyone waited for Kalon to react to this indirect reminder of that tragedy, and my nose told me that several of us were ready to run, but after one angry ear-flick and a single growl, Kalon returned his attention to his plan. "That's a sound suggestion – and one more reason why we must strike during the melt, when the weather on the Expanse is less predictable. Taral, your training area is here?" He brought the pointer down on a representation of the low peaks to the south of the Expanse.

"Further east, Lord." Taral extended a claw to scratch a mark on the map. "Near the coast, in the mountains beyond the southern bay."

"So you'll have sight of the *Spirax* and the plateau?"

A shake of the head. "There are other peaks between our training area and the bay. From the ground, we can see the ocean, but not the *Spirax* peninsula."

"But from the air? Under cover of darkness?"

Taral dipped an ear. "We'd be able to see the plateau, the *Spirax,* the entire southern bay, and the southern edge of the Expanse."

"Good. So you'll need one night to get to the orenvine grove, another to the Copper Hills and...what? One night to the training area? Two?"

"It'll be a long flight, but I think we'd better aim to do the last stage in one night, especially as we'll have to wait for rain."

"What about patrols?"

130

Jotto's question drew a sigh from Taral, and his ears angled toward regret as he answered: "There's a possibility that the few guardflight left on the Expanse might intercept us, or that the Elite Guard have sufficient numbers to cover the borders now. But I think we can avoid being seen – unless the patrol patterns have changed drastically since I left."

"What about the Koth?" said Veret. "Surely, if you fly through the hills beyond Paw Lake and Far-river, you'll draw their attention?"

"The Koth will not attack a large flight of armed drax." Taral all but spat the words, his contempt for the Koth rising from every hair. "They never have. They are too cowardly to take on those who are capable of fighting back."

Manel chimed in, her voice a growl, her ears and scent betraying long-buried rage. "They prefer to prey on helpless farmers, who try to stop them carrying off a fattened groxen and get their throats ripped out for their trouble."

I was a little startled by her outburst, but Taral dipped a respectful ear her way and said, "The attack on the Paw Lake farm, yes. That was your dam and sire, as I recall? I was a mere youngling at the time, but I remember my dam's regret that she could do nothing to avenge them."

Manel's paws were clenched, her voice tight with fury. "I was Guardflight myself when it happened. I'd been on patrol there earlier in the day, but..." She shook her head, clearly still too upset to say more.

Taral finished the thought for her. "But as usual, the Koth waited till the patrols had passed."

"We will finish the Koth," Kalon snapped, his patience with the aside at an end, "once we have dealt with my shell-brother."

Manel subsided, ears set to contrition, though I could still smell the grief she had nursed, and Kalon turned to Taral.

"So, from Falls Camp you will need two nights to get to the Copper Hills. Once there, you'll wait for the first rainy night to complete the journey," he said, returning the discussion to its main agenda. "You will need time to rest and recover once you arrive at the training area. Is there somewhere that you can stay out of sight?"

Taral nodded, and tapped a claw against the mark he'd made on the map. "There are caves in the mountains where we shelter during our training flights," he said, and I recalled the story he had once told me about how as a youngling he had forgotten the firestick, and the entire training group had had to eat cold food. "The Elite Guard hadn't been near them, up to the day we flew to join you, Kalon. I don't think they even know about them. If we take sufficient food supplies, we can stay in there for days." He glanced over at me. "We'll have to eat cold food, though – can't risk drawing attention by lighting campfires."

"It will suffice," said Kalon. "As for those of us who can't fly, we will need to walk over those high hills that lie between Falls Camp and the upper reaches of the Ambit. Varel, send a nine of flyers there today to begin cutting a route through the vines."

"Uh...I'm not sure we actually know where the upper reaches of the Ambit are, Lord?" Varel ventured, timidly. His fur was on end and his shoulders hunched in anticipation of a bark, or even a bite, but he hadn't finished making his point. "Uh...also, the water will need to be wide enough and deep enough for the floats—"

"Then have someone fly from Falls Camp to the Ambit, and fly upstream till they identify the best spot for our floats to launch downriver. The nearer to Falls Camp the better – remember, those floats will have to be carried over the Forest."

"Yes, Lord." Varel bent his head over his own moontrap leaf and scratched another note.

Kalon waited a few beats, glaring round to see if anyone else would dare an interruption.

No-one did.

"Once we have a pathway cut," he went on, "that part of the journey shouldn't take more than a nineday, Spiral willing. We'll have enough flyers with us to transport our floats from the Falls to the Ambit."

"And from there, you'll be going with the current," said Jotto. "If there's a favourable wind, it may only take one night to get all the way to the Ambit estuary."

"And if you make camp on the northern side of the Ambit peninsula," Taral added, "You won't be seen, not even by the patrol around the *Spirax* plateau."

From there, even I could work out that they would be able to make their way along the coast, by float – the same coast where I had spent so many painful days with the wingless as we walked toward the Forest. If only we had had some wind-catching floats back then! How much time, energy – lives – might we have saved?

Shaya glanced at Kalon to see whether further discussion would be welcomed, then ventured: "An attack from two sides. The wingless from the north, and the guardflight and females from the south." She paused, ears twitching as she thought, then said: "The wingless will be able to climb the plateau, Lord, but how will *you* join the battle?"

"I won't be taking a float," said Kalon. Heads swivelled, ears flicked, Hynka paused in her note-scratching. Kalon stepped toward the table and, after a momentary hesitation, placed a paw on Dru's shoulder. "Dru, my current heir, will lead the wingless in their floats. He—"

Dru's eyes rolled and his mane stood on end. The last time he had had a Vision at a council meeting, he had fallen at Kalon's feet, howling about betrayal and death. This time, he made no sound, and Kalon held him upright on his stool for the several beats it took till Dru shook himself and looked around. Running a paw through his white mane, he was panting hard, and I snatched up his beaker and poured him a drink.

"Take a few beats," I said, "and a few deep breaths. Then tell us what you Saw."

Dru gulped down the contents of the beaker and refilled it. "Nothing useful," he said. "Blood, howls and confusion, mainly…" He lifted his head, ears upright, proud. "And I Saw the wingless climbing the plateau, just as Shaya described." He swivelled on his stool to look round at the map, and got to his feet. "When you fly," he said, glancing around at those of us who had wings, "the noise of the wingbeats carries for spans."

"The Elite will hear us coming," said Taral. "There's nothing we can do about that."

"And I have taken it into account in my plans and calculations," said Kalon.

"Of course," said Dru, making the necessary gestures of acquiescence. He turned from the map to face us, impatient to continue. "But don't you see? When the wingless climb, we can do it quietly, with stealth. I suggest that we should begin the attack, by climbing the *Spirax* plateau. With your approval, Lord—" he dipped an ear in Kalon's direction "—we could time our climb to reach the top of the *Spirax* plateau by sunrise on the appointed day. No-one will have heard us approaching. If we can get to the top with throwing-nets before the flyers press home their attacks, we might prevent the Elite from even taking off—"

"And the flyers would be in position to strike while they are still trying to disentangle themselves!" said Jotto.

Taral nodded. "You will not be able to net all the Guards, though. You will be vulnerable to attack from the ones who are able to take off, or run at you."

"Only until the rest of you arrive," said Dru. "And we've been taught well – Shaya and her hunters, Jotto, Culdo – and you, Taral, with your guardflight – you've all helped us learn how to survive, how to use our weapons. We will not be defenceless."

Kalon raised his head, looking about and sniffing for any dissent. There was none.

"It is agreed," he said. "Dru and the wingless will lead the attack, in the way shown by the Vision the Spiral sent him."

Dru dipped a respectful bow, and resumed his seat. Jotto leaned toward him, hopeful, and murmured, "Did you See who was winning?"

"No." A tiny tail-quiver, a twitch of his whiskers. A lie. I knew the signs by now, but if Dru had chosen not to share everything he Saw with the council, I had to trust he would at least tell me, later.

"As I was saying," Kalon rumbled, weary now with the discussions, "Dru will lead the wingless contingent down the Ambit. Wait on the estuary side of the peninsula, where you can't be seen from *Spirax*. At moon-end, when the night lacks the moon's light, proceed along the coast to the plateau, and be in position to start the attack at dawn the following day." He jabbed his pointer at the map once more, indicating the orenvine grove. "While Dru and the wingless float down the Ambit, I'll take a vlydh to the orenvine grove with the non-flyers – there are enough vlydh for each of us – and the remaining flyers. One night after that, we'll fly to the Copper Hills, and at dawn following moon-end I will howl the advance, and move south-east toward the *Spirax*. I will have a battle-banner made, and have it unfurled when I lead my contingent in formation over the Expanse. We'll fly in at low level to call to every drax in every cluster to join us. On the *Spirax,* the winged will attack from above, the wingless will climb from below. Between us all we'll crush any resistance. Kalis and Fazak and their Elite Guards won't know where to mount a defence."

He made it sound so easy. So painless. So swift. I knew it would be none of those things. As Kalon moved on to discuss the logistics of moving everyone up Death River to Falls Camp, I looked around, trying to commit the faces, voices, and smells of everyone present to memory. Even without the Vision Dru had had, I was sure they would not all survive the battle – was not sure that I would – but in the hope that I might, I thought it important that someone should remember the drax at that meeting, and tell their tale some day.

Nineteen

For the second time in a cycle, I flew upriver. It took half a day for the wingless to paddle upstream to the tongue of land where we had first landed, exhausted and soaked, after our encounter with the rapids. Their floats were left for the river to take, for none of us intended or expected to return. New floats, sleeker, lighter, with shaped paddles and detachable posts for wind-catchers, waited on the banks of the river upstream from the gorge.

Flyers guided vlydhs laden with packs of hide-wrapped weapons and panniers of food. The zaxel, surprising us with a tentative melt sprouting, had been cut, and its small red cobs pulled from the ground. Avalox, chalkmoss, and kerzh-grass had been bundled into jars and bags to add flavour to the fish stews the river would provide, the stubble and stalks and melt shoots left to grow wild.

I had waited for the last floats to set off from the lake, while I circled on a warm northerly and looked back at the place that had been our home for an entire cycle. How long, I wondered, before the rough vinewood dwellings rotted? There was still smoke climbing from a few of the chimneys, and for a beat I worried that the untended hearths might spark a fire. Then I realised it didn't matter. We would be alive and living on the Expanse, or we would be dead – or worse. Whatever happened on the *Spirax* plateau, we would never see, never need, those dwellings again.

I spiralled a paw across my tunic as I bade the lake and its islands farewell. It had been good to us, this place, a Spiral-sent refuge at the end of a terrible journey. Here we had rested, remembered our lost friends, rebuilt our shattered lives. It was not home, it would never be home, but it had been a haven, a place I would always remember with gratitude.

With a last glance north, to where the Crimson Forest resumed its march to a distant sea, I'd turned and headed upriver.

It took another day for the wingless to make their way through the scrubby vines that lined the tops of the canyon cliffs. Their legs and purple tunics were coated with fine red dust from the dry soil they'd bounded through, and as they reached the riverbank campsite beyond the gorge, some of them took the opportunity to put their feet in the water and wash.

Those of us on the wing had already prepared the camp, on a bend near the towering walls where we had first been swept into the rapids a cycle ago. Thanks to all the vine-cutting and float-making, the vineline had been pushed back for spans in a great semi-circle, and there was room enough for everyone on the stump-strewn ground. Over ninety new floats were tethered side-on to the bank, bobbing on the current in three neat rows. The poles for the wind-catchers were stored in the bottom of each float, while the wind-catchers themselves doubled as blankets. As the sun plunged toward the western horizon and a bank of cloud smothered the remaining daylight, we lit the campfires, and a line of protective flames set at the edge of the Forest. Damp tunics, washed in the river along with the dusty wingless, steamed on poles, and we didn't want for food, as the first to arrive had busied themselves fishing once they'd deposited their carry-pouches and set the kindling.

Kalon, who had journeyed by vlydh and pronounced himself pleased with the ride, found a vine-stump at the top of a small rise, stood on it, and roared for attention: "Remember," he barked, when all had fallen silent, "from here on, there will not be enough clear land between the river and the Forest for all of us to camp together. We travel from here in the three groups Varel has organised, and rendezvous at the Falls a nineday from now."

I had asked Taral if I might travel with his troops, though I was not sure that I would be able to offer much assistance in a battle. "I'm a terrible shot," I said, "and I'm not sure I can actually bring myself to thrust a spear at a fellow-Drax – unless perhaps it's Fazak."

"You are Fate-seer, Zarda," he'd said. "To have you flying with us will be an honour and a blessing."

So I flew upriver with the guardflight, and the armed females selected to fly with us. Shaya and Jotto would fly at the wingtips of Kalon's vlydh, while Dru of course led those in the floats, their wind-catchers unfurled to catch the breeze, which blew helpfully from the north. Cavel was with him, his float tucked in right behind Dru's. There was Ellet, steering her float in their wake with a sure touch. I recognised Chiva, Nixel, Oztin, and Dugaz. I saw Ravar, Shaya's pup, leaning forward in his float as it glided upstream. So many young wingless, all looking determined, confident.

I thought of Dru's Vision of the battle to come – blood, howls, confusion – and of the lie he had told when Jotto asked him if he Saw who was winning. I'd confronted him about it after the council meeting, when he and I were safely in my dwelling, out of earshot of anyone else. "You did See who won, didn't you?" I'd asked.

And then was sorry I'd done so, when Dru replied: "I Saw Kalon. He was dying."

I'd had to take a few beats to think about what that might mean, and had remembered the Vision I'd had when the float tipped over: my broken spear, the Elite Guard, the hopelessness. But.... "That doesn't mean we'll lose the battle, Dru," I'd said, eventually, "only that Kalon will fall."

But as we left the wingless and their floats behind on the twisting river, and flew a straight course southward, it was difficult to be positive when Taral called, "Do you truly think this plan will succeed, Zarda? Have you Seen anything that will help?"

Telling Taral about Dru's Vision, or mine, would hardly boost morale. Instead, I said: "Hold on to the Vision of Dru, Taral, the one that Vizan and Dru and I have all Seen. He will survive to defeat the Koth, and plenty of guardflight with him – I know a red tunic when I See one."

Perhaps, I thought, I might even be able to go to the Dream-cave when this battle for the *Spirax* was over, and summon the Vision again. I had not Seen it since I last visited the cave, over a cycle ago, and it was not as clear in my head as it used to be. Had that truly been me with Dru at the top of the mountain? How did that reconcile with what looked like certain death for me at the hands of an Elite Guard?

I would stay close to Taral, I decided, as I watched the muscles in his shoulders move his broad wings with long, powerful strokes. If anyone could keep me safe to see my Vision come to pass, it was Taral.

Just so long, I whispered to the Spiral, as my survival was not at the cost of his own.

"No-one flies from Falls Camp tonight." Kalon stood on one of the rocks in the middle of the pool at the base of the falls, both arms and his single wing spread as he roared his message over the noise of the water. Looking up at the lights of the Spiral, already visible in an unblemished sky as the sun dipped toward the mountains, he spiralled his paw over his tunic. "The Spiral and the moon make it nearly as bright as day, and we can't risk anyone being seen."

The arrival of Kalon on his vlydh, and the flyers accompanying him, had completed our numbers that after-zenith. The clear ground at the foot of the Falls, that had seemed so wide and empty when I had first seen it, was now crowded with drax on both banks of the river. Taral, Shaya, and Jotto had conferred with Kalon, and agreed that it was safe to light our campfires, but for those travelling on foot to the Ambit, this would be the last night they would have hot food till...

Till after.

The guardflight had spent the after-zenith cutting thin vines and sharpening them. Once the wingless had rested from their journey, the guards showed them how to angle the stakes into the ground, to provide some defence against Forest creatures while they camped along the newly-cut pathway to the Ambit.

I'd flown above the path the previous night – a narrow strip of ground that smelled of cut vinewood and trampled mulch, it wound over hills and valleys like a dry river. With barely enough wing-clearance for a flyer to skim down and land, it would hardly be the safest part of the journey for the grounders, and I was glad that I would not have to rely on a sharpened stick and nightly lookouts for the next part of my journey. Still, compared with the conditions we had stumbled through on our journey to Death River, the cut pathway would be an easy stroll, Spiral willing. The guardflight and hunters who had been tasked with carrying the floats from the Falls to the Ambit were the ones I didn't envy. Special harnesses had been fashioned for the task, and each load would be shared by two flyers, but still, it seemed a long way to fly with such a burden.

A single glump surfaced at the edge of the pool, croaked with alarm at the sight of so many possible predators, and plopped back into the water. Even over the crash of the falls, I could hear the vlydh, tethered to a couple of spindly orenvines on the eastern bank, munching happily on the snack that the leaves provided, while along both banks of the river, floats bobbed and danced in tethered lines. The tumbling water a few spans from where I stood next to Kalon provided a constant drum-roll against which the hum of conversation ebbed and flowed, but nothing could disguise the overwhelming smell of apprehension that emanated from every drax. Except for the guardflight, a mere pawful of these drax had thrown a spear in anger, or fired an arrow at anything other than a target. Those who had done so had been aiming at Forest creatures: serpents, creepers, spiny slugs, gumalix.

And of the guardflight we had with us, only Taral, Jisco, and Veret had ever killed another Drax, and that had been a very small skirmish indeed. Internal conflicts on the scale we were about to attempt were the stuff of a history so old it was practically legend. Yet, just a few ninedays hence, we would all be expected to fight, and to kill.

I raised my snout and tested the air again. There was no doubt here, no-one questioning that we were doing what we must. But the fear was tangible, not just in the smell, but in the careful way everyone moved, the quiet murmurs. The silences.

"We should perform the ancient pre-battle ritual, Lord," I said, pulling my attention back to Kalon. "It's a perfect night for it, and it will help calm everyone's nerves to know that the Spiral has blessed our endeavours."

Kalon folded his arms and gave me a questioning look. "Do you know it?"

I pulled a torn and rather crumpled leaf from my tunic – one of the many notes I had stuffed into my carry-pouch before leaving the plateau so many moons ago. "Vizan wrote it down," I said. "I've learned the incantation. Getting the moves right on the ground might be a bit of a challenge, but I think we can do it. In fact, I think we must – and before we split up again."

It took some time but, with a little jostling and careful aerial direction, we managed to get the three battle-groups each formed up in a tight spiral, spread over the moss and rocks on the eastern side of the river. With the carry-pouches stacked in the floats out of the way, there was just enough room for the ritual manoeuvres, which were carefully explained and, with the guardflight's help, rehearsed.

The waning moon was setting by the time I judged us ready, and some of the younger drax kept sitting down near the edge of the river to take a little doze, but at Kalon's word everyone moved into position on the western bank. When I was sure they had formed the necessary three tight spirals, with the leaders at the outermost edges, I took off, taking care to hover below the vinetops. As I began to chant, the drax beneath me moved together, twisting and blending with scarcely a wrong move, till they had re-formed into one large spiral, to represent the unity of the groups.

Once the moves were complete, I took a quick glance at my notes, and spoke the final invocation as I flew low over the tightly-wound ranks. Taral held the centre, his black mane a half-head higher than the drax around him. Shaya's pale fur stood out even with my night-vision, while Dru's white mane and cream tunic made him as visible as Kalon, whose white tunic marked the outermost edge of the spiral.

There was so little space left, with everyone on the same bank, that I had to land with my feet in the pool. "It is done!" I called, trying to ignore the pain that shot up my legs from the chill of the water, "The Spiral hears our prayers. The lights—"

I looked up as I spoke and what I saw shocked me so much that I toppled backward into the water. I sat on slime-covered rock, up to my waist in water, too amazed to heed the cold as I pointed a shaking finger skyward.

"The lights have sent us a sign."

I heard the awe in my voice echoed a ninetyfold as everyone looked up. At the edge of the Spiral, blazing in the sky to the south-east, one of the lights had exploded to a dazzling blue-white. It was brighter than the tierce moon, and I felt my heart flare with it. I was shivering as I stood up, my feet were numb, and shooting pains climbed my legs, but none of that mattered. We had a sign, a clear, bright, beautiful signal that our mission was blessed.

Kalon himself helped to pull me out of the water and handed me a blanket. "I doubted you, Fate-seer, after the Night of the Two Moons. But this!" He swept an arm upward toward the brilliant light near the Spiral's edge. "You have true power, Zarda, the Spiral listens when you chant." He lowered his arm to clap me on the shoulder, almost pitching me back into the water, and raised his voice so that everyone could hear his next words. "If Zarda is with us, Kalis and his Elite Guards have no hope! Tomorrow night, I will lead the wingless on the first steps of our path toward Drax territory, and let no-one here doubt that we have the right to take it. The Spiral itself lights our way!"

Twenty

The caves where I sheltered with Taral, the guardflight, and the ninety others who had flown alongside us were damp and cold, and smelled of unwashed fur. Wrapped in my blanket, with my head on my carry-pouch, I struggled to get comfortable on the unyielding rock floor, while a steady dripping noise, somewhere toward the back of the cave, provided a constant irritation. I tried flattening my ears against it, but the taps continued, faint but relentless.

Giving up on trying to sleep, I opened one eye and looked out past the cave entrance to the sunlit view beyond.

From where I lay, the peaks to the north hid the *Spirax* peninsula – and hid us from those who occupied it – but a dip between two of the mountains allowed a glimpse of the Expanse's southern bay. The Hollow Crag where Fazak watched over the record leaves was, like the *Spirax,* hidden from view, but just knowing it was all so close made me feel warm – then cold as I realised how far away we still were.

At least our luck had held so far. Truly, the Spiral had heard my incantation that night by the Falls. Our transfer of floats, supplies and arms to the Ambit had gone without a hitch. The wingless and grounded had reached the Ambit without losing anyone to Forest predators, and our own flight to the orengrove on the Ambit's southern bank had been blessed with a dark, clouded night that hid even the Spiral's new light. When the clouds rolled away, the white glow to the south-east was visible even at zenith. By night, it still outshone the moon, and we had been forced to spend a second night in the orengrove, our space limited, our food cold. I detested having to wait there – the place held such bittersweet memories: my juvenile adventure with Doran, my arrest by Murgo, and rescue by Taral. Rolling dead bodies into the clinging, stinking Deadlands marsh.

I'd smelled Taral's distaste too, read discomfort in the postures of Jisco and Veret who had fired their own arrows, killed their own targets that night. I'm sure they were all as relieved as me when the clouds brought darkness and showers of rain on the third night.

After that, the weather had favoured us. Heavy rain had swept in from the mountains on our second day in the Copper Hills, and at nightfall Taral had led us over the hills beyond Paw Lake, turning east with the Far-river and matching its course toward the coast.

"Won't the guardflight patrol this far south?" I'd asked, as I'd moved alongside Taral and matched my wingbeats to his.

"Not this side of the hills. Not after dark," he said, and I'd remembered the Koth and their wicked curved blades, and shuddered.

As for the Koth, perhaps they didn't see us, or perhaps they decided there were too many of us to tackle – they were, after all, cowardly creatures who preyed on isolated farms and lone Drax for the most part – but we reached the Guardflight's training caves without incident after a long night of unbroken flight. My wings hadn't been so exercised since I'd flown with Taral to check the ice on the Manybend, and my shoulders had ached as I'd touched down outside the cave-mouth to find a space inside the entrance of the cavern for my blanket and carry-pouch. The cave itself was huge, its ceiling too high to see even with night-vision, and twisting tunnels and passages at the back led through the mountain to other, smaller, caves. Strange cone-shaped rocks hung overhead and protruded from the floor, some of them joining midway to form columns that appeared to be holding up the roof. It was a damp, cold, dark place to wait, but it was safe, there was fresh water nearby, and there was room for all of us inside.

I had been so tired that I hadn't even bothered to eat, and sleep had come easily for a while. When I'd woken it was after zenith, and everyone had spent the remaining daylight hours sharpening spears, knives, and claws, testing bow-strings, and discussing the plans for the attack in low murmurs. The next day had passed in similar fashion, and a third. But today was different. The coming night was moon-end, and it was the realisation that this would likely be the last sunlight, the last day, for nines of Drax that allowed me no sleep. The dripping water, the uncomfortable ground, were incidental. I wondered and worried about Dru's group of wingless on the far side of the Ambit peninsula, and Kalon's group, who should be in the Copper Hills by now in readiness for their dawn flight over the Expanse. There was so much that might have already gone wrong…but no, the Spiral had sent the sign. Surely we would prevail?

I sighed and sat up.

No-one else seemed to have had difficulty in drifting off. Apart from that nerve-stretching drip of water, all I could hear were the deep, sighing breaths of drax in slumber.

The one exception was Taral. His blanket lay rolled up next to my uncomfortable resting-space, his carry-pouch and weapons neatly stacked against the cave wall.

Giving up on sleep, I stood up, stretched, and went outside to find him. The rain that had masked our wingbeats three nights ago, and persisted through the next two days, had finally stopped, leaving behind the smell of soaked moss and damp earth. Clouds still hung heavy over the mountains to the west, but the steady breeze from the ocean was pushing them back from the coast and allowing a few rays of morning sun to dodge through them. I'd left my blanket in the cave, and regretted it in the cool shade cast by the peak to the east, which sat between us and the sea. But to glimpse the Expanse again, even under such circumstances, lifted my spirits.

"Up here."

I turned at Taral's quiet call, and saw him perched on a rocky ledge that jutted from the side of the mountain, just above the cave mouth. It was a short flap to join him and, as I settled myself beside him, he said, "This time tomorrow, we'll be on the *Spirax* plateau."

From the higher vantage point, it was possible to see a little more of the southern bay. I could even see a couple of fishers skimming the water, their net held between them, and wondered whether anyone on the Expanse would see their catch. Did the drax there have enough goods to trade for even a solitary sea-fish now? "I keep going over it all in my head." There was a patch of lichen under my right paw and I scratched at it with a claw, dislodging tiny clumps and releasing a faint, tangy smell. "I keep thinking of everything that might go wrong."

"Have you Seen—?"

"No." I barked out the single word too sharply, too quickly. A glance, a sniff told me Taral didn't believe me, and I waved a paw to dismiss his concerns. "Nothing of use," I amended. No point in telling him about my Vision of the Elite Guard raising a spear to strike at me. It had no bearing on strategy or tactics, and concerned no-one but me.

The set of his ears told me Taral was still sceptical, and I expected him to press me further. But, after a beat or two, he said instead, "You know, you don't have to fly with us, Zarda. You don't have to carry a spear or bite anyone. You're a Fate-seer – our Fate-seer. You should stay out of harm's way till the fight's over."

My whiskers twitched at the memory of young Nixel saying something similar, moons ago, during one of our training sessions. How easy it would have been then, to retire gracefully from the coming fight, to hide behind my black tunic and wait till the battle was done.

How easy it would be now. But… "Taral, I'd like nothing better than to stay out of harm's way and wait it out. The Spiral knows I'm hopeless with a bow and clumsy with a spear. But this is my battle too." My ears and hackles rose as I remembered all the injustices, the slights, the losses I'd seen and endured. I had friends to avenge, and no-one, not even Taral, would keep me from fighting in their memory. I sighed. "Besides, what sort of message would it send to everyone flying with us if they see their Fate-seer loitering at the back of the formation? Especially after I summoned the Spiral's new light. They'll think I know something terrible is going to happen, and if they believe that, then the battle is half-lost before it even starts."

Taral acknowledged the truth of that with a flick of his ear, and we sat in silence for a few beats, listening to the gurgle of the nearby spring, and breathing in the fresh smell of the damp meadow-moss that cloaked the slopes around us. Raising his head, sniffing the breeze, Taral said, "The wind's changing. Spiral willing, there'll be cloud again tonight."

After zenith, carry-pouches were raided for a cold meal of salted fish patties and dried serpent-meat, washed down with fresh water from the spring. The caves echoed with mutters and murmurs, with a snap here and a bark there as tension thickened and tempers wore thin.

"I hate this waiting." Azmit stood near the cave entrance, nose quivering as she leaned toward the daylight, sniffing for the scents of home. Her slender frame was taut as the bowstring she kept plucking at, and the claws of her toes drummed on the unyielding rock floor. "Give me a hunt any day."

"Even for serpents?" Rewsa, crouched, ears almost flat, pulling at her tail.

"Even for serpents. There's so many things that—" Azmit glanced at Rewsa, stopped whatever she was about to say and said instead, "That we have to remember."

Hariz and Marga, sitting at Azmit's wingtips and securing seatach-bone tips to their arrows, both chimed in to agree, but it was too late. Rewsa wrung her tail, and whimpered, "That's not what you meant. You were going to say how many things might go wrong." Raising her snout and her voice, she howled, "We'll die! We'll all die!"

It had been clear to everyone for moons that our venture was a dangerous one, fraught with difficulty, but it had always been a distant threat, something to worry about in a moon's time, or a nineday, or tomorrow. Now, with 'tomorrow' almost upon us, the difficulties and dangers were crowding everyone's thoughts, and nines of others joined their howls to Rewsa's, their whimpers and cries echoing back through the vast cave system.

A shadow blocked the light at the cave entrance, bringing more squeals and whimpers – and, for those of us close enough to smell it, the odour of anger and annoyance. Taral strode into the cave, wings half-raised, and roared for silence.

He got it. Only that insistent drip of water at the back of the cave could be heard as he stalked through the outer cave, kicking at any weapon or pouch that wasn't dragged out of his path. "I know it is hard to wait and think and worry." He halted in the middle of the damp rock floor, speaking with resolve and authority, turning where he stood to make sure his gaze travelled across every group, every drax. "But howling won't help anyone – and if we all do it, who knows how far the noise might travel? Do you want to bring the Elite Guard this way? Or the Koth?" He took a deep breath, set his ears to reflect a confidence his scent didn't quite match, and went on: "There are very few of us here who have ever shot at another Drax. Let me tell you, it isn't easy – not even when that drax is threatening others, not even when he deserves to die. But we have a good plan here, using a form of attack the Elite will never anticipate, and it has every chance of succeeding – provided we all do what needs to be done." Pacing back toward the cave entrance, he pointed outside in the direction of the *Spirax* peninsula. "Remember what those drax over there have done. Remember what they did to you, to your younglings, and to the friends you lost." Growls and angry barks answered him, and he raised his paws for quiet, dropping them as the mutters died away. "You'll all find the strength to fight tomorrow, and you all know how to use the weapons you have in your paws. We have the Spiral's blessing, we have surprise on our side, we have a Fate-seer – and we have more armed drax than Kalis can dream of." Glaring at Rewsa, he barked, "We will not all die. We will fight, and we will win." A pause. "But if it will help relieve the tension, you can leave the cave in groups of nine to stretch your wings, once it's dark outside."

A flight around to the southern flank of the mountain and back was just what I needed. Once again, I breathed in the scent of the meadow moss, a healing smell that lifted my heart. On the near-vertical face of the mountain to the west, I caught sight of a kervhel with its tiny youngster, both bounding along as though the ground beneath their hooves was level. The distant wash of the ocean carried on a light north-easterly that had, as Taral predicted, brought a shroud of high cloud to cover the lights of the Spiral. Our wingless half-growns would have the blessed cover of darkness as they left the Ambit peninsula and raised their wind-catchers to use the now-favourable wind, steering their floats along the shoreline. The Spiral was clearly still with us.

My brief excursion must have calmed me, because for the rest of that night I slept. Despite the discomfort, the dripping, and the anticipation of battle, I slept dreamlessly and soundly, until Taral shook my shoulder and hissed: "It is time, Zarda. Eat. Be ready."

He moved on along the row of sleeping drax, while I sat up slowly and sniffed the air. The smell of fear was obvious, certainly – I felt it crawling about my own insides – but today it was tempered with anticipation, determination and – faint, but distinctive – with hope.

The cold meat I chewed on that morning seemed tougher and drier than anything I had ever eaten before, but I supposed that was due more to my own mood than to any problem with the meat's preparation. Forcing it down, I got to my feet, rolled up my blanket, and moved out of the cave.

The clouds that had – I hoped – concealed the wingless and their floats as they made their way toward the *Spirax* plateau were beginning to thin and shift. Here and there, the lights of the Spiral shone through – and there was the new light, Vizan's Light as it was becoming known, still brighter than any moon as I stretched my arms and wings and raised my snout skyward to murmur another prayer. As I finished, and spiralled my paw across the front of my tunic, I heard feet brush against the moss behind me, and turned to find Taral approaching.

"May the Spiral protect us," he murmured, spinning his own paw across his tunic – though, as ever, I sensed that he did so

149

more from habit than conviction. To me, he said, "Have you Dreamed at all? Do you sense anything I should know?"

I shook my head. "I had no Dreams, and I have not Seen anything beyond a broken spear and an Elite Guard – and neither of those concerned you." I folded my wings as we both looked toward the bay beyond the mountains, a pool of black, dappled with shimmering reflections where the Spiral's lights shone through broken cloud. "I still remember my Vision of Dru on Cloudsend mountain, celebrating the defeat of the Koth. But when I try to bring it into focus, to See who else is with him and how he reaches it, I get no more than an aching head." I turned to look at Taral. "I can't tell you if you'll survive today's battle. But I don't need Visions to know that you will fight well, and fight honourably." I bent my head, felt him touch his forehead to mine in a gesture of friendship that was given to very few. "May the Spiral watch you and keep you," I said.

He straightened, and tugged at his tunic, smoothing its overnight creases. "Be safe, Zarda," he said. "If the Spiral wills it, I will see you in the Audience Chamber of the *Spirax* before zenith."

I dipped an ear, and took another glance up at the Spiral. "Let it be so."

Twenty-One

As the eastern horizon began to shade to a paler grey, we took to the skies in nines. It was too early even for the Fishers to be out, and our wingbeats sounded loud in a clear sky. Only a couple of floaters, glowing in the clouds to the west, shared the breeze with us as we formed up into three sections and headed toward the *Spirax*. Jisco took three nines to fly low over the clusters near the river, skimming over the chimneys to howl: "Kalon has returned! Join him! Come and fight the Elite with us!"

Veret and three more nines took the upper winds, flying above and behind Taral's vanguard, which was formed of the best archers and four nines of the best spear-throwers.

I flew behind and to the left of Taral, catching the air currents his wings disturbed, feeling them ripple beneath my wings as they bore me up and onward, hearing the snap of my own wings as I sent the airstream on to the flyer behind.

Once over the peaks that had kept us so well hidden, there was nothing between us and the *Spirax* peninsula, save the south-eastern edge of the Expanse and the curving shoreline of the southern bay. I glanced east toward the Hollow Crag, the squat hump of rock in the bay where the Record Keeper maintained every note, every leaf, every scratching in the Drax archive. It was in there that Fazak had found the ancient shell that had proved the Night of the Two Moons ceremony had been carried out incorrectly for generations. That had been the excuse Kalis had needed to banish the wingless and their dams. Now the Spiral was with us, with Kalon, and we had returned to reclaim our lives, our dwellings, our destiny.

Ahead of us, at the end of an undulating, mossy peninsula, the *Spirax* plateau squatted like some vast black creature. The sheer sides of the massif, which fell away into the ocean at their easternmost point, looked to be much higher than anything the wingless had climbed before. Even the Tusk, which Dru and Cavel had scaled when they were just a few moons old, had not been as tough a proposition as the black cliffs of the plateau. Could the wingless really get to the top using nothing but paws, toes, claws, and the strength of their limbs? Or would they tire, retreat, fall?

I wanted to be flying near them, net in paws; I wanted to turn tail and flap back to the cave.

I wanted this to all be over.

I flew on, my right paw aching from gripping my spear too tightly, my carry-pouch heavy with nets and ropes. The wind was carrying the sound of our wingbeats away from the *Spirax*, but surely it would not be long now before someone heard us?

No-one spoke. Save for catching occasional snatches of Jisco's howling chorus below and behind us, I could hear only our wingbeats and the hiss of the ocean on the shore. Lights showed through the see-shells of the Fishers' clusters, and one or two torches on the plateau behind the *Spirax* marked where the early risers were already about their work. I scented 'home' – the sea, the rocks, the plants near the shore, the moss on the plateau – and had to swallow back a heartfelt howl.

The sun peeked over the horizon to our right, and I blinked from night-vision to normal vision in the haze of a purple dawn.

Abruptly, the lights on the plateau went out, and figures in maroon tunics began to run about, some of them pointing in our direction. They'd heard us, and now they were hurrying to rouse reinforcements from inside the *Spirax*. We were still too distant to make out individuals, but it was clear from the way they moved that many of them were carrying bows or spears.

"There are so many of them!" I counted three nines, four – and still more maroon-clad drax emerged from the *Spirax*'s eastern entrance to deploy across the plateau where the nine Council dwellings lay. How many Elite had Fazak recruited?

How many had joined the ranks simply to get enough food, and how many would be willing to shoot us out of the sky?

"They've seen us!" Manel was on Taral's other wing, and she nocked an arrow into her bow as she called.

"Probably heard us coming, as we anticipated," he called back, "but I don't think they've seen the wingless!"

He pointed, and I caught a flicker of movement on the vertical rockface below the flat summit of the plateau. Here and there, I saw shadows moving from rock to rock, powering upward with the speed and sureness of the kervhels I'd seen the previous night.

"We must make sure we keep the Elites' attention on us!" Taral barked. "Archers – ready! Fire high, make sure you don't hit the wingless. Loose!"

With the wind in our snouts, we were too far away for the first volley of arrows to reach the plateau, but they had the desired effect of ensuring the Guards kept their gaze skyward.

Close enough now to pick out individual snouts, I snarled as I recognised Difel, one of the Elite who had been with Murgo on the day they shot down our unarmed females. He was barking orders at a nine of maroon-clad drax who were still fastening tunic straps and stringing bows as they stumbled out of the *Spirax* entrance. Beyond them, on the northern side of the plateau, Elite Guards were lining up to take off into the breeze, and Taral urged us to fly faster. "Quickly! Before they can fly too high! We must maintain the advantage of height!"

It was then that the first of Dru's wingless climbers reached the top of the plateau. Ravar, Cavel, Nixel, and then Dru himself pulled themselves over the lip of the plateau, and Ellet's white-striped snout appeared over the edge on the far side, alongside Dugaz' bushy grey mane and Chiva's russet ears. Below us, figures in maroon tunics who, a moment before, had been flapping their wings to take off, suddenly halted as purple-clad strangers appeared in their path. A few tried to veer away, but the wingless had the advantage of surprise.

Nets were flung, throwing-nets Chiva had devised with weights at the corners and along the edges. They appeared to hover like floaters for a beat or two before descending over the heads and wings of the Elite nearest the cliff edge. As we drew closer, shrill howls carried to my ears from some of those struggling in the nets.

"They've got their attention!" cried Taral, and I saw that the Elite's ranks of archers were in disarray – no longer looking upward to gauge the best moment to loose their arrows, but looking around to see where the attack had come from. "Descend!" Taral ordered. "Loose arrows as soon as you are in range! Take those in the centre of the plateau, make sure you don't hit one of our own!"

I dipped a wing and angled my tail to begin my downward glide. Taral was already below me, his wings angled back as he hurtled downward in a stoop I regarded as 'reckless' at best, and 'suicidal' at worst. The entire formation dived after him, wings set back, bows drawn, spears ready.

Already some of the Elite were rushing for the cover of the nine council dwellings that spiralled around the centre of the plateau; others scuttled back toward the entrance of the *Spirax,* getting in the way of reinforcements who were trying to get out. A few were attempting to regroup, pointing about or loosing arrows in our general direction. Their shots fell short, plummeting off the plateau before they so much as grazed our tunics, but we were firing downward. Our shots had greater range, greater impact, and as another volley was loosed toward the Elite, maroon tunics fell all over the red moss of the plateau.

They began to retreat, backing toward the western side of the plateau and the base of the *Spirax,* but as they did so they were met with another volley of arrows, this time from Veret's nines, who sent up howls as they plunged from the sky.

I landed on the plateau's eastern edge. A span to my right, Cavel was struggling to hold two of the Elite in a single well-thrown net, and I dropped my spear and dumped my carry-pouch next to it, tugging at the straps to pull out a bundle of cord.

The two netted Guards stormed and cursed, jaws snapping. They reeked of anger and hate as they savaged the net with unsheathed claws, trying to scratch and bite. In the absence of other weapons, they hurled insults – fur-curling curses, terrible names for the wingless – twisting and kicking as they strove to free themselves. Azmit the hunter fluttered down beside me, and she helped Cavel wrap the rope around the net, and around their legs.

"Push them over," Azmit barked at Cavel. She jabbed at the netted guards with the blunt end of her spear as she spoke, and they toppled over as they tried to dodge the blows. "Two down," she crowed, stepping on the swearing guards as she turned her spear and ran at an unnetted Elite who was nocking an arrow.

I barely had time to give Cavel a nod of acknowledgement before he too bounded off to find someone else to fight, and I looked about to see what else I might do to assist.

All around me, Elite struggled and cursed in tightly-bound nets. As they were overpowered, so the smell of hatred was replaced with the odour of distress and frustration – and the coppery smell of blood. Everywhere I looked, drax in purple tunics were striding about, prodding an Elite here, sparring with one there. There were shouts, howls, whimpers of pain, screams of agony, all competing with the rasp of flying arrows and the crack of spearshaft on spearshaft.

I caught sight of Dru amid the melee. He was fighting paw to paw with a burly male whose dark fur and mane seemed familiar. With a shock I recognised his opponent as Hazul, the nest-mate of Dabri, the gatherer who had betrayed me to Murgo. He was bigger but Dru was quicker, and he leaped in, bit hard, then leaped away while Hazul growled and snapped, and swished a mighty paw at empty air. Ravar jumped on Hazul's back and slashed at his wings with a knife, gripping his mane as the bigger male spun and howled, lifting his head, exposing the throat.

It was all the invitation Dru needed, and as he closed for the kill, the wingless behind him sent up a howl of triumph.

"Zarda!"

I jerked round at Taral's warning cry, found a snarling female in maroon bounding towards me, spear raised. I looked around for the spear I'd dropped, saw the shaft protruding from beneath the two Elite that Azmit and Cavel had pushed over, and knelt to snatch it up. It snapped in two as I lifted it, the point and half the shaft crushed beneath the weight of the netted Guards.

The female was still pounding toward me, wings raised in challenge, teeth bared, spear poised to throw at me.

It was my Vision – and it was surely my end.

Twenty-Two

Still on my knees, half a useless spear in my paw, all I saw were bared teeth and unsheathed claws, all I smelled was hatred – and my own terror as the female Elite Guard bore down on me, spear raised for a killing thrust.

It never came.

She crumpled, eyes wide with surprise, as an arrow embedded itself in her throat, and I gagged on the smell as blood spattered my tunic. I looked up to see Taral soar over my head, nocking another arrow.

"Look to yourself, Zarda!" he called. "Never mind watching the others!"

It was fortunate for me that Taral had not been following his own advice, but I would have to save my thanks for later – more Elite were emerging from the *Spirax*, and in any case Taral was already too far away to hear me above the shouts, howls, and clatter of wings that assailed my ears.

Picking up the spear that the dead female had dropped, I began to move, dodging nets and bodies on the ground, holding the weapon ready as we had all been taught, ready to throw or thrust. To my right, on the northern edge of the plateau, Veret's drax were landing, the crash of spear-staves replacing the noise of their wing-beats as they joined the wingless in pushing the Elite back toward the *Spirax*.

A large black-maned male rushed toward me, wings extended, fangs bared. There was no time to think, to concern myself with consequences: I could only react. Dropping to one knee, as I had learned to do from the wingless, I had the advantage – the Elite had not worked out how to adjust to this strange method of combat. My adversary came straight on, his wings catching the breeze as he snapped his jaws where my snout should have been, had I fought in a more traditional way. But I was below him, thrusting my spear upward, and its point ripped into his side, spilling blood and hitting bone.

He fell, wings crumpling, and I tugged the spear free, accidentally banging the butt end hard into the jaw of another Elite Guard and knocking him cold. I moved on, my ears flicking around instinctively, though there was too much noise to make sense of where danger might appear next. There was no-one ahead of me, and I glanced upward, saw females clad in purple, and the red tunics of Taral's and Veret's troops.

We had gained the sky, and were gaining the plateau, as more and more Elite fell back toward the *Spirax*. Taral landed beside me, breathing hard, his upper arm smeared with drying blood. "Kalon is coming," he said. "Listen."

I turned my ears to the south, where we had left Jisco and his nines to gather support, and twisted one west, where our view was hidden by the black bulk of the *Spirax*, which shone purple in a shaft of early sunlight. Floating to us on the breeze, faint but unmistakeable, was the sound of cheering, of nineties of wingbeats – and the sweet, clear notes of *spirorns*.

The fight went out of the remaining Elite. As Kalon landed his vlydh on the eastern edge of the plateau and dismounted, a great howl of triumph erupted from every purple-clad drax, and every drax from the Expanse who had answered the calls of our non-combatants.

Kalon planted his banner in the plateau's thin soil and held it as it unfurled in the breeze. It was a magnificent piece of work, completed by the weavers and dyers just a few days before we'd set off from the lake. A single black wing, stark against a purple background, the design was a unique, simple representation of Kalon in cloth.

Handing the banner to Galio, who had landed just behind him, Kalon roared his thanks, and began to make his way across the plateau, paws and ears raised in gratitude and celebration. Jotto and Manel moved through the crowds to flank him, spears in paws, and the nines in front of him shuffled and shifted to form a curving path that led to the *Spirax* entrance. Some of the wingless dragged netted Elite out of the way of the crowd and left them on the spiralling pathway that wound between the nine council dwellings. The Fate-seer's dwelling – my dwelling – had been in the middle of the little cluster. Who lived there now? Was it even occupied?

As the overnight clouds fled with the dawn, nines of hovering flyers produced flickering shadows all across the plateau. I found myself outside the outermost dwelling, the one that had been Fazak's. Its door hung open, and a quick sniff – gag-sweet avalox, trampled zaxel stems, a musty nest – told me he was not inside. Perhaps it was just as well. The spear in my paw shook as I imagined what I would have done to him if I'd found him there…but no, running him through would be too merciful, too quick.

Shouts from overhead ripped my thoughts from vengeance, and I glanced up to see Jisco and Veret rallying other guardflight to encourage the airborne crowd to fly a little higher. On the ground, young Tonil dashed past me to greet her sire and dam, her spear bloodied, Taral fluttered up to the top of Fazak's dwelling, nursing his arm, and Dru picked his way over the fallen to wait with me for Kalon to pass by.

A chant started somewhere above me, growing louder as it spread through grounded and flyers alike. It took me a few beats to realise what they were chanting. Then, as I understood, I set my wings and ears in acclamation and joined in, hearing Taral's voice roar over my left ear as he too began to bark:

"One-Wing! One-Wing!"

As he passed me, Kalon looked as though he could have been borne aloft by the cheers. He looked and smelled more than triumphant: he was excited, pleased…

No. He was *happy*.

"Join me, Dru," he rumbled, magnanimous, as the half-grown bowed respectfully. "The wingless have proved their worth – this is your victory too."

As Dru and I stepped forward to join the procession, and Taral flapped down behind us, Kalon pressed on toward the *Spirax*, paws waving left and right to acknowledge the chants and the cheers as he moved closer to his goal.

He was still several spans away from the yawning entrance when a white-maned figure in a white tunic emerged from it to stand at the base of the *Spirax*: Kalis. As the cheers and howls died away, I stepped to one side and raised my snout to peer over Jotto's shoulder. The red crystals in the Prime's badge-of-office glittered at Kalis' throat as he raised his snout, baring his teeth in a snarl of defiance.

"I should have slashed your throat, not your wing."

As gasps of shock travelled through the sky and across the plateau, and murmurings from the crowd relayed his words to those who hadn't heard them, Kalis strutted toward his shell-brother. He looked well-groomed and well-fed, though somehow he seemed smaller than I remembered. His ears were rigid with anger, and he made no move to bow or kneel, but even so, with his head lowered and his wings folded, he didn't look like a drax who was about to rally his forces and continue the fight.

Accompanied by the clatter of wingbeats from those hovering overhead, Kalon extended his remaining wing, and raised his voice: "The Spiral saw your betrayal, brother, and sent the Sickness to punish you, while I found food and shelter in a haven far to the north. You blamed the wingless for your troubles and banished them, but I would never have overcome your Elite Guards without them. The *Spirax* is mine, Kalis." He gestured around, indicating the nineties at his wingtip. "I was first out of the egg. I have the drax with me – the drax you banished, punished, neglected, intimidated, and starved. I am Prime here, and that tunic, that badge-of-office, are mine."

Calls and howls of support resounded across the plateau as he held out a paw for the badge, and stepped forward to accept Kalis's surrender.

It never came.

With a roar that could be heard over the rush of sea below and the beat of wings above, Kalis spread his wings in challenge, pulled a knife from his tunic belt, and leaped to stab at Kalon.

Kalon jerked away, the blade slicing his arm as a howl of protest and disapproval rippled through the crowd. Jotto, Manel, and Shaya all started forward, and a twist of my ear told me Taral had spread his wings, but Kalon halted them all with a bark and a wave of his paw. "To the death then, brother," he growled, and drew his own blade from his belt.

If Kalis replied, I didn't hear it – there were barks and yips, wingbeats and scrabbling feet, as everyone jostled for a better view of the fight. As a space cleared around the growling shell-brothers – both in white tunics, both wielding knives, each so like the other that only their manes set them apart – I got a better look at the weapon in Kalis' paw.

It was the Koth blade I had seen on the wall of the Audience Chamber, the day Dru had hatched; the blade I had Seen dripping blood. So this was what my Vision had meant! The knife had not yet finished the deadly work it was fashioned for.

Kalis lashed out with a snarl, and Kalon dodged aside, snarling insults, snapping his teeth. In front of me, Jotto winced and called, "Careful, Lord!", as Kalis extended his wings, flapping wildly as he ran around Kalon in an effort to take off. Kalon slashed at the nearest wing, drawing a howl of fury and pain from Kalis as the membrane tore, forcing him to remain on the ground.

"Now we're equal." Kalon darted to take another swipe at Kalis' damaged wing, twisting away as Kalis lashed out with his own blade. Both were panting with effort as they weaved and dodged, slashed and bit, claws scrabbling on the trampled moss. Kalon landed a bite on Kalis' left shoulder; Kalis lashed out with a foot, raking his claws down Kalon's thigh. They drew apart, circled each other, closed again…and as Kalis brought his knife down, Kalon stumbled and fell.

Howls, barks, whimpers of alarm. A familiar voice calling, "He'll die!"

And Kalon rolled, reached out a paw, tugged at Kalis's left leg, and pulled him to the ground. As Kalis thrashed, howling with shock and pain from the fall, Kalon threw himself on top of him, bit at his throat and stabbed the arm that held the knife. Kalis, gurgling and struggling, dropped the blade and, lifting his head with a roar of triumph, Kalon plunged his own knife into Kalis' chest and twisted it.

"I take back what is mine, brother," he roared.

In the stunned hush, it was Manel who turned to me and hissed: "The rite of succession, Fate-seer, quickly!"

Could I even remember it? I squeezed between Jotto and his nest-mate and hurried across to where Kalon stood over his shell-brother's twitching form – just in time to hear Kalis' last words. They were little more than a growl through gritted fangs, but they were enough to make me stop where I stood and whimper with horror:

"You will not be Prime for long, Kalon. My blade…was poisoned…"

His eyes closed, his tongue lolled, his body stilled. Blood stained the front of his tunic and spilled from his throat.

But at his neck, the badge-of-office sparked as the wingbeats overhead allowed a shaft of sunlight through.

Fur on end, I pulled my gaze from Kalis' still form to Kalon. His ears signalled victory, but his tail swished with alarm as he clutched at the cut on his arm.

"Let me see it, Lord, I may be able to make a poultice…"

But no. The moment I pulled the fur aside and got a good look at the wound, I knew it was hopeless. Kalis must have smeared his blade with rotberry juice, the same cruel poison Murgo had boasted he'd used on his arrows. Kalon's limb was already swollen, the wound and the flesh around it turning black.

Kalon must have read the distress in my posture and the set of my ears, smelled my shock, my regret. "How long?" he said, voice level, his scent exuding disbelief, pain, and something akin to fear.

I shook my head. "The poison is fast, Lord. Even if I had a poultice ready, it would just prolong the pain and delay the inevitable. I'm sorry."

I wasn't sure what I should do – chant the rite? Try to make Kalon comfortable? He was already beyond my help, but perhaps I could ease any pain at least.

"I should have known," he growled. "My brother was ever the coward." Then, raising his head, he called, "Dru! Come!" As the half-grown moved across the trampled space where Kalis's body lay, spiralling a paw across his tunic as he briefly paused to press a paw to his sire's chest, Kalon raised his voice so that as many as possible might hear. "I am poisoned by my shell-brother's blade. My arm is dead already, it will not be long before I follow. You must swear fealty to Dru. He is now the rightful successor."

"Lord!" Varel pushed through the crowd and across the scuffed moss as fast as his limp would allow. "Allow me." He reached out a paw, took Kalon's wounded arm, and gave it a sniff. Ears drooping with sorrow, he shuffled round to stand alongside the bigger drax. He hadn't let go of the arm, though if Kalon leaned a little heavily toward his adviser I thought it prudent not to remark on it.

"Fate-seer, quickly!" Kalon snapped. "The rite…" He winced with pain, but the set of his ears and resolute odour told me he was determined not to succumb to Kalis's poison until the ritual was done.

"I…" I glanced around as I gathered my wits. The crowd was pressing closer, and there was scarcely room to spread my wings. Catching sight of Taral bearing down on the stricken Prime, I called, "Taral, I need to take off."

"Clear a path! Clear a path for the Fate-seer." Taral, cradling his own wounded arm, marched toward the drax on the southern side of the plateau, barking at them till they moved aside or took off and joined the others in the air. Spreading my wings, I took off along the cleared pathway and I glided clear of the hovering crowd to climb a few spans higher. As I turned on the breeze, Kalon was on his knees, next to Kalis' body, Varel standing over him, still clutching his Prime's paw. I felt for the air currents, angled my wings for lift, and spiralled upward, chanting the incantation, asking the Spiral to take both Kalis and Kalon into its care. Then, with a twist and a flick of my tail, I turned to spiral down the opposite way, still chanting, till I landed at Dru's feet and dropped to one knee, folding my wings and bowing my head.

To my left, Kalon crumpled, breath rasping, his collapse slowed by Varel's steadying paws.

Lifting my head, I looked around for a fable-spinner, and saw Swalo being ushered through the crowd by Jotto.

"Kalon the Courageous." As he knelt beside the dying Prime, Swalo's grey ears showed respect and sorrow. Only his swishing tail betrayed his nerves. "Your life will be remembered, your tale will be spun. Prime with one wing, your name will be spoken with gratitude and respect generations hence."

Kalon grunted acknowledgement, sighed...and lay still. My tunic flapped in the breeze, the sea plashed against the base of the plateau and nineties of wingbeats clattered above.

And Dru raised his snout to the sky and began the death-howl.

"Drax! Tomorrow two Primes will be taken to their final nests in the Deadlands." A table had been dragged from the *Spirax* and positioned just outside the capacious entrance as a makeshift platform for Dru. As he roared his message, the cavernous chamber behind him caught his words and reflected them back across the plateau, helping his voice carry further. "Let their deaths mark the end of Drax fighting Drax." He gestured south and west, in the direction of Cloudsend Mountain, blocked from sight by the bulk of the *Spirax*, but ever present in our minds. "We have a greater enemy to conquer." Lowering his arms and setting his ears forward, he looked down at the Elite who had been lined up in front of him. Nines of them were still in nets, others were on their feet clutching minor wounds, and several lay unconscious. At least nine were dead. "The Elite Guard is hereby abolished."

The announcement was greeted with howls of joy, and he waited for them to die away before he raised his paws for silence and went on: "Any Elite wishing to join the Guardflight will be welcome to do so. The rest of you – I believe there are plenty of clusters in need of good drax." He looked around again, his gaze searching, and I realised there was a drax missing: the drax who had been responsible for everything – the persecution of the wingless, their banishment, Kalon's dispossession, the hunger on the Expanse, the deaths of so many.

Taral, a poultice on his wounded arm, and a grim set to his ears, led eight of his guardflight across the moss from where they'd been guarding the Elite. "He's not on the plateau, Lord," he called. "Nor in the Hollow Crag with his archives."

Dru raised his paws again, to still the murmurs that had started up. His fingers curled into fists as he dropped his arms and roared with frustration and anger.

"Where," he thundered, "is Fazak?"

Twenty-Three

"I didn't know there were so many chambers!"

Taral's observation mirrored my own thoughts as we hurried after Dru, who led the way up the *Spirax*'s main passageway. Every few steps, he would stop to open a door, or duck along a side corridor, all the while roaring for Fazak to come out and face him. Behind us, Shaya and eight guardflight clattered up the slope, spears in paws, claws scratching against the rock with a noise like rainfall on stone. Everyone else had been ordered to remain outside, where the rest of the guardflight had begun to prepare the dead for their last nest. Healers, and others who'd learned to mix a poultice or bind a wound, were tending to bites, bleeding, and bruises. As Fate-seer I could have opted to assist with that, but instead I'd lent my carry-pouch and my salves to Hariz.

I had to go with Dru, had to confront Fazak. He'd belittled me, sneered at me, urged Kalis to ignore my advice. The results of his own counsel would be mourned for cycles – and had to be avenged.

"Now we know what happened to all those tithes," I said, a little breathless from trying to keep up with the new Prime. The *Spirax* storerooms were overflowing with grain, beans, berries, fruits, herbs, and dried fish. Chambers which might once have held candles or platters or polishing cloths were now stuffed with grain, zaxel, and salted meat.

Taral shook with rage as we opened yet another door to find the room beyond stuffed with food. "All those drax out on the Expanse, going hungry! Look at it! No wonder so many were opting to join the Elite Guard!"

I nodded, and dipped an acknowledging ear, though my stomachs rumbled as my nose detected the sweet smell of loxcakes. "We'll get it all redistributed," I said, "after we find Fazak and take the dead to their last nests."

Taral slammed the door shut on the enticing smells and hurried to catch up with Dru, who had paused near the top of the main passageway. Snout raised, he sniffed at the corridor to our right, ears upright, listening. "Can you smell that?" he said, as we caught up to him. "Avalox. Remember how Fazak likes to smother his fur in it to mask his scent?"

"Maybe it's just another room full of supplies?" Taral peered cautiously along the passageway, which led off toward the middle of the *Spirax*.

"No." I put out a paw to touch the smooth black wall. "This leads to the Nesting Chamber. Morel took me along here the first time I acted as Fate-seer – the day you hatched, Dru."

"The Nesting Chamber?" Taral spiralled a paw across his tunic. "Spiral forbid that Kalis and Morla already have a hatchling."

"That would complicate things." Shaya's voice, behind us. "Still, there are ways of dealing with unwanted hatchlings."

"Shaya!" Taral, appalled. "Hasn't there been enough of that?"

"Just stating a fact."

"We need to find out first whether there *is* any hatchling." Pulling his knife from his tunic belt, Dru moved cautiously along the passageway, the rest of us following in pairs, filling the width of the corridor. Outside the Nesting Chamber, Fazak's sickly-sweet odour clung to the walls of the passageway, overlaid with a distinct whiff of fear. The door to the chamber was closed and Dru pushed it open, slowly, the hinges creaking as the vinewood shifted. We listened and sniffed, switching to night-vision to peer into the gloom beyond the doorway.

"Nothing," Taral murmured. "But I'll go in first, just in case—"

Dru wasn't listening. Ears alert, eager to confront the drax who had made his life so difficult, he brought his knife up in readiness and stepped into the chamber.

"Dru!" Taral plunged after him, I followed, and Shaya brushed my wingtip as she hurried through the door.

An empty nest. A discarded carry-pouch on the chamber floor, spilling grain from splitting seams. An odour of fright.

A squeal of terror.

For a moment, just for a beat, I thought we'd found him.

But it wasn't Fazak who stood beside the empty nest, whimpering. It was his eldest offspring, Morla, the female who Miyak had nested with after Doran was banished.

Morla who had hatched a proving-egg with Miyak.

At sight of Dru's knife, she held out her paws to show she was unarmed, and backed away till her wings pressed against the rock wall on the far side of the chamber. "Fazak-fa isn't here." Her voice was ragged, ears set flat, and she smelled of panic, rage, and bewilderment. "He waited in the Audience Chamber for Kalis to return. When he got word that the battle was lost, he came here." Her voice rose to a howl. "He's taken the egg!"

"Egg?" Dru stepped forward a pace, but lowered his knife. "What egg?"

"My egg. Kalis' egg." Morla's anger and defiance overcame her anguish, and she glared from Dru to me to Taral and Shaya, then returned her sulky stare to Dru. "Kalis took me as nest-mate two moons ago, he needed...he wanted..."

"He wanted an heir with wings," said Dru. He sheathed his knife but bared his teeth as he stalked across the chamber toward Morla. She cringed away as he snapped his jaws together a whisker from her snout. "Where's Fazak going?"

She shook her head and wrung her paws. "I don't know."

Dru growled and opened his mouth for another snap. Or perhaps an actual bite.

Morla squealed like a wounded gumalix and slid down the wall, paws raised above her head. "Don't bite me, I don't know, he didn't tell me! He said he'd keep it safe till it hatched," she said, words tumbling. "He said he'll return in a moon's time with the true heir."

She shook her head, whiskers quivering with shock and fright, but as Dru closed his teeth and turned away from her, I realised there was only one chamber where Fazak could have gone. As I looked across at Shaya and Taral, I read by the set of their ears that they'd worked it out too.

So had Dru. "To the Audience Chamber," he said, striding past to lead the way again.

I nodded, already turning in my tracks. "He's going to take off from the balcony."

The Audience Chamber had changed little since I had last set foot in it, though the council table I had once sat at had been turned on its side in a desperate effort to impede our progress, and the stools were all upended across the floor. But stems of zaxel were scattered underfoot, just as they had always been, and logs had been set in the great hearth ready to be lit. The slimecrawler shells were still in place along the right-hand wall, their iridescence glowing in the sunlight that poured through the see-shell.

Dru leaped over the table and, by the time everyone else had scuttled around it, he had reached the platform where the throne-stools stood. A heartbeat later, he threw himself to the floor, and I flinched as I saw a knife spin over his head and bury its point in the arm of the Prime's throne-stool.

"Fazak!" Taral charged across the Chamber toward the open balcony door, heedless of the danger of further weapons that Fazak might have.

But it seemed Fazak had been interested only in trying to kill Dru. With the egg he'd taken tucked under one arm, he had already jumped off the balcony by the time Taral reached it and, as I gained the platform, he had spread his wings and was flapping frantically towards the southern mountains.

"Go after him!" Dru shouted, and Taral needed no second bidding. With Shaya close behind him, he followed Fazak off the balcony, barking for his guardflyers, and I was about to follow them when Dru gripped my arm. "No. Fetch a vlydh for me. I want to catch that cracked shell myself."

It didn't take long for me to fly around the *Spirax* to the plateau, where the vlydh who had carried the maimed into battle were munching on well-earned branches of orenvine. I tugged on one harness, then another, snatched away the leaves, dodged snapping mandibles, and finally induced one of them to take off. I don't suppose it took more than a few beats, but by the time I had led it round to the balcony and persuaded it to hover next to the narrow platform, Fazak and his pursuers were already beyond the peninsula and crossing the line of avalox bushes that marked the boundary with the Expanse.

"Throw me the reins!" Dru leaped on to the vlydh, unmindful of the gap between the hovering vlydh and the balcony, or the distance to the ground, and grabbed a knot on the harness to steady himself.

"Be careful, Dru." I tossed the leading-rein into his paws, and within a beat the creature he rode had resumed its flight. "I'll be right behind you." I had no intention of pacing the plateau or the corridors of the *Spirax* while Dru hurled himself after the architect of our misfortunes, but the vlydh had four wings and I had only two. Eight guardflight had answered Taral's bark and were flying close behind their chief and the purple-clad hunter. Dru's vlydh chased hard and began to gain air on them, but flap as I might, I fell behind the chase.

I glanced up to make sure the scattered clouds were free of floaters, and climbed higher, feeling for a favourable wind that would help me fly faster. Finding it, I set my jaw against the ache in my shoulders and flapped on.

"Don't shoot him!" Dru's roar carried faintly against the breeze, but those ahead of him didn't appear to have heard it. The guardflyers had caught up with Taral and Shaya, and flew in a disciplined V formation behind them. Seeing them begin to nock arrows to their bowstrings, Dru leaned forward on his vlydh, as though urging it to fly faster.

Ahead of Taral, the distinctive flash of Fazak's bright green tunic was easy to see. He was heading for the western mountains, it seemed, though whether he had some plan beyond that I couldn't guess. He was beating his wings frantically, but Taral, Shaya, the troop behind them, Dru, even me – we were all gaining on him, and as we drew closer I realised why: Fazak was huge.

His tunic had been so easy to spot because it was almost twice the size of normal outfits. It had to be. He was enormous.

"Grown fat on all those tithes, while he sat around in the *Spirax* spreading his poison," I muttered to myself. As I closed the distance and descended, panting with effort, I heard Dru shout again and this time the guardflight heard him. Taral waved a paw, and the arrows were returned to their pouches, though the formation continued their pursuit. Dru's vlydh caught up with them, and at his shout they moved aside to allow him to overtake, and fly on ahead.

The gap between the vlydh and Fazak narrowed to less than a span.

But what could Dru do without wings of his own?

As Dru guided his vlydh to a position just above and slightly ahead of Fazak, Taral's horrified bark carried to my ears: "Dru – Lord – don't do it! Leave it to us—" He reached out a paw as if to steady Dru or catch him, though he could have done neither, then barked an order to the guardflight behind him: "A net, quickly!"

But already Dru had moved to kneel between the vlydh's front wings, one arm out for balance, the other paw holding the creature's harness, swaying slightly as the wings beat up and down. He clearly wasn't prepared to wait for anyone to unravel a net. On the ground below, the ninety-nine stone dwellings of an artisan cluster were busy with drax in copper tunics. Some were running and flapping, taking off to join the pursuit; others stood on the spiralling pathway between the dwellings, roaring and banging pots or clutching howling hatchlings. If Dru should fall…

I angled my wings back and dived toward him. "Dru, no!" I roared. "You're the Prime now, you can't—"

With a howl that mixed triumph with sheer exhilaration, Dru jumped from the vlydh and, for one heart-stopping moment, plummeted earthward. I saw Taral change course to dive beneath him, presumably in the futile hope of catching him if he missed his target. I took a single deep breath and held it, fur on end, wings juddering as nines of terrible possibilities chased through my mind. The howls from the cluster below increased in pitch; one or two ducked back into their dwellings, hatchlings in arms.

But Dru's leap had been true, and in a beat he had landed squarely on Fazak's broad back.

Something arced away from Fazak; a small purple ovoid something that seemed to hang in the air like a tiny float bobbing on the water.

It fell.

It was the egg, and as it plummeted groundward Fazak howled and plunged after it, as though he might somehow catch it and prevent it smashing on the stones of the dwellings beneath us. Dru held onto his wing-struts just where they joined the shoulders, and Fazak's flight became erratic, jinking from side to side as he struggled to throw Dru off. As the Egg splashed to pieces, scattering shell and liquid across the cluster and drawing squeals of distress from those nearby, Fazak roared with rage and defiance. "I'll fly over the mountains," he shouted, beating his wings faster in a futile attempt to gain height. "I'll tip you off over the highest point I can reach and leave you for the Koth, you freak!"

But Dru simply clung on tighter and his weight, allied with Fazak's own extra bulk, began to force the big drax groundward. Taral and the guardflight were circling down after them, and I set my wings back and followed, all the time spiralling a paw over my tunic in fervent prayer for Dru's safety.

Fazak landed awkwardly on the chalkmoss that lay between the artisan cluster and the traders' cluster to the west. Thudding onto his own shadow with a force that drove him to his knees, he sent Dru tumbling from his shoulders and stumbled on, still flapping his wings in an effort to take off again. Dru roared as he rolled clear, jumped to his feet and bounded after him. Fazak, overweight as he was, began to get airborne, and Taral signalled to the guardflight to be ready with the net they were still unrolling, but, with a leap that no winged drax could have accomplished, Dru grabbed Fazak's trailing right leg and pulled him down.

Fazak kicked and struggled, roared and howled. He used his wings to beat at Dru rather than to fly, but Dru was equal to him. Drawing the knife from his tunic belt, he slashed at Fazak's wings once, twice, three times. The membrane ripped, Fazak yelped with pain and anger, and Dru signalled for the guardflight to descend with their net.

The chase was over.

As I glided down to land, I heard more wingbeats overhead, and looked up to find nines had followed us. Some were in the copper tunics of the artisans we had just flown over, others were in the pale blue of traders, but flying in from the east there were at least three in Elite Guard tunics, a couple of fable-spinners, and several nines of purple-clad drax from Kalon's Lake who I had last seen on the plateau.

Fazak was still struggling and cursing in his net, and I folded my ears against the whine of his high-pitched bleat. Taral put a stop to it by pushing him over, placing a foot on his chest, and bending low to roar: "Be quiet, Fazak, or I swear I'll have your tongue as a snack." He spread his wings in a challenge for good measure, and Fazak took the hint.

"You'll have your chance to speak," Dru assured him, as Taral stepped back and two guardflight hauled Fazak to his feet, "in the Audience Chamber."

There were howls and protests from the hovering crowd. "Kill him now" – "There's plenty of drax died because of him, they got no say" – "I want to see him suffer".

But Dru extended his arms for silence and raised his voice as he issued his orders: "I will not begin my Primacy by behaving like Fazak. He will have his chance to speak, as will those who aided him. Taral, have the guardflight check every cluster, every dwelling. I want Sifan, Hapak, and Broga in nets by nightfall. I want those who shot down our unarmed females identified and captured."

"What about Miyak?" said Taral. "Don't forget he sided with Fazak when it came to that crucial vote."

Dru shifted his gaze to the purple-clad drax who had flown from the plateau, and I guessed that his thoughts were with his wingless friends, and especially Cavel. "Leave Miyak alone," he said. "If we punish every drax who wanted us exiled, there'll be very few left."

Taral bowed, and stepped away to give orders to his guardflight, while I went to stand beside Dru. "That was well done," I said, "but please, Lord, don't ever try jumping from a moving vlydh again – you all but stopped my heart up there!"

He snuffled a little and waggled his ears. "If I'd not been so angry I would never have done it," he said. "All I could think of was catching Fazak – and I had to be the one to do it. I had to prove I could best a large, winged drax, even without wings of my own."

I dipped my ears in acknowledgement. A Prime without wings was unprecedented. Dru was right that he'd had to prove he was worthy. "Your vlydh is still heading for the mountains," I said, pointing west toward the unguided vlydh, which was still diligently flying in the direction it had last been set. "You'd better send someone to fetch it, if you're going to get back to the *Spirax* by sunset!"

A cheer from the hovering crowd made me turn. Fazak, secure in the net, was being lifted skyward by two drax in maroon-and-blue Elite Guard tunics, and two crimson-clad guardflight troops. He reeked of anguish and pain, rage, and fear, but I couldn't find any compassion in my heart for him – he had cost too many lives, ruined others, brought this all on himself.

"What will you do with him?" I said, as the net and its escort circled upward on the breeze.

Dru bared his teeth and set his ears forward, his eyes following the direction of the carry-net and its burden. "I'll do what I must," he said. Then, tilting his head as he used to when he asked a question as a youngling, he met my gaze, and I smelled the hatred and contempt for Fazak that poured from his fur. "Will the Spiral forgive me if I enjoy it?"

174

Twenty-Four

"See to the wounded, Zarda," said Dru, as we reached the plateau and he jumped down from his vlydh. Looking around, it seemed there was little left for me to do: Hariz and the other healers had done a fine job of licking wounds and applying poultices and ointments, though some of the more badly wounded would benefit from an extra tincture or two. The dead had been set side by side at the base of the *Spirax,* and I spiralled a paw across my tunic at the sight of the bodies. Most of them were Elite, but there were purple tunics in among the maroon, and I fought a howl as I recognised the wiry grey form of Azmit, the torn remains of Peren, Winan's sturdy body, and the wingless half-grown Dugaz among the casualties.

Not far from where they lay, Taral stood watching as a group of whooping wingless emptied Fazak's dwelling of all his goods and furniture. Fazak – sitting at Taral's feet, still bundled in the net – whined in protest: "Those leaves are private! Be careful with that, it's valuable! Those tubes contain important records from the Archive, you oaf! What are you doing with my table?"

The table, its elaborate carved legs bearing testament to the level of craftsmanship Fazak had been able to trade for, was set down on the scrubby moss outside the dwelling, and the remainder of Fazak's belongings piled on or beneath it – stools, shells, record tubes, knives and spoons, candles, lamps, pots, beakers, overflowing containers of branmeal and loxcakes, a haunch of meat, blankets, even the logs from his hearth. All were unceremoniously bundled outside.

Taral glanced across, acknowledged Dru with a dip of his head and answered the question I had been about to ask: "We need somewhere to put Fazak till we have time to deal with him," he said. "It won't hurt for him to spend a night or two fretting. His friends can join him in there when my guardflight have found them."

I nodded, satisfied with the idea of Fazak and his anti-wingless cronies kept together under guard in a single dwelling, blaming each other, squabbling among themselves, and worrying about what might await them. I turned my gaze to the nines of wounded drax and the healers scraping the last of their ointments from well-used pots, then looked past them along the spiralling path that led to the dwelling I used to call home.

And I felt tired; so tired, so utterly spent, I doubted I could raise a wingflap if my life depended on it. I had planned and Seen and waited and fought to return home – for all of us to return home – but now I was within sniffing distance of my threshold, and I wasn't sure I had the energy to set foot in it.

Perhaps I was just a little afraid of what I would find there. It had been over a cycle since I left. The Fate-seer's dwelling had surely been reassigned, probably to whoever led the Elite Guard after Murgo's death. There would be nothing in there for me now.

I took a step, hesitated, took another. Halted.

"You have to live somewhere, Zarda," said Dru. He placed a paw on my shoulder, and raised his snout to sniff as he peered along the pathway toward the dwelling at the centre. "That place was the Fate-seer's for generations. It should belong to the Fate-seer again."

"Come on." I turned to find Shaya beside my left wing, a bloodied spear upright in her right paw, ears set to indicate respect and friendship. "I'll give you an escort."

She signalled to Marga, who hurried across to join me on my other wing, and Dru moved away toward the *Spirax*. As I resumed my journey along the path, he startled me with a loud and insistent bark. "Drax – be still. Stop what you're doing. Welcome your Fate-seer home."

I couldn't believe it. From all sides, from the plateau around me and the air above, there were yips of delight, cheers of joy, the odour of relief and thankfulness. Drax in every colour of tunic lined the pathway, squeezing between the dwellings, hovering overhead. I saw young Ellet bouncing with glee, Varel spiralling a paw across his tunic, and Jotto finding space to fly a backward loop. My tail spasmed with embarrassment, but I set my ears in acknowledgement and gratitude, gave a few self-conscious waves to those I knew well, and made my way slowly around the path.

There was a drax in an Elite Guard tunic standing on the entrance-stone.

"I haven't touched your things," he said, "nor did Murgo." He spun a paw across his tunic. "It's Fate-seer's stuff, I didn't want to…in case…well, anyway, I just have a couple of tunics and my own beakers inside." He was nursing a cut on his jaw, pressing a blood-soaked cloth against his face, and I recognised him by the white stripe through his amber mane. It was Bolby, the third drax who had been with Ordek and Murgo moons ago when they'd chased and teased Cavel across the meadows near Paw Lake. He'd rather lost his swagger, I was pleased to see. "I'll move them out once I've had this cut seen to."

I put a paw on the door and pushed. It sagged open. I took a breath, and stepped inside.

Home. I was home. After so many moons, so many terrifying days and nights, so many losses, so many hopes.

Home.

So why did I not feel more excited, more satisfied, content? The dwelling itself was unchanged – the spiralling stone walls, the see-shell, the hearth. The reed screen was the one Vizan had used. A stubborn blob of branmeal still clung to the scrubbed vinewood table, surrounded by scratches where I had tried to pry it loose.

But the smell was wrong. Bolby's scent clung to the nest behind the screen, and maroon tunics hung from the hook behind the door. I had left the Fate-seer's ritual tunic there – where was that now? The herbs that had hung from the shelves and the roofstones had vanished, along with their distinctive aroma.

Moving further inside, I picked my way around Bolby's unemptied waste bucket, trying not to gag on the stench, and reached up to pull down a couple of the baskets that lined the shelves. Canox in the first. Dried zaxel roots in the next. My supplies, untouched.

The jars on the shelf near the hearth were mine too – but their contents weren't. Berrywine, loxcakes, dried fish, avalox, branmeal…so much of it, and all for one self-important young drax. "There's food in here," I called. Shaya's snout appeared round the doorframe, nostrils sniffing, ears upright, and I hefted one of the jars onto the table. "We should check all the dwellings on the plateau – make sure all the food's added to the supplies for redistribution."

With a last sniff round, I headed outside, blinking as I stepped into the sunlight. Bolby stood off to my left, wincing as Hariz dabbed a camyl salve on his bloodied jaw. "Have your things out of here by morning," I called, "and leave the door open when you leave."

I didn't wait for him to reply, or even to acknowledge my instructions, but set off along the pathway again, back toward the *Spirax*, with Shaya and Marga at my wingtips. The crowds had begun to disperse, thank the Spiral, so it was a more relaxed perambulation than the walk there had been.

Shaya held her peace till we were crossing the trampled moss near the base of the *Spirax,* heading toward Dru and Taral. "If you're not going to stay in your own dwelling tonight," she said, voice loud enough that everyone around must have heard, "where are you going to sleep?"

Dru looked round, a querying ear raised.

"There's too much of Bolby in there right now," I said, my glance taking in Dru, Taral and Shaya. "Once he's cleared out his things, and it's had a good airing, it will feel more like home."

"Yes." Shaya was persistent. "But tonight?"

I indicated the dead, spiralling a paw across my tunic and dipping an ear in Dru's direction. "I'll have work to do tonight. And tomorrow…"

There was scuffling and howling off to my right, where four guardflight were lowering a net to the moss. A greying muzzle, a dark blue tunic, a whiff of salt and fish. Broga. Chief Fisher, member of Kalis' council, ally of Fazak, fanatically anti-wingless. Even as the guardflight wrestled her into Fazak's empty dwelling, she howled insults in Dru's direction, and the odour of hatred poured from her every hair.

Dru watched, his gaze, his scent, speaking more of sorrow than anger. "Tomorrow," he said, as the dwelling door slammed, muffling the howls, "we deal with Fazak and his allies."

Twenty-Five

"Fate-seer, it's almost time."

Time for what? Where was I? Oh yes. In a makeshift nest in the *Spirax,* with Morel the First Herald shaking me awake. And it was time to pronounce judgement on Fazak and his cronies.

"It's zenith already?"

With so many dead to send to their last nests, I hadn't crawled under my blankets till near dawn. While the dead Elite had been despatched with no chanting or ceremony, those who had fought with Kalon had received the honour and respect they deserved. Flown in nets to the shore near the Cleft Rocks, they'd been laid out on the sand side by side, while I spoke the incantations and removed the hearts. A clump of brambletrap that had not been used before had been identified just inland from the Rocks, and there our fallen were sent to their last nest together. From there, we had flown across the Deadlands to the clump of brambletrap designated for Primes. Neither of their hearts could be shared –

Kalis' was unworthy and Kalon's was poisoned – but at Dru's request, both were given the traditional chant before being sent to their last nests.

It had been a long and difficult night, after a long and difficult day. It was little wonder I still felt tired, even as Morel scurried round the chamber lighting torches. "Bolby brought your ritual tunic last night, while you were still in the Deadlands," he said, dropping the last torch into a sconce. By the look of him, Morel had not overindulged in the supplies stuffed into the *Spirax* – he wasn't overweight at least – but still, he'd been better off than those on the Expanse. Even so, he smelled of anticipation, of hope, and I realised he'd lost the odour of fear that had always clung to his fur. Kalis had not been kind to him; perhaps he was relieved to have a new Prime to serve, even if he still had doubts about Dru's lack of wings.

Lifting the beautiful black tunic from a stool near the door, Morel gave it a sniff. "It was horribly creased, and there were grease marks down the front, but I've done what I can with it. I think it's presentable now, at least."

"It looks better than I remember, Morel. Thank you."

The grease marks had probably been my fault, some of the creases likewise, but as I fastened the tunic straps around me and smoothed a paw over the shell trimmings, and the neatly-stitched goldthread that spiralled across its front panel, I was overwhelmed by gratitude, and sent up a prayer of thanks to the Spiral that I was alive to wear it.

When I entered the Audience Chamber, the place looked much neater than it had the day before, when we had chased Fazak through the *Spirax*. The table had been righted and moved beneath the see-shell, where it had stood on the morning I presented a newly-hatched Dru to the waiting cluster-criers. There were no platters of food on it today – just the stools which the council used, stacked on top of it to clear more space in the chamber, which was crammed with drax.

Flattening my ears against the din of nines of conversations, which filled the room and rebounded from the smooth black walls, I made my way through the crowd to the platform at the far end, ignoring the murmurs of 'Fate-seer', and the paws that spiralled across tunics as I passed. My attention was on the throne-stool, and the young drax who occupied it.

Dru sat straight, ears pricked, wearing a clean cream tunic and looking every hair the Prime he now was – save for the colour of the tunic, which would be remedied as soon as the weavers and dyers produced a white one that fitted. His fur and mane had been washed and combed, and the badge of office that I'd last seen pinned to Kalis' tunic now glistened red at Dru's throat. Ranged along the platform behind him stood his new Council: Taral stood behind Dru, with Jotto and Shaya to his right, and a preening Varel to his left, along with Yaver and Tonil, who had reached maturity less than a half-cycle before. Hynka stood to their left, with Galio behind her. At Dru's right shoulder a space had been left for me.

As I stepped onto the platform and turned to take my place, Taral leaned in from my left. "You should see the assembly area outside. There's nineties out there around the Tusk, waiting to hear what happens."

I glanced toward him, dipping an acknowledging ear, and noticed the space on the wall beyond – a space where the carved-handled dagger had once been – and I spiralled a paw over my tunic as I remembered the damage that blade had wrought.

In front of us, the chamber was awash with whispers and murmuring. The smell of anticipation was palpable. Daylight from the see-shell slanted across the room, making the torches that lined the walls redundant. The breeze that entered through the open balcony doors brought welcome fresh air, and the sound of wingbeats as Heralds and Cluster-criers hovered outside in readiness to start relaying proceedings to the rest of the waiting drax.

The murmuring stopped as the main door opened, and Fazak, Sifan, Hapak, and Broga were brought in. The eight guardflight who escorted them – four in front and four behind – had all been with us on the Lake and had fought with us the previous day, but now they wore clean, untorn scarlet tunics, and smelled of pride rather than bitterness. Halting at the base of the platform, in front of Dru, the guards bowed and stepped back. Sifan, Hapak, and Broga lowered their heads and twitched their ears in what might have been grudging acknowledgement.

Fazak, I noted, made no obeisance. He looked outraged, ears set upright, torn wings braced out almost in challenge. He'd not been able to rub avalox on his fur today, and in the absence of its over-sweet scent, he reeked of hatred and defiance. In the quiet that had descended on the room, I heard him growl.

Dru stood, taking a pace forward to stare down on the ambitious, scheming drax who had caused all of us – and Dru in particular – so much misery. For a moment they stood snout to snout, each breathing hard, ears set and teeth bared. Just when I thought Fazak would continue his show of defiance, he gave a snort of contempt and settled his wings. "Taral," said Dru, without moving, his gaze still on Fazak, "explain to these four drax why they are here."

Only then did Dru back away from Fazak and return to stand in front of his throne-stool, while Taral produced a sheaf of leaves on which Hynka had set out every grievance, every crime Fazak would be charged with. As he read them aloud, each indictment was echoed by the heralds and criers outside: "...aiding and abetting in grievous harm...cutting the wings of Kalon and his companions...fomenting unrest...compelling exile...causing deaths...increasing tithes to a level that caused hardship..." The list went on, with each item greeted by grunts of agreement, jeers, and growls from the drax within and outside the chamber. Charges for Sifan, Hapak, and Broga followed, as the mood of anticipation shifted, and moved from bitterness and grief toward justice and vengeance.

There was a disturbance outside, a clatter of agitated wingbeats, a shout: "Half the drax in our cluster died in the last freeze thanks to you and your tithes, Fazak! I hope they feed you to the Koth!"

At a nod from Taral, two guardflight hurried out onto the balcony, but already the wingbeats of the wrathful male were falling away as he flew groundward again. "Just so he knows!" he called, in a parting shot. "Fat slug!"

There was more murmuring, angry shouts directed at Fazak, a shuffling in the crowd in the chamber, and Dru held up his arms and barked for silence.

He got it, though the scents of animosity and anger were not so easily dispelled.

If Fazak smelled the hostility, he gave no sign of it. After all he had done, all he had coaxed others into doing, he had the audacity to plead for mercy, claiming that his every move and utterance had been for the good of the Drax. "I should be thanked," he said, his high-pitched bark becoming a whine, "not punished for doing what needed to be done. Surely you must see that!" He wrung his paws as though beseeching us to understand, though I noticed he hadn't bothered to use Dru's title. "The Drax fly! We have always flown. To allow those who cannot fly to contaminate our blood-lines is to deny what it is to be a Drax. I—"

"Enough!" Dru's command was growled rather than barked, but his voice nonetheless carried clear to the back of the chamber. "You ask for mercy," said Dru, "though you have shown none. You helped Kalis cut Kalon's wing along with those of his guards and his friends, and left them to die. You manipulated Kalis into exiling the wingless to what you hoped and believed was certain death. You have grown fat on the tithes of hard-working drax while they starved, but have shown no remorse for any of this. You drew others into your flight-path, whispered poison in Kalis' ears till he was blind to the rightful way of doing anything, and *you are proud of it*." Drawing himself to his full height and setting his ears forward, Dru raised his voice as he turned his wrath on Hapak, Broga, and Sifan: "You three were the first to fly alongside Fazak. Your own prejudice against the wingless allowed you to back his desire to see them exiled, but what in the name of the Spiral were you thinking when you continued to aid his flight-path to oppression?"

He paused, waiting for a response, an excuse, a blustering reason. But Hapak, Broga, and Sifan lowered their heads and looked at each other, as though each was waiting for the others to reply. Though the males' manes were unbrushed, and Broga's tunic was still torn and scuffed from the previous day, the three of them looked almost as well-fed as Fazak, and I could well imagine that they enjoyed the power and the privileges that must have come their way as a result of their choice to leave Fazak and Kalis unchallenged. It felt good to see them squirm and, to judge by the low growls and murmurs around me, I was not the only one who felt that way.

But what would Dru do with them? Until yesterday, we had assumed it would be Kalon, not Dru, who pronounced sentence. With his death, our discussions after Fazak's capture had been edged with shock and sadness, as well as bitterness and anger. Still, for all their faults, Hapak, Broga, and Sifan had been followers, not leaders.

The murmuring stopped, and all was quiet, save for the heralds' wingbeats as they hovered outside, listening for the decision.

Dru raised his arms in lieu of wings, and he spoke with an authority in his voice I'd not heard before. "Hapak, Broga, and Sifan: your wings will be removed, and you will be exiled as we once were. You will live in the Abandoned Cluster, with groundeels for company. Perhaps they'll make good eating."

Cheers, barks of laughter, and cries of "serves 'em right!" echoed round the chamber, carried to our ears from the crowd outside, while six guardflight seized Hapak, Broga, and Sifan by their arms and wings.

"Just in case they were thinking of flying anywhere," Taral murmured, though by the look of them – heads bowed, ears drooping – they didn't look as if they were about to give any trouble.

Fazak regarded his allies with contempt, his own ears still set in defiance, his snout wrinkled as though he smelled something bad. It was as if he had forgotten that his own fate was about to be pronounced. Only when Dru raised his arms again and the room stilled once more did he deign to look at the wingless Prime. Only then did I detect a faint whiff of fear from him, as though the finality of the situation was only now occurring to him. Had he truly believed that his slippery words of justification would fool Dru into releasing him? If so, he was about to receive a terrible refutation.

"Fazak, your wings will be removed, and you will be taken by net to the Crimson Forest." Dru's words drew gasps and yips of approval, but he hadn't yet finished. "There, you will be lowered through the vine canopy to the ground and released, to take your chances with the mouldworms, the spiny slugs, the sucker-ferns, and the other forest creatures."

Dru had to raise his voice to a shout, so that it carried over the roars of acclaim that resounded within the chamber, and – a few beats later – from outside, as the message was relayed by the heralds.

Fazak's fur stood on end, he folded his wings tight as if that would protect them and, as two guardflight stepped up to seize his arms, he began to shriek and howl. "You can't do this to me! You have no wings, no authority! You're not the Prime, you freak, you can't be, tradition dictates—"

His words were snapped off as Taral stepped off the platform, placed his paws around Fazak's jaw and snout and squeezed his mouth shut. "I think we've all heard enough from you." Taral glanced round at Jotto. "Would you like to assist?"

"With pleasure." As he moved to Taral's side, Jotto pulled a seatach-gut binding from his tunic pocket and wrapped it around Fazak's snout, clamping his jaws shut.

Taral turned his head in Dru's direction, seeking permission to proceed. The swishing of Dru's tail was the sole sign of nerves. His bearing was upright, his scent edged with the faintest whiff of sadness. Perhaps he thought of his dam, Varna, and the pain and suffering she had gone through after Kalis had her wings removed, or perhaps he thought of the sort of life he was condemning Fazak's three main followers to. After all, no-one understood the limitations of life on the ground better than a wingless drax. Dru was making the right choice, the only choice – but even so, it was right that he should be apprehensive, given the gravity of what he was about to say.

Everyone had stilled. Only the wingbeats outside and the ragged breaths of the captive anti-wingless broke the silence – everyone else seemed to be waiting for permission to breathe again.

Dru dipped his snout, flicked an ear. "Ground them."

Taral raised a paw, then brought it down in a swift, chopping motion, and Fazak and the three drax alongside him were pushed to their knees, their guards keeping firm hold of their arms and wings. Hapak and Broga struggled and writhed, making little whimpering noises, while Fazak growled as best he could with his mouth strapped shut. Sifan was silent, but his mane stood on end and his ears and whiskers twitched with distress. As Taral drew his knife, I shuddered, and instinctively folded my own wings tighter against my back. The rustling around the chamber told me everyone else was doing the same.

Taral cut Sifan's wings first, then Hapak's and Broga's, and their wings clattered to the Chamber floor while the dewinged drax snarled and howled. Pulled to their feet, they were half-carried, half-marched from the Chamber, still howling. Claws clicked on stone and the smell of crushed zaxel rose from under their feet as the cheering, jeering crowd moved aside, and barks of joy floated through the open doors as the heralds and criers reported what had happened.

The chamber door slammed shut, muffling the howls, and Taral stood straight, bloodied knife poised, waiting until the murmuring and shuffling had ceased before he turned his attention to Fazak. He bent low, pushing his face close to Fazak's as Dru had earlier, and I had to strain to hear what he said: "This is going to hurt."

"Wait, Taral."

Dru stepped down from the dais, and for an eyeblink I thought he had changed his mind about Fazak's punishment. Then I saw his outstretched paw, and realised he wanted the knife.

He was going to cut Fazak's wings himself.

Leaning down to press the knife against the right wing-strut, Dru took a deep breath, spiralled his free paw across his tunic, and began to saw.

As the blade sliced through fur, skin, membrane, and muscle I felt – Spiral forgive me – a surge of triumph and satisfaction. At last, the drax who had caused so much misery and suffering was getting a taste of how it felt to be hungry, in pain, and facing certain death. I wondered whether, even now, Fazak truly understood what he had done, and edged nearer to him to check his scent.

No. Not a sniff of remorse. Hatred, pain, contempt, and anger all emanated from him in waves, but of sorrow or regret there was nothing.

Dru wrinkled his snout too, obviously smelling the same self-pity I detected, and handed the blade back to Taral. With a snarl of triumph, he raised Fazak's severed wings in his paws for all in the Chamber to see – and I realised that this was the Vision I had

had moons ago in the storm-battered seavine grove, when we were still journeying to the Forest.

While I spiralled a paw across my tunic, Taral pulled a cloth from his tunic pocket to wipe his blade and his paws, handing it to Dru when he'd finished. "Net!" he called, as he tucked his cleaned knife into his belt, and two more guardflight hurried across, unrolling a net.

"Take off from the balcony," said Dru, rubbing his paws with the bloodied cloth and ignoring the mewling noises Fazak made as they wrapped him in the net. "I don't want his stench contaminating the *Spirax* for a moment longer than it has to."

Taral, Jotto, and the guards manoeuvred the net and its writhing contents toward the balcony doors, and Dru followed, Shaya and I at his heels. There was no room on the balcony for all of us, so Shaya and I halted in the doorway, and I tucked my wings tight as everyone in the room headed for the dais, hoping to glimpse the take-off.

A roar beneath us preceded a clatter of wingbeats, as some of those who had been waiting on the ground took to the air. A phalanx of guardflight and heralds formed a line of red and grey between the balcony and the hovering crowd, but no-one was trying to get close: they simply wanted to witness Fazak's humiliation.

"Take him away," said Dru, and the four guards, each gripping a corner of the net securely, spread their wings and took off. Dru raised the bloodied wings again, and the crowd's ecstatic howls drowned anything Fazak might have whimpered from behind his gag. I caught sight of Swalo, hovering at the edge of the crowd, scratching at a leaf. Making notes for a new fable, I realised. Yes, this was the stuff of legend.

As the four guards beat their wings in a steady synchronised rhythm, and circled higher before heading north towards the Deadlands and the Forest, I moved outside to stand beside Dru and thought again of all the trials and tribulations Fazak had caused: that terrible journey, the despair, the terror, the deaths. I remembered with a shudder the shadows, the strange noises, the smell of rot and decay beneath that crimson canopy, and thought again of Jonel, Manda, and the others who had died there. Of

Varna, Flori, and all those who had drowned in the rapids, including Doran.

Dear Doran, who had been a friend to me since we hatched. How she would have enjoyed this day.

The crowd was still howling, hurling insults at Fazak long after he'd been carried out of earshot, and cheering Dru as he stood on the platform, watching the guards flap steadily on with their burden. Already they were distant enough that the scarlet of their tunics was barely discernible. With his ears set upright, shoulders squared, and severed wings still in his paws, Dru looked confident and supreme, though the wind that ruffled his mane also carried the scent of his nervousness to those of us close enough to smell it.

"We have Difel under guard in Fazak's old dwelling," he said, as we stood watching the grim procession recede into the distance. "Taral says we'll have the names of the others who were with him very soon."

"Bolby?" I was horrified at the thought that my dwelling might have been occupied by a cold-hearted killer. "Was Bolby with them?"

"He swears not," said Dru, "and he smelled sincere enough when he said it, but we'll have the names from Difel soon enough."

"You did well, Dru," I said, "but now the hard work will really begin. There'll be food to distribute, Elite Guards to reassign, eggs to hatch—"

I broke off, suddenly conscious that the shouts of the crowd had changed, and the wingbeats that had been as steady and rhythmic as the tide were now a mass of undisciplined flapping.

"Smoke!"

"Over to the south-west – look!"

"A raid!"

"The Koth!"

The cry of "Koth!" spread swiftly through the whole crowd, and I heard Taral utter an oath under his breath. As he picked out a nine of guardflight and took off from the balcony, I looked south-west toward where the crowd was pointing.

"Taral told me this might happen," said Dru, his ears drooping as he turned towards me. "He said that there were not enough guardflight left to control the crowds today, deal with Fazak and the others, and patrol the borderlands. We hoped that the Koth wouldn't notice their absence for a half-day or so, but..." He looked again at the purple smoke in the distance and the red-tuniced figures making air towards it. "We have to deal with them, Zarda. Once and for all."

Twenty-Six

"It will take days to reach the foot of Cloudsend." In warm late-melt sunshine, fur barely stirring in the desultory zephyr that blew from the north, Jotto stood on the *Spirax* balcony beside me, staring across the Expanse to the indigo smudges on the western horizon where the mountains pierced the clouds.

Dru stood between Jotto and Taral, the top of his mane almost level with theirs, though he still had another half-cycle of growth before he reached his full height. His left ear dipped in Jotto's direction. "The Koth will see us," he agreed, "but they won't expect to be attacked. They know you can't fly high enough to be a threat to them."

Taral nodded. "Even so, we should be prepared for possible aerial assaults and ambushes."

Jotto snorted. "The Koth won't attack a large, armed group," he said. "They never have. As Manel always says, they're cowards who'll only take on isolated Drax in the outlying farms and clusters."

Two moons had passed since the Battle of the *Spirax,* as the fable-spinners called it. Fazak had been lowered, whimpering, through the canopy of the Crimson Forest, and had been heard howling in terror as the guardflight flew away. Difel had given up the names of the Elite who had flown with him and Murgo on that deadly morning near the Ambit, and the younglings – half-growns now – of those they'd killed had been given the pleasure of removing their wings before the howling killers were netted to the ocean. The rest of the ex-Elite had been given scraps to eat, and tasked with distributing the hoarded food to everyone else. Some had returned to their previous clusters, ears and tails drooping with shame and apology; others had been assigned to the Guardflight. The females who had been discarded by disappointed nest-mates and exiled by Kalis found new mates to nest with, or empty dwellings to settle into, while their half-grown wingless offspring astounded those who had remained on the Expanse with the range of skills they'd learned on their journey.

With the warming of the weather, eggs had been laid, and nestlings – both winged and wingless – hatched, while a renewed sense of hope had spread through the clusters like hacklebrush.

Distrust and resentment, blame and grudges, still lingered, and would likely take cycles to wear away, but my hope was that by leading winged and wingless together in a fight against the Koth, Dru would not only fulfil his destiny: he would reunite the Drax in common purpose.

I glanced across at Dru, wondering whether he felt the weight of expectation on his young shoulders. If he did, he masked it well. Ears alert, sniffing the wind, he took a cautious step, his toes gripping the edge of the balcony. Taral and Jotto immediately edged forward too, ready to stoop after him if he should fall. Never had I been more aware of the unguarded edge of that narrow platform, and I resisted the urge to step behind Dru and hold onto his white tunic. "It all looks so peaceful."

I nodded. Below the ledge we stood on, the black rock of the Tusk gleamed in the after-zenith sun. Beyond it and around it, the red moss of the assembly area stretched, untrampled, along the neck of the peninsula, while to either side the waters of the bays lapped gently against curving shores. Beyond the green stems of the avalox bushes that marked its eastern border with the peninsula, the Expanse stretched into the distance, the smoke of cooking fires issuing from nineties of chimneys. In the nearest clusters, drax in various tunic colours scurried from dwelling to dwelling, and in the distance a couple of traders, distinctive in their pale-blue tunics, flew low as they made their way to another cluster. Life, it appeared, was clawing its way back to some sort of normality.

For the moment.

"I wonder," said Taral, "if perhaps our own attack came just in time."

"Taral?" Dru's tone reflected my own bafflement, but Jotto was nodding.

Taral gestured toward the distant mountains. "It must have been obvious to the Koth that Drax numbers were dwindling – the chimney smoke, or lack of it, would tell them that. They knew that the defences were weak. If we hadn't attacked when we did, I'm sure the Koth would have done so. As it is, they are still carrying out their land-and-snatch raids, but they might reassess the situation in a few moons."

Dru stepped back and I mirrored the action, resting a paw on the smooth black surface of the *Spirax* rock. Taral and Jotto turned, but remained where they were – between Dru and the sheer drop to the ground. "You mean the Koth might still decide to carry out a larger strike?" Dru's tail quivered with alarm. "Before we can fully recover our numbers and strength?"

"It's what I would do," said Taral, "if our positions were reversed."

Dru looked from Taral, to Jotto, to me, and I knew by the set of his ears that he'd made his decision. "We don't have a choice," he said. "We've always known we must take the fight to the Koth one day." A dip of the ear. "That day has arrived sooner than we'd like, but we must attack, and attack now, before they do."

Turning, he led the way back into the Audience Chamber, where the other councillors were just arriving. As they took their seats, Morel fussed round them with beakers and jugs. A younger herald, Perak – who had been 'half-grown and half-trained' when last I'd seen him – brought in a bowl of kerzh fruits which he set in the middle of the table. It was clear from the lightness of the heralds' steps and the set of their ears that they were content with the new regime.

Light streamed through the see-shell and the open doors of the balcony, and a puff of breeze ruffled my fur as I pulled up a stool diagonally opposite Taral and poured a beaker of berryjuice. Shaya, Jotto, and the rest of the new council occupied the other stools, while Dru ignored his throne-stool on the dais and stood to my left at the end of the table. Between us all, on the well-scrubbed surface, Hynka, the new Record Keeper, unrolled several glued leaves on which a map of the route to Cloudsend had been scratched.

"This looks very old." I noted the cracked edges of the leaves and the discolouration of the scratches. "You did well to find it, Hynka."

She twitched an ear in acknowledgement. "The older shelves do need a bit of tidying," she said, "but the index is straightforward enough."

I was astounded. "There's an index?" How much easier Fazak could have made my own searches if he had seen fit to help!

Hynka nodded and opened her mouth, as though to expand on the theme, but closed it again as Taral seized the map and drew it nearer to his end of the table. "It doesn't matter how old the map is," he said. "The mountains haven't changed, nor are they likely to." He traced the scratchings with a claw and Jotto, beside him, nodded.

"It should be possible to fly between some of the smaller peaks," said Jotto, as he looked up from the map. "With plenty of vlydh and a fair wind, we could penetrate almost to the base of Cloudsend on the wing."

"The problem is that once we get there, the Koth are not only bigger than us and stronger – but they can fly higher." Galio kept his wings carefully tucked back as he spoke, to emphasize that he was stating a point – albeit an obvious one – rather than presenting a challenge.

Dru acknowledged the truth of the statement with a brief ear-flick, then leaned down to brace his paws on the table as he looked at each of us in turn. "But none of you have ever seen them use a bow," he said, "only knives and spears." There were grunts and nods of confirmation around the table. "They cannot throw their spears so far as our guardflight or our hunters can fire their arrows – and however big they are, no Koth is immune to a well-shot arrow."

"True." Taral straightened on his stool, the set of his ears reflecting the pride in his voice. "Raids on the outer clusters have ceased over the past moon. The guardflight are still under-strength, but we have more flyers than I did a cycle ago. With the nine of wingless half-growns we've taken on patrolling the Expanse on their vlydhs, I've been able to set patrols to the west and south in the old pattern."

"And the ex-Elite?" said Dru. "Are any of them still causing problems?"

Taral shook his head. "None that a few well-placed nips don't solve," he said. He gave a little snuffle of laughter. "I think they find the Guardflight a relief, after the sort of discipline Fazak expected from them."

Jotto snorted. "We'll have to be harder taskmasters," he said, but the set of his ears told me that he spoke in jest. "Those who didn't really want to join us were rooted out before a moon had passed and sent back to their home clusters." He scratched his snout and flicked his ears. "Of course, that didn't always end well…"

He looked over at me and I confirmed his words with a nod and a dipped ear. "I had to treat quite a number of ex-Elite during the first moon or so for bites and slashed wings," I said, "but not so many in recent days. The feeling seems to be that once they've been punished they should be allowed to return to their old trades. The Spiral knows, we need them to!"

Shaya chimed in. "So many clusters without healers, gatherers, artisans, and criers. Even with our new system, it will take cycles to get back to our optimum numbers."

Our new system. My fur inadvertently stuck up every time someone mentioned it, and I'd had some sleepless nights worrying about it. Generations of tradition, of drax learning a single trade and learning it well, set aside. Instead, the half-growns we had, and the hatchlings to come, would learn a major trade, plus several supporting skills. Apprentice hunters would also learn to gather and to heal minor scrapes, apprentice guardflight would also learn to hunt and heal, while apprentice healers would learn to gather and to weave. Each trade, each skill, would learn from the others, as those who had been exiled had been forced to do. New tunics would be fitted with collars and belts of a colour that reflected the additional skills. Already, Shaya wore a band of Healer green-and-black around her neck, and a belt of Gatherers' brown, while Jotto's ochre collar and copper Artisan belt were bright against the scarlet of his guardflight tunic.

Varel coughed politely, and ran a paw through his own startled mane, smoothing it to an untidy quiff. "Perhaps we should wait till our numbers have increased, before committing our best drax to pursuing the Koth. Allowing two hatchings for every nest during this cycle will—"

"No." Dru stood up straight, shook his head. "The Drax have suffered too many raids over the cycles. If the cold seasons continue to be as harsh as the last two have been, we'll need all the crops we grow for ourselves."

"And we'll need reserves," Yaver put in, from his stool to my right. He glanced round, his trepidation at speaking up at a council meeting palpable in his raised fur and nervous odour. "We can send flyers back to Kalon's Lake to gather any crops we left there, which will help, but if the raids go on – or get worse – we'll struggle to feed ourselves, especially if the river fish don't return."

"I agree," said Shaya. "We need to strike at the Koth now, but the problem of their greater altitude remains." She stood and jabbed at the map. "We cannot get above them. We can't even pursue them further than the snow-line."

Dru rocked on his heels, stroking his whiskers as he raised his snout and ears. He glanced at Taral and Jotto, who looked and smelled equally smug. Clearly they had already discussed how to get to the top of the mountain. "We can't get there on the wing, no," he said, "but we can climb up there, surely?"

In the silence that followed, I recollected my Vision of Dru, raising his arm in victory amid the swirling snow and, at last, I understood. "By the Spiral! Since the wingless began to hatch, drax have been asking why such a thing should happen. I've never been able to give them an answer, though it was there in my Vision all along."

"You are a gift," breathed Galio. "The Spiral sent us a gift and we rejected it. Kalis sent you away – and none of us stopped him."

I took a beat or two to consider the weaver's words. "An accurate assessment," I said. "But it's also true that without the exile, and everything we learned on that journey, none of us would be the drax we are today – including Dru."

"You're saying that terrible journey, and the deaths and horrors and the hardships were a *blessing*?" Shaya looked as indignant as I had ever seen her, ears set forward, whiskers twitching. "You'll forgive me, Fate-seer, if I find it hard to see it that way."

With a sniff, and a snap of her teeth, she sat back, paws clenched together on the table, to indicate she hoped that would be the last word on the subject.

Taral rescued the debate, steering it back to the matter at paw. "At the moment, the wingless are the only climbers we have," he said, "but we can't send them to mount an attack on the Koth by themselves." The set of his ears indicated that the statement wasn't up for debate. "The guardflight will need to climb too."

"So will the hunters," said Shaya. "We'll be coming too – you'll need everyone who can wield a bow or a spear." She looked around the table as though daring anyone to suggest otherwise, but Taral merely tilted an ear in thanks and, after a moment's hesitation, Dru did the same.

I shivered at the thought of what I had to say, weary at the very idea of scrabbling up that mountain, but it would have to be done as the Spiral willed. "I must learn to climb too." I remembered the freezing nights we had spent on frozen ground, huddled under open skies and flapping seatach hides on our journey north, and wondered how long we would have to spend on Cloudsend mountain. Even now, there was snow visible on its peak when the wind tore the clouds. However warm it was on the Expanse, it would clearly be treacherous with ice up there.

"You, Zarda?" Taral's whiskers twitched with amusement. "You are no fighter. You proved that in the battle of the *Spirax*."

"I know." I fingered my badge of office, proudly displayed at the neck of a clean black tunic, and sat straight. "But a battle must be blessed and you will need a Fate-seer to do that."

"And the Vision in the Dream-cave showed Zarda would be with me," Dru added, "at the end of the battle."

I nodded. "The *triumphant* end of the battle."

Dru's dipped ear acknowledged the truth of that, and he turned to Varel. "The Vision also showed a banner raised in victory," he said. "I don't want to use Kalon's, it's not fitting. Would you arrange the production of a new one, please?"

Varel looked gratified to have been tasked with something so significant. "I will liaise with the weavers and dyers, Lord." Already taken up with the idea, he began to plan: "I suggest a white background to represent your mane and tunic. And some purple, I think—"

"Not now, Varel." Shaya looked more amused than annoyed, but Varel huffed a little as he subsided, his odour distinctly offended as he hunched down on his stool.

"On a more practical note?" Taral looked down at his fingers as he flexed them, as though contemplating how well he might grip a rockface – or an ice wall. "Perhaps we can all start by climbing Guardflight Rock," he said, his voice firm, though my nostrils detected his reluctance. "Its sides are steep, but they're not vertical like the plateau cliffs or the Tusk."

Dru nodded affirmation. "Perhaps the Hollow Crag and the peaks around your training-cave, too, Taral," he said. "The wingless will help."

Taral scratched at his beard. "We'll need at least a couple of moons to practice."

"One moon," said Dru. "For five ninedays, all those who are going must spend either a morning or an afterzenith climbing. For the sixth nineday, we'll climb after dark, by the light of the Spiral."

"Agreed." Taral held up a paw to indicate he hadn't finished. "On the understanding that we review the situation before we start night-climbs. Let's not have anyone hurt because we're trying to move too quickly."

It was agreed, and scratched for the record by Hynka, while Jotto sat forward, eagerly, and turned the map to examine it again. "Then all we have to do now is work out our plan of campaign."

For the next moon we honed our plans, practiced with bow and spear, gathered everything we needed – and those of us with wings learned, hesitantly and painfully, to climb.

"I thought my legs ached when we walked to the Forest," Shaya grumbled, rubbing at her thighs as she sat by my hearth-fire waiting for me to mix a poultice for her skinned foot, "but that was nothing compared to trying to get up that wretched rock." She half-extended her wings and rolled her shoulders, limbering and stretching. "Could the Spiral not have sent the Sickness to the Koth, so they couldn't fly down the mountain any more, instead of sending us the wingless and making us climb up it?"

Standing at my worn, scratched table, crushing camyl leaves in a bowl, I paused, unsure what to say, but she waved the question aside with a dismissive paw. "Don't worry, I'm not expecting an answer."

"I have one anyway." I set the bowl down beside the low flames to warm, and stirred the pot that bubbled over the heat. "Tea?"

I filled two beakers, handed one to Shaya, and pulled up a stool opposite hers, glancing round at my dwelling while I took a sip. The tea was strong and sweet, just the way I'd enjoyed it before harsh necessity had forced me to take it weak, bitter, or not at all. Healing herbs hung from the shelves, and my baskets and jars were slowly being replenished; Bolby's nest had been swept away and with it the last of his odour. The place was a Fate-seer's again, with all the smells and tastes and supplies that belonged there.

It was possible my nest needed a change of moss, though. The aroma from behind the screen was just a little too fetid.

"The Spiral sent the Sickness so we might learn," I said. "All of us." I held up a paw as Shaya opened her mouth to protest. "I know you don't like the idea that our journey was necessary. I mourn too, Shaya – there's not a day goes by that I don't think of

Doran, or Galyn, or Milat. Every night I pray to the Spiral that their lights will shine on us always. But we *did* learn, all of us. We learned to work together better, we learned new skills, and how to apply old skills to new situations." I took another sip of tea and leaned towards her, cradling my beaker. "And we learned about the Koth – that they didn't always live in the mountains, that they grew avalox, and built in spirals just as we do."

"And what use is that? So what if they built in spirals? So what if they still do?"

"Then perhaps we can find common ground with them."

"Common ground?" Shaya stood up, her injured foot forgotten. Tea sloshed as she took an angry pace to the table and banged her beaker down. "Common ground! With Koth?" She extended an arm, pointing westward in the direction of Cloudsend. "Your Vision tells us we're going to defeat them. Why would we need to find common ground with them, for lights' sake?"

"Because once we defeat them, what then? Should we wipe them out? All of them? Hatchlings and younglings included?"

"I…" Shaya scratched delicately at her snout, picked up her beaker and limped the few steps back to her stool. "I'd not given it much thought."

"I have. Tell me – do you believe they will agree to stay in their eyries in future and not raid us again?" I set down my beaker and picked up the bowl I'd set down by the fire, gave it a sniff and a stir. "Here, this is ready – smear it on your foot and I'll bind it with a canox leaf to speed the healing."

Shaya handed me her beaker, and set about rubbing the poultice over the cuts and tears on the sole of her right foot. "I don't see why the Koth should agree to anything. Why should they?" A sigh. "But I'm not comfortable with the idea of slaughtering hatchlings either, or any that are unarmed, come to that." A faint shudder, a swish of her tail told me she was remembering what happened to Milat and the others when they flew to parley with the Elite Guard.

It hadn't been pretty to watch, and I'd already told Dru that I'd have no part in any action that repeated such barbarity.

"Then what do you suggest we do with them?" Shaya asked – just as Dru had. Wiping her paws, she reached to take her beaker again, then tilted her head and flicked a questioning ear. "Always assuming that we do actually win, of course."

"We know we'll win, Shaya," I assured her, reaching down to pick up my beaker. "Vizan Saw it, I've Seen it, and so has Dru."

"But what did you See?" She turned an ear, eager for my reply.

Despite my promises to myself, I'd still not taken the time to visit the Dream-cave since our return, and it had been some time since I'd Seen the Vision. I closed my eyes for a moment as I called it to mind again. "Snow," I said, "swirling and blowing around us. Dru. Myself. Red tunics around us. A banner held aloft. A dead Koth on the ground below us."

When I opened my eyes, Shaya was sitting back, ears twitching with scepticism. She smelled unconvinced. "That's it? One dead Koth?"

"And a banner raised in triumph."

"Are you sure? Where are the other Koth? What if you've Seen the beginning of the battle, not the end? What if there are Koth hidden in the snow waiting to counter-attack?"

"It's the end of the battle," I said. "I'm sure."

Except that suddenly I wasn't.

What if Shaya was right? What if the Vision did not show victory? Might it be a warning? What if there were more Koth hidden by the snow and the limits of my Sight?

What if we were not destined to win after all?

Twenty-Seven

I kept my doubts to myself. As word of our plans had spread, every cluster and every drax on the Expanse sent support. Clusters almost got their wings tangled as they competed to see who could send the sharpest arrows, the straightest spears, the most tightly-woven nets to the *Spirax*. The Fishers, under their new Chief, Roban, insisted on providing as much dried fish as we could carry, and asked nothing in exchange, and the Hunters flew all the way to the Crimson Forest to catch a nine of vinecreepers. Gatherers sent sprigs of healing herbs and vineleaves to add to my supplies, Farmers sent melt-harvested avalox and haunches of fresh-slaughtered groxen, and Artisans made nets, vlydh harnesses, bindings, and tethers.

Best of all, the nines of wingless hatchlings which emerged from melt-laid eggs were welcomed and embraced by their whole communities as a blessing from the Spiral.

At least twice a nineday, Dru would fly a vlydh from the plateau to the Expanse, to visit different clusters and see for himself how they were faring. "Kalis-fa stayed in the *Spirax* and listened to the lies Fazak told him," he said, as I accompanied him to the dyers' cluster one afterzenith. "I don't want to make the same mistake. I have to see what's happening for myself."

"The dyers' cluster wasn't very welcoming the last time we visited, Dru."

That was an understatement. Telin, the welcomer, had reeked of dislike and disapproval for the wingless pup who'd travelled with me, and I had had to remind her of his status as Kalis' heir before she'd deigned to answer his eager questions with something approaching courtesy.

"All the more reason I should go and see them. Besides, the orenvine plantation is close by, I can go and see Cavel afterwards. I've hardly set eyes on him since his sire..."

Since Miyak had flown to the ocean, rather than submit to rule by a Prime with no wings. A few nines had taken the same course, and I couldn't help but wonder whether they would end up being eaten by some sea-monster, like the unfortunate female we'd found in the belly of the seatach that had washed up on the Ambit peninsula.

The youngling Miyak had sired with Morla – her proving-egg – had been gathered up by his dam and taken to the Guardflight cluster that spiralled out from the base of Guardflight Rock. *"They'll be safe with us,"* Taral had assured the council, *"and we'll be happy to take the youngling as an apprentice when he's a little older."* The vlydh and the orenvine plantation that nurtured them had been left without a keeper; Cavel had been the obvious candidate, and accompanying him back to his old home had been a wonderful moment, albeit one that had been laced with poignant memories.

"You've both had a lot to do." I said. "With the wingless finding their places, there's more demand than ever for vlydh-hire, and Cavel's tending them on his own."

"Not for long," said Dru, whiskers twitching with adolescent amusement. "Not if Ellet has anything to do with it."

"They have another half-cycle before they can become nest-mates," I said, "and that's assuming that what Rewsa said was true." I sighed, wishing it had been Doran who had told me such gossip. I pictured her cradling a beaker of bitter-brewed avalox tea by my hearth, ears twitching, every hair alive with pride as she told me her news, her hopes.

My thoughts were interrupted by a shout from Dru, and I realised the dyers' cluster was just beyond the next meander of the Manybend, near the loop that held the orenvine plantation. I angled my wings, called the descent warning to those below, and managed a graceful landing on the moss, just behind Dru's vlydh.

"Lord Dru, Fate-seer Zarda. I welcome you on behalf of all at the Dyers' cluster. Will you rest and take tea? Please follow me. Narva will take your vlydh to the nearest orenvine." It was Telin, the welcomer who had treated Dru like groxen-droppings on our previous visit. She'd had fur-clump by the look of her patchy fur and, like most of the drax I'd seen on the Expanse, was thinner than I remembered. I crushed the thought that she'd deserved a little suffering, and instead set wings and ears to respect and greeting.

"We're honoured by your visit," she grovelled, dipping bows as she backed up along the pathway. "We're eager to show you how many cauldrons are back in action, and how quickly our wingless apprentices are learning the trade."

The last time we'd followed Telin along the spiralling path through the cluster, doors had been closed, and only those few drax with wingless pups had greeted us with any enthusiasm. Now, as soft melt moss cushioned our footsteps, and an unclouded sun warmed our backs, the pathway was lined with drax, all yipping a welcome. There were barks of thanks for distributing the food, howls of joy, and an overwhelming smell of amity.

"If only I'd understood the Spiral's purpose when the wingless first hatched. You might have been greeted like this on our first visit here, and everything we went through could have been avoided."

I was behind Dru's left shoulder and leaned forward a little to murmur my regrets into his ear. He dismissed them with a shrug and an ear-flick. "None of us Saw the purpose, Zarda, till the Spiral willed it so. Not even Vizan. Besides, do you really think Fazak would have rested content, even if we had?" He nodded left and right, waved a paw at those hovering over their dwellings, acknowledging the cheers. "Besides, if I'd been greeted this way as a pup, I'd probably have been as insufferable as Urxov. As it is, I know exactly what these cheers are worth."

"They are good to hear all the same."

"Yes. Imagine how they'll greet our victory over the Koth!"

"There'll be many a hoarse throat and a sore wing once those celebrations have finished." Yet behind my reply, that seed of doubt that Shaya had planted had taken root. Was it a victory we'd Seen? Or a lull in the fighting, a false hope?

As Telin ushered us into the zaxel-strewn interior of the Welcome Place and offered freshly-pressed berry juice, avalox tea, and loxcakes, I knew I had to confront my doubts. The best way to do that was to visit the Dream-cave and breathe the Dream-smoke.

"You mean you've not been back there since the battle?" Dru spoke around a loxcake, spitting crumbs.

I licked my fingers, resisted the urge to wipe my own sticky paws on my tunic and pulled a cloth from a pocket. "It's not been a priority, Lord. There have been wounds to heal, illnesses to tend, and climbing to practice." I held up my left paw and extended a broken claw. "It's not as easy as you make it look. Besides..." Time for a small lie. "I thought it best to wait till we were almost ready for the next battle before I breathed the Dream-smoke. Perhaps it will reveal more of what is to come, now that the time is so close."

So it was that, while Dru travelled to the orenvine plantation to spend time with Cavel, I flew once more to the Dream-cave. How many days of pain and effort had it taken us to reach the Cleft Rocks on foot – nine? Ten? When I reached the Cleft Rocks, after a flight across the south-eastern Deadlands that took less than a quarter-day, I hovered and looked south. Before, my attention had always been caught by the *Spirax* plateau, its bulk dominating the horizon beyond the Manybend estuary and the Northern Bay. Now, I noticed the dunes that edged the sands – no more than undulations of shadows and light from where I hung on the wind. The cliffs, seavines and rocks we had struggled over and through were just varicoloured marks on the landscape – dots and slashes that might have been scratched on a map. There was the cliff I'd fallen off; beside it, stretching inland for spans, was the seabramble the wingless and grounded had had to walk around. I spotted the seavines where we'd sheltered from the storm, and spiralled a paw, murmured a prayer, remembering.

The Dream-cave itself, unchanged since I had last been there over a cycle before, felt comforting in its quiet solidity. As my torch hissed and guttered in its sconce, I sat still, listening to the wash of the ocean beyond the outer cave, and breathing in the smell of damp rock, Dream-plants, and the last lingering hints of the Dream-smoke as it dispersed.

The Vision in the smoke had not changed. Still it showed Dru, the banner, the scarlet guardflight tunics surrounding the Prime, myself beside him. It had to be the battle's end, surely?

"Great Spiral," I murmured, "do not desert us now. For so long we have believed in this Vision, that you show us victory over our enemies the Koth. If it not be so, please send me a sign, a Seeing, a better understanding of what this Vision means. We have come so far, lost so many, suffered so much. Please don't let those sacrifices be in vain."

I waited, sniffing again at the ashes of the Dream-smoke, but nothing happened. I thought again of Vizan and his ability to control what he Saw and when, an ability he had promised to teach me but had not been able to before he went to his last nest.

I sighed. "You Saw it too, Vizan, and you called it victory," I said, raising my snout. The roof of the cavern stretched into darkness, hidden even from my night-vision, but my thoughts and prayers stretched beyond it to the lights in the Great Spiral, and to one in particular: the dazzling light that had blazed so bright in the south-eastern sky, prior to our fight for the *Spirax.* Vizan's Light, which, though its brightness was fading, surely looked on us still with kindness and wisdom. "If you had any doubts, you never voiced them." Standing up, I brushed the sand from my tunic and collected my torch from the worn sconce. "Victory it must be."

But still I couldn't quite banish my niggling doubts.

Twenty-Eight

"The Koth will notice that we're gathering our forces."
Dru stood in the middle of our small group, on the crest
of a low hill overlooking Paw Lake. Once, moons ago,
I had taken Dru there as a tiny youngling, to show him the full
extent of the Expanse, and to test his knowledge. Then, he had
been small enough to carry in a harness, strapped to my chest like
a carry-pouch; now, he was taller than me, his chin was lined
with white where his beard had grown in, and he'd been carried
there by a vlydh.

As he stood gazing out over the Expanse that was now
rightfully his territory, I stood to his right with Taral, while Shaya
and Jotto flanked his left, where his wingtip might have been.
Spiralling around the hillside below us, ninety wingless half-
growns in various colourful tunics mingled with nines of scarlet-
clad guardflight and ochre-tuniced hunters as they moved or
stood or sat around campfires, from which the smell of roasting
meat and stewed fish carried on thin smoke. On the lake shore,

where the orenvines grew thick, branches shook as the vlydh grazed on the leaves, the constant rustling reminding me of waves on a pebble beach. Overhead, the sun was a suggestion of brightness hidden behind a haze of pale clouds that stretched to the horizon, barely moving in the still air which was thick with murmured conversations. An occasional bark of laughter floated up the hill, and I noticed Taral turn an ear eastward as the snaps and snarls of a minor dispute intruded on the calm.

"Someone prefers his tea sweeter," he murmured, after listening for a moment. "The female he threw his beaker at has told him to make it himself next time." A shrug. "If they start biting each other I'll send a wingflyer to intervene." Turning to answer Dru, he extended a paw to indicate the steep grey walls of rock to the west where the mountains swept upward into the clouds. "If we can't see up through the cloud, they can't see down either," he said.

Jotto dipped an ear in agreement. "Even if they do see us – and at some point they will – they know we can't fly higher than the snow line. They won't see us as a threat, no matter how many of us there are."

"Do we have enough vlydh?" I'd flown in late after tending a case of fur-clump in one of the river clusters, and the pack-creatures had already been making themselves at home in the orenvines by the time I arrived. "They'll have to carry the wingless, our supplies—"

"And enough orenvine leaves to keep them going." Jotto waved a paw dismissively. "There's barely a vlydh left on the Expanse – and the ones we've left behind are either too small or too old to risk on a journey like this. Don't fret, Zarda, it's all been taken into account. Varel worked on the logistics personally."

I knew that. I'd been there at the council meetings when all this had been discussed. I knew that Varel was not only capable enough to work on the numbers for vlydh and supplies, but was trustworthy enough to be left in charge at the *Spirax* in Dru's absence. The old adviser had accepted the role with a whimper of such heartfelt gratitude it had been almost embarrassing to witness. "*I won't let you down, Lord,*" he'd said, kneeling at Dru's feet as the Badge of Office was pinned to his tunic. "*I won't let any of you down. I have the inventory of everything stored in the* Spirax*, and notes on what's already been distributed. I'm just waiting on confirmation of the melt harvest, and what can be salvaged from Kalon's Lake. Cavel has already provided statistics on the vlydh...*"

I'd stopped listening at that point, but I didn't doubt that Varel – and Jotto and Taral – had worked out exactly what was likely to be needed.

It was the nagging doubt about my Vision that bothered me.

I shook my head to try to dislodge it, and flicked an ear in apology before turning to Shaya. "I know you've been busy with the seatach hides, Shaya," I said. "May I see one?"

"Of course. They're with the vlydh packs. What about you, Jotto, are you coming? Taral?"

Taral shook his head and gestured toward our own campfire, which his wingflyer Veret was tending just a few spans away on the western side of the hill. "I've seen them," he said, "and by the smell of it the food is almost ready."

"Don't be too long," Jotto called, "or we'll eat your share too."

I took off after Shaya, and we glided down to the lakeside, where the large carrypacks for the vlydh had been set down. Shaya called a greeting to Ravar, her half-grown, who sat with Cavel, Ellet, and six other wingless at a campfire close to the orenvines. They were tucking into a haunch of groxen that was roasting on a spit over the flames, pulling chunks from the sizzling flesh and gobbling them down with barely a pause to chew. "How many times have I told you not to bolt your food?" she scolded, the teasing set of her ears belying the edge in her voice. "Don't come whimpering to me if you choke on your cud."

Ravar waved a sticky paw to acknowledge his dam, dipped a courteous ear in my direction, and popped another gobbet of meat into his mouth. The other half-growns called greetings, and Cavel made to stand up before Shaya waved him back to the log he was sitting on. "We're just going to take a look at the hides," she called. "Carry on with your meal." To me, she added, "Remember those awful thin stews we had to eat while we travelled to the Ambit? If we'd had just one groxen to roast..." She shook herself and smoothed her fur, the brief, regretful memory banished as she led the way across the springy chalkmoss to the nearest carrypack. She gave it a sniff to identify its contents, undid the straps, and pulled out an armful of something that resembled a strange folded rock. "You see?" Carrying it to a rocky stretch of lake shore, she unfolded it and spread it on the ground, tucking back an edge to show me the underside. "Seatach hide – but we've stuck dust and sand and tiny pebbles to the outside. Take off again, Zarda, see how it looks from the air."

I did as I was bid, and circled up till I was above the orenvines. When I looked down, I was amazed to see that the hide was almost invisible. If Shaya had not been standing next to it, waving, I might have missed it completely.

"Impressive," I said, folding my wings as I landed beside her. "Once we're in the mountains, we'll be able to disappear underneath those when we make camp."

She nodded. "I've had smaller ones made, too. Here, help me fold this, and I'll show you."

Returning the folded hide neatly to its carrypack, she pulled another from the pack next to it, and held up a circle of camouflaged hide with a hole in the middle. I tried to work out what it was for, and Shaya must have seen the puzzlement on my face. "Head goes through here..." She demonstrated for me, the folds of the hide draping about her as she squatted. Instantly, she all but melted into the ground, and I saw the potential at once.

"For our lookouts? Or are there enough for all?"

She stood up and pulled the hide off, folding it neatly as she answered. "They're too heavy to wear on the move," she said, "especially climbing those slopes. But we'll need to post lookouts when we make camp, and there's no use them sitting about in green or red or even ochre. That'll just be asking for a Koth attack."

"What about fires? It'll be freezing up there." I felt cold just thinking about the snow that lay beyond the clouds, beyond the point where we'd be able to fly.

Shaya glanced upward, though there was nothing to see but cloud. "We'll have to judge it day by day." The concealing hide crackled and snapped as she rolled it, and I wondered how far aloft the vlydh would be able to carry such things before their wings failed too. "If there's enough cloud between us and the Koth, we might risk a fire, I suppose, but only for a short time, and we'll have to keep them to flame rather than smoke. If we start by flying under this cloudbase, and stay under the hides as much as possible when we make camp, we should at least be able to get to the base of Cloudsend without the Koth noticing, Spiral willing." She knelt to push the hide back into its carrypack. "Whatever Taral might say about them not expecting an attack, there's nothing to stop them coming down for a look if they get curious. They'll have the height advantage, so we need stealth, if we can manage it."

I looked up at the towering edifices where the freeze reigned even now, in the middle of the growing season. "I hope we've got enough furs," I said.

As Shaya had suggested, we travelled beneath the cloudbase, the better to avoid being seen by Koth scouts – though as we drew nearer the foot of Cloudsend, I feared that they would long since have heard our wingbeats, for they seemed to echo from the rock ridges and rubble-strewn gorges of the mountains that towered around us.

My fears about not having enough vlydh had vanished as soon as they had emerged from the orenvines. We had vlydh to carry the wingless, vlydh to carry orenvine leaves for them all to feast on, and vlydh to carry our own food and weapons. I couldn't help but reflect that it was a pity the beasts could not help us with the actual fighting. Alas, we would have to leave them behind once we got above the snow-line, as they would not be able to fly any higher.

The route through the mountains took us through steep-sided valleys, where lichens and mosses softened the piles of grey rock, and hacklebrush grew thick on boulder-strewn slopes. We flew over steep ridges, sharp and unforgiving as axe-blades, where kervhels picked their way from one scrubby bush to another. As with the Forest, the mountains had sounds and smells that I'd never experienced before and had no names for – dark rumblings that seemed to issue from the mountains themselves, ancient musty smells, peculiar cries from unseen beasts.

Here, too, we had to be constantly on the lookout for floaters. Our flight path took us almost to the base of the clouds at times, and the scouts had been issued special orders to watch for anything that glowed. Fortunately for us, it appeared that the creatures did not like to be too close to the bigger peaks, and we saw just a single dangerous cloud, and that distantly.

"We can't take the vlydh much further," Cavel said, as we made camp on our second day. He pointed upward, toward a fierce, angular slope where patchy snow clung to rocky crevices. "Once we're past the snow-line they'll think the freeze has come, and start spinning their cocoons."

I was standing next to a seatach hide that had been spread across ground lined with pebbles, tufts of scratchy grass, and grey dust. Its centre bulged upward where it had been draped over a boulder, and its edges were being pegged down firmly against a buffeting southerly wind.

Jotto and Taral must have overheard his remark, as they dropped the pegs they were holding and hurried across to join me. Shaya, busy helping with another hide, noticed them move and murmured something in Ravar's ears before scurrying over, and Dru stopped collecting moss from a nearby patch of muddy ground.

"So soon? I was hoping to get them at least to the next camp." Taral glanced upward as he spoke, but there was little to see beyond the snow-patched slope, as we were once again shrouded with cloud and mist that hugged the mountain and – praise the Spiral – hid us from the Koth.

"They'll freeze," Cavel snapped. Then, dropping his ears and moderating his tone, he added, "Or they'll spin their cocoons, as I already said. I don't know which. Both, perhaps."

"Well, we can't risk that," said Dru. "I don't want those of us without wings to have to walk home." He still clutched the bag he'd been dropping the moss into, and I wondered how many pawfuls it would take to cover the unyielding ground beneath the hide. Rather more than the muddy patch would supply, I feared. Ah well. We'd slept in worse places.

"Can they survive if we leave them here?" Shaya wiped her paws on a cloth before smoothing her tunic.

Cavel nodded, flicked an ear. "I think so, provided it's not for long." He pointed to the outer curve of an overhang, beneath which the vlydh had been herded. Sheltered from the worst of the elements from above and on two sides, the creatures seemed content enough, huddled together and chewing the orenvine leaves Cavel had given them. "They'll be warm enough under there for the moment. I can climb to get snow to melt for water, and we've still got plenty of orenvine leaves in the carrypacks, but I'll have to keep enough aside for the journey back."

Jotto, like Taral, glanced upward before he spoke, as if trying to see, or guess, what lay beyond the clouds. The map Hynka had found had brought us so far – but beyond this point, the scratchings were vague, and marked simply, 'more mountains'. Whatever lay beyond the clouds, beyond the snow-line, we would be the first Drax to see it. We would have to trust to the Spiral that there would be room enough to camp, and slopes that wouldn't be too hard to climb. "If we leave their food here," said Jotto, "and get them to fly just a little higher, I think they could help get us within striking distance of the summit."

Cavel looked stricken, wringing his paws as he looked across the camp to the nines of tethered vlydh. "But—"

Jotto held up a paw, forestalling the half-grown's protest. "We can turn them around once they've been unloaded and bring them straight back here."

"I don't know, Jotto." Taral's ears twitched with thought as he tugged on his beard. "We've no idea how much further up any of us can fly, and we don't know where we might be able to land and make camp." He indicated the busy camp with a wave of his arm. "Some are already struggling to fly – some are even struggling to breathe. Perhaps we should fold our wings and climb from here."

"No." Jotto was a picture of stubbornness, ears set, posture erect, a smell of impatience emanating from his fur. "I think we should at least try to fly higher."

"I agree." Dru's intervention squashed further debate, but his agreement was not unequivocal. "However, I don't think we should risk all our flyers and all our vlydhs in a blind flap. Taral,

Jotto, once you've had something to eat and some rest, perhaps you would fly through those clouds to see what awaits us, and find a place where we can all land safely?"

As the two guardflyers dipped ears in acknowledgement, Dru turned to Cavel. "I'm sorry," he said, "but you'll have to stay here. Someone must tend the vlydh while the rest of us climb."

Cavel's ears drooped. *He* drooped, his entire body slumping in misery and disappointment. "We can leave food for them—"

"And have them scoff the lot before we get back here?" Dru shook his head, put a paw on his friend's shoulder. "You know they'll need to be rationed and watched. It's important, Cavel – we can't get home without them, you know that."

Cavel didn't smell very mollified, though he gave an ear-twitch of agreement. "I know it. I just hoped..." His fur stood on end and his head came up as another thought struck him. "What if you don't come back?" He looked at each of us in turn, and swept an arm to indicate the entire camp. "Any of you? How long should I wait?"

"We'll be back," said Dru, certainty in his tone, posture, smell. "I've Seen our victory, remember? So has Zarda, so did Vizan."

Cavel, cushioned by abiding friendship with the drax who was now his Prime, dared to rephrase his question. "But did you See how long it would take?"

Dru sighed, put his bag of moss down, and folded his arms as he straightened. "How many days' food do you have for the vlydh?"

Cavel had his answer ready. "Almost two ninedays, but we'll need to keep enough back for the return journey."

Dru nodded, dipped an ear. "Then we'll be back here in a nineday," he said. "Less, if the Spiral grants us a swift victory. For now though, let's get these shelters secured. Then we can all get something to eat."

"Get under the hides now. Quickly!"

It was just past dawn, and I'd scarcely emerged from our seatach hide when the call came from the sky. I recognised Jotto's voice, and looked up as his words were repeated by Taral.

The two guardflyers, who had flown off on their scouting mission just after moon-zenith, were returning in a hurry, stooping from the swirling grey clouds that hugged the mountain.

"Koth!" Taral barked. "Douse those fires, and get back into the shelters now!"

I gawked at them, and glanced around in the early light. The vlydh were cloaked in shadow beneath their sheltering overhang, and I hoped they were all still asleep and would remain quiet. The few nines of Drax who were already up had lit fires to melt snow, and my nose detected the aroma of branmeal and reheating stew. I hoped they were not in the same pot.

As if that mattered when there were Koth coming! I cursed my slowness of thought, and turned to head back under the flaps of the camouflaged hide, wondering how far behind our guardflyers the Koth might be. I bumped into Dru as I scurried inside, almost knocking him over, and he caught my arm as he peered outside:

"What's going on?"

"Koth coming. Behind Taral and Jotto."

Dru gave a nod, but stuck his head out of the shelter anyway, and it was my turn to hold on to him as I seized his shoulder and said, "Don't go out there, Lord!"

"I just want to make sure the fires are out."

"Taral and Jotto will see to it. Get under the hide now." Hearing movement and grunted questions from the nines who shared our shelter, I turned my head to make sure none of them were trying to get outside. "Stay still and quiet," I said. "There's no point hiding ourselves if the Koth can hear us moving and talking."

Somewhere to my right, Shaya gave a low chuckle. "Good to know my hunting lessons were not entirely wasted on you, Fate-seer."

The shelter fell silent then, save for the thudding of my heart which I was sure would carry to the ears of the Koth. I took a couple of deep, slow breaths, sat down next to Dru, and turned my ears to listen for hints of what was happening outside.

Wingbeats. Feet running to a halt. That would be Taral and Jotto landing – I hoped. Taral's voice: "Jisco, Veret, Culdo, get out here and relight this fire. You four – stay where you are so the Koth can count nine of us. The rest of you stay under the hides and keep quiet." Grunts. Scrabbling noises, footsteps.

Jotto, saying: "Here they come. Unsling your bows and nock arrows. Let them think we're patrolling."

More wingbeats. Not Drax this time – the sound was different. Not like pebble on stone, more like…what was it they reminded me of? I remembered a storm, long ago it seemed, when I'd taken shelter with the exiled females and younglings in a grove of seavines. Vine branches had cracked and snapped in the wind as they broke in pieces, driven by the gale. Yes. Breaking branches. That was the sound the Koths' wings made as they beat the air over our heads.

Roars. Barks. The twang of a loosed arrow. More roars, loud and deep-throated, from directly overhead it seemed. Those snapping wingbeats, rhythmic, incessant, petrifying. Within the shelter, the overwhelming scent of alarm from the adults, and something closer to terror from the half-growns. My fur was on end. I needed a waste-pit.

Snarls. Gruff noises that might have been derision.

And the Koth flew away, the sound of their wingbeats receding eastward, no doubt heading for the Expanse and another raid we could not prevent. Well, it would be the last time they did that, Spiral willing.

Winding a paw across my tunic, I crawled from the shelter, smoothing my fur as I went.

"They didn't see us," said Dru, following me out. "The hides worked, just as Shaya said they would."

Around us, nines were emerging from beneath the shelters, many smoothing their fur, others spiralling paws across their tunics. Cavel hurried to the smaller hide beneath which the vlydh-panniers and packs were stored, and emerged a few beats later with arms full of orenvine branches. Murmurs of relief swirled on the breeze, along with the aroma of rekindled fires and warming food.

Taral and Jotto picked their way past the adults discussing our escape, and knots of chattering half-growns, to report to Dru. "We found a ledge, above us and slightly to the northern side of the mountain," Taral said, dipping a bow. "We believe it's big enough to hold all of us for a night—"

"Vlydh included," put in Jotto.

"—but we didn't have the time to check. We were just about at our flying limit as it was, but then we heard those Koth coming, and flew back to warn you all."

Dru flicked an acknowledging ear, though he'd turned his head to look east, in the direction the Koth had flown. "They'll likely come back this way later, once they've raided our territory," he said. "We'll have to be careful they don't catch all of us out in the open."

Manel had emerged from our shelter and hurried across to greet Jotto, in time to hear this last remark. "Let them see us," she said, her ears signalling contempt. "It's not as though we have to worry about them attacking us. They wouldn't even attack the nine guardflyers Taral kept out in the open, because our troops were armed."

"It's not an attack we have to worry about," said Jotto. "Seeing so many of us where there were only nine would make even the Koth curious, wouldn't it? And the last thing we need while we're trying to get up this mountain is a gaggle of curious Koth checking on our every move."

Manel shrugged. "Then let's just kill those few when they come back. It's not like they're out for a morning glide – they've gone to raid one of our farms!"

It was Taral's turn to shoot down Manel's suggestion. "And what would happen when the rest of the Koth start to wonder what's happened to their raiding party? They'll come looking, as we would do. And next time, we may be too high to fly ourselves. Do you really want to be fighting off Koth while you're trying to climb?"

Dru held up a paw as Manel raised her ears and opened her mouth again. "Manel, we will be fighting soon enough, in strange territory and without benefit of flight. The main advantage we have is surprise. Let's not lose that in a fit of pique." Turning to Taral, he said, "It will take those Koth the morning at least to get to the Expanse. We won't go any further up the mountain today – the delay will give you and Jotto a chance to rest, anyway. Let's all have something to eat, and spend the morning stretching legs or wings. At zenith, all but the lookouts and nine guardflight must be back under the hides, and the vlydh concealed, in readiness for the return of that Koth raiding-party." He raised his head to look around at the rest of the camp, and looked at each of us in turn as he said: "Tell everyone that we'll rest this afterzenith, and tonight, we'll fly as high as Drax wings or vldyh can take us."

That night we flew on, following Taral and Jotto as they led us upward toward the 'snowy ledge' they had found on their scouting foray. The ground beneath us rose ever more steeply, and we had to beat our wings harder and faster to stay aloft in air that made everyone pant for breath.

"How much further?" My words came in wheezy gasps as I flapped frantically with the effort to stay aloft and keep up with Taral, Jotto, and their vanguard of guardflight. "When will we get to Cloudsend?"

"We're there," Taral called over his shoulder, his words almost lost in the chill easterly that gusted and snapped at our struggling wings, as though the wind itself wished to hurl us against the mountain. "That broken ice below us is on its lower slopes,"

"*Lower* slopes!" I looked down and around, able now to see that the ice field below us curved down the mountain like some giant frozen river. Hemmed in on each side by sheer cliffs of bare rock, it ran from the base of a great grey slab that rose like a wall ahead of us. I looked up, through wisps of cloud that swirled around the mountain as though afraid to linger near it for any length of time.

Above the rock wall was an icy slope from which crags jutted. Above that was snow, ice, grey rock, and more snow, angling up into the clouds. My head spun at the thought of making our way up there on foot – surely there weren't enough winter tunics in existence to keep us warm enough!

Near my left wing, Dru sat astride a panting vlydh, and I sympathised with the creature's obvious discomfort as I saw how hard it was beating its wings. Dru pointed, and I saw through the misting clouds a vertical fold in the wall of rock, creasing the mountain's south-eastern face. "I think that's the shelf there," he called. "Taral and Jotto said it was a sloping wedge between two rock walls."

They'd also said it was big enough for us all to land on, but my first impression of the area Dru pointed at was of a small pile of snow lying in a corner. The buttresses that sheltered the spot angled up on either side, the rock walls a dark threat that blotted out the lights of the Spiral as I glanced up – and up. We still seemed a long way from the top, though we were above the lower, thicker clouds now. We had been fortunate to escape the attentions of the Koth raiding party the previous day; if any more flew from their eyries now they would doubtless see us, and our chances of beating off angry Koth while clinging to a rock face would be slim indeed.

Shaya's voice, behind me, brought my thoughts back to the moment: "That can't be it, surely?"

"Well spotted, Dru," Jotto barked, ignoring – or perhaps not hearing – Shaya's remark. "That's the place. Not much further now."

"Thank the Spiral for that," I called, "I'm about at my limit here."

"I think we all are," called Manel, flying behind her nest-mate, her wings beating faster than Jotto's as she strove to keep up.

Up ahead, Taral dropped onto the shelf, knee-high in snow, flanked by Jisco and Veret. The three of them waded off in different directions, using their unstrung bows to poke at the drifts, clearing shallow paths for the rest of us to land. After a few paces on the flat, Taral's path toward the cliffs took him uphill on a slope that would have been considered gentle back on the Expanse. Watching him struggle and flounder upward, extending his wings for balance, it was clear that our journey by wing was at an end. We would not get any higher than this except by climbing, and I spiralled a numb paw over my winter tunic as I looked up at the towering edifice that would be our pathway up the mountain. "Great Spiral give us strength." My words were lost in the wind, and I could but hope that they had been carried far enough for the Spiral to hear them. Whether they would be heeded…

On the snow-laden rock shelf, Jisco and Veret had reached opposite ends of the flat, and were toiling up the slopes toward

Taral. The patterns of their footsteps in the snow made a shape like a glowshell, but I couldn't summon the energy to point it out. It wasn't important, anyway. All that mattered was that the space within those footprints was large enough to take us all.

It was a relief to see Taral signal for us to land – though actually setting down on a snow-covered slope was never easy. We sent the vlydhs in first, and as they floundered in the snow the sound of their mandibles clicking in distress rebounded from the cliffs. The decision to send them back down the mountain once they'd been unloaded and fed had been the right one – they could certainly go no further, poor beasts.

In the swirling wind that threatened to smash me against the mountain at any moment, I landed hard and skidded, though managed somehow to stay on my feet. Others flapped into drifts or plopped onto paws and knees, everyone gasping for breath, several unable to move from their landing-spot and needing to be helped clear so that others could land. What with the altitude, the squally wind, and the increasingly-crowded space, we were fortunate that no-one fell off the ledge or crashed into the shoulders of rock that it clung to.

"I suggest we put the wingless as far from the edge as possible," Taral said, as he stood beside me, peering over the sheer drop, wings extended to help him balance. "That precipice must be at least twice the height of the *Spirax* plateau. If they fell off here, they'd end up splattered like Fazak's egg."

I wrinkled my snout at the memory, and the idea, and told Taral to come away, too. "We're at our own limits, Taral. If you fall off, you might not be able to gain control of your flight fast enough."

We set Dru's command shelter at the back of the rise, against the bluff, where there was some relief from the buffeting wind, and suggested that numbers beneath each camouflaged hide were doubled for warmth and safety.

"Is it safe to light a fire?" I asked, as Taral and Jotto, wrapped in thick fur-lined tunics, finished their checks around the camp and ducked into Dru's shelter.

Taral shook his head, pulling a blanket across his shoulders as he sat down. "The thicker clouds are below us now, and daybreak isn't far off. We've set warning stakes near the edge of the precipice, advised everyone to keep to their shelters, and told them they'll have to make do with cold food from here on."

Manel, bundled in a blanket, was cuddling a couple of flasks under her fur-lined tunic. "We can't even have a drink till this water's melted." Her breath hung in the air like thin mist. "Personally, I'd like a pool of it big enough to bathe in. And the thought of hot water..!"

"We'll be warm enough in here." Jotto stuck his snout out of the shelter as he spoke, raising his voice so it would carry to the shelters beyond. "But we can't risk lighting any fires. I'm sorry."

Cavel scrambled inside to join us, just as the melted water and dried meat were being passed round.

"Smell it, did you?" Manel teased as she collected his empty beaker to pour his share – though my nostrils tickled with the scent of her concern. Cavel's fur was rimed with ice, and he shivered as he pulled his blanket from his carry-pouch and sat down beside Ellet to rub his paws and feet. "I've got the vlydhs under a shelter near the bottom of the slope. They're dozing off now, but they'll start spinning cocoons if they stay up here much longer – they think the freeze has come."

"You're the one who's freezing just now. Come under this blanket next to me and get warm."

"Thanks, Manel." Cavel's paws shook as he took the slice of meat she handed him. Melted ice dripped from his snout as he sipped water from his beaker and looked over its rim, his eyes travelling from Ellet and Jotto on his right, past Shaya, Dru, me, Taral, and on to Manel. "The vlydh have to go back at nightfall. They can't even breathe properly up here."

"None of us can." Shaya took a sip of her water and gestured around with a raised beaker. "We're all gasping like fish on land. We need to rest, catch our breath, and recover from struggling to fly."

The others nodded agreement. "The vlydh have done well," said Dru, "getting the wingless and our supplies this far. We'll send them back down the mountain tonight, with Cavel and our strongest flyers, as agreed. The rest of us will wait for the flyers to return." He glanced at his friend, whose ears were drooping again. "I'm sorry, Cavel."

"I trained to fight." There was resignation in Cavel's protest. He knew nothing he said would make any difference.

"And you did," said Dru. "At the Battle of the *Spirax* there was no-one more fierce, but your skills with the vlydh are more important now."

"I know. It's just…" Cavel's glance around took in everyone, and even my still-numb nose smelled his anxiety from across the shelter. "I don't know when I'll see you all again."

It was clear from his scent that his worry was not when but if he would see us again, and it was clear from everyone else's scent that they knew it. For several beats no-one spoke, then Ellet said, "I'll come back with you, Cavel. I can help with the vlydh, and you won't be on your own."

A few adult ears were flicked in amusement, but no-one spoke against the idea and Cavel looked relieved as well as pleased.

I wondered whether Rewsa would approve, if she'd been with us, but before I could voice the thought Tonil, seated next to her sire, flicked her ears and, with forced cheerfulness, changed the subject. "Well, at least some of us will have a few days to rest, while we wait for Jotto-fa and the others to return from taking the vlydh."

"I for one will be grateful for that," I said, reaching a paw up to rub at my aching shoulders.

Taral grunted. "So long as the Koth don't spot us. The hides help, and lookouts have been posted, but they'll have to be relieved every sun-width or moon-width, otherwise they'll freeze."

"By the time the flyers return from the lower camp, the wingless will have worked out the best route up the mountain," said Dru. "We'll start to scout beyond the camp at nightfall, and—" His eyes rolled, his head went back, and I grabbed for his beaker as I realised what was happening.

"He's having a Vision." The shelter stilled as I spoke, all attention on Dru, the scent of surprise and anticipation mingling with the aroma of dried meat.

"*Two wings, two ways, two routes.*" Dru gasped, blinked, shook himself. I handed him his beaker and he seized it in both paws, took a long swallow of the cool liquid.

"Two wings?" I prompted. "What did you See, Lord?"

Dru drained his beaker and set it down. There was a distinct smell of excitement on his fur, certainty issuing from every hair as he sat upright, ears pricked, tail twitching. "There are two routes up the mountain from here," he said. "One follows a natural crevice that winds up and around to the north face; one takes a steep incline to the south. We can split our forces, attack the Koth from two different points. When we reach their eyrie, some will be on their right wing, some on their left. Two wings. Two ways to victory. Two routes to the top."

There was silence in the shelter for several beats, then Jotto spoke for all of us: "Right now, I'm having difficulty believing there's one route up this mountain, let alone two!"

"Dru's Seen it," I said. I kept my voice firm and positive, though I too found it hard to believe. My heart clenched as the reality of the impending climb and confrontation struck me anew. We were in unknown territory, at the limit of our flying abilities, counting on wingless half-growns to lead us up a snowbound mountain face, where the wind blew constantly but never steadily. Once on those slopes, ice would chill our feet, blown snow would mist the air, and – unless thicker, higher clouds rolled in – we would be without hope of cover. Already we were short of breath, and I wondered if we would be able to breathe at all if we went much higher. But we were committed and, in any case, "There must be routes to the top – remember, Vizan and I both Saw that we defeat the Koth. We can't do that from down here."

I caught a whiff of scepticism from Shaya, but the set of her ears mirrored mine and she turned her snout to look past me at Dru: "Did you See which way we go from here, Lord?"

"Ways." Dru closed his eyes, remembering his Vision. "The route splits here." He opened his eyes, took another sip of water from his beaker and outlined his plans for our climb: "While the vlydh are guided back down the mountain, I'll send wingless climbers to scout for the fissure that leads to the south face, and the crevice that leads north. Once the main climb begins, Taral will take half-a-ninety of wingless and half the Guardflight, and take the route to the south. Everyone else will climb around to the north face. We'll each take one night to move as far around and up the mountain as we can, and rest by day. On the following night, we will all start to climb as soon as it's dark enough to need night vision. By dawn we should be near the summit. After that…"

"…may the Spiral be with us all," I murmured.

For however carefully we had planned this, and however well we fought, the fact remained that we would be attacking our enemy from below, in unfamiliar territory, and without any possible way to take to the air.

If anyone fell off the mountain then, winged and wingless alike, we would fall.

Twenty-Nine

"Flap your wings," I said to Bolby, who was just ahead of me, clinging to a shoulder of bubblerock which the wingless had scrambled up and over with ease. "It won't be enough to take off in this thin air, but it will give you enough lift to make it easier to climb."

"I can manage," he snapped, though clearly he couldn't. Clad now in Guardflight red, the young male who had once led the Elite Guard smelled mainly of terror – till his odour soured as Nixel, lying on his front, leaned over the top of the rock and put out an arm.

"Take my paw!" As the wingless half-grown reached to help, Bolby's fur stood on end. He likely wondered if the wingless drax whose dam had been shot out of the sky by Elite might pick this moment to take some terrible revenge.

But as he hesitated, Dru's snout appeared above Nixel's. He must have been sitting on the other half-grown's legs, anchoring him. "Use your wings, Bolby. Check your pawhold again before putting any weight on it. Then flap – and take Nixel's paw."

A last beat of doubt, another moment of hesitation, then Bolby did as he was bid and his upward progress surged. He might even have muttered a thank you to the wingless half-growns who'd helped him, but with the wind battering my ears, and my own claws scraping for a hold on the rough bubblerock, I couldn't be sure.

I flapped my own wings, reached a little higher, scratched a toe on the rock as I scrabbled desperately for purchase, and finally, with Nixel's help, hauled myself another half-span up the mountain.

The wingless were all ahead of us, their longer, stronger legs an asset as we clawed our way up steep, icy slopes, edged across snow-lined ridges, and pulled ourselves from rocky ledge to rocky ledge.

The wind was a constant, bitter roar, with a chill that had little regard for fur, whether it be our own or our tunics' winter linings. It picked up snow from the slopes around us and flung it in our faces, managing to find eyes and snouts and ears no matter which way we turned our heads. Thirsty, I hung out my tongue to gather a few flakes, but it numbed so fast I feared I would never be able to speak again.

It was our second night after leaving the relative shelter of the rock shelf. The previous day had found us huddled together in a tiny depression in the rock, which only the most optimistic eye would have called a bowl. With a couple of hides pulled over us, we had whispered prayers that we would not be seen from above, and muttered curses at anyone who needed to scrape a waste-pit. I may have dozed, though I'm not sure how; I was sure that the smell of fur-raising fear would carry to the noses of the Koth.

We had spent three days on the rock shelf – though Shaya, Jotto, and the other flyers who had flown down with the vlydh, had had just a single day to rest. Once past the almost-vertical nightmare of the fissured bulwarks that had enclosed the encampment on three sides, the slope had eased slightly. As we'd scrambled up hummocky bubble-rock, where claws scratched for a hold and tiny tufts of kerzh-grass and moss poked from sheltered crevices, I'd realised I had probably climbed sand-dunes that were steeper. But up there, every step, every paw-hold, needed several breaths and an effort of will. Legs and arms, backs and shoulders, howled for rest, fingers and toes protested at the work they were expected to do in such cold, while the wind stole what breath we had, and the thin, high clouds, mist, and spatters of wind-whipped snow dampened fur and clothing.

On we climbed, the lights of the Spiral and a sliver of moon showing the way through the high clouds that furred the sky like nines of white tails. I was taking three breaths for every movement I made, and my feet and fingers were numb. The odour of sheer terror swirled in the wind, and my focus narrowed to the next painful step, the next paw-hold, the next tiny ledge.

Until the moment came when I saw, through the wind-blown snow a line of wingless, standing shoulder-to-shoulder up ahead of me, along a horizontal ridge-line, unmoving.

"Dru?" With what felt like the last of my strength, I heaved and pulled and crawled those last few spans till I was on my knees and paws beside him. Head down, chest heaving, I took a nine of deep, gulping breaths, raised my head to peer over the ridge – and understood why we had stopped.

The Spiral had heard us, and I found the strength to move a paw across the front of my tunic as I gave thanks.

For what we had thought was the summit of Cloudsend was actually the rim of a great natural basin. We were at the highest point on the mountain – and the Koth eyrie was below us, at the bottom of the bowl, their dwellings spiralling out from its centre.

That was the first shock. The second made my fur stiffen with surprise and disbelief. "There can't be more than ninety dwellings down there," I bellowed into Dru's ear, making sure he heard me over the noise of the wind. "Where are the rest of them?"

Where indeed? I blinked away snow, shook my fur, looked again at the scene below. Most of the dwellings were mossy hummocks, roughly the size of a drax Welcoming Place. In the centre, as with a Drax cluster, was a larger structure, which I guessed might be their leader's dwelling. The smoke that issued from holes in the centre of each dwelling must have made the interiors both smoky and warm, for little snow settled on them, though it lined the floor of the sheltered bowl. It was a big space, surrounded by steep sides but flat enough in the centre. It was large enough for several Drax clusters and a field or two as well – but what an inhospitable place it would be to try to cultivate anything! Spindly vines grew in clumps, blown almost to horizontal by the prevailing wind, their branches clinging to each other as they fought the elements. Here and there, tufts of zenox fought their way through the soil, their red stems vivid against the falling snow. On the far side of the eyrie, roughly-hewn blocks of bubble-rock had been set in a circle to create an enclosure for several nines of huge horned beasts.

I pointed. "Those things look like giant kervhels," I barked. "I Saw one in a Vision, cycles ago. The Koth use the horns to make their knives."

"Look at the fur on them," Dru yelled. "Right down to their hooves. They must be a lot warmer than we are!"

Chiva, on Dru's left, barked something I couldn't quite catch.

"The Koth?" Dru's reply supplied the missing question. "Still asleep, by the look of it. Who can blame them in this weather?"

I looked up. The lights of the Spiral were half-hidden as wisps of furry cloud raced overhead, driven by the same vicious gusts that hurled snow at us and threatened to pull us from the mountain. Surely nothing could fly in such weather – not even the Koth.

All our fears of attacking them from below were groundless: we were above them. We had the benefit of the high ground. And unless there were more Koth hidden somewhere, there were fewer of them than I had dared hope.

What if...?

No. It was too late for doubt. Too late to do anything but believe that the Vision showed victory. For the Spiral had given us the wingless.

The wingless had shown us the way up the mountain.

And now we had the advantage.

On the far side of the snow-lined bowl, the jagged ridge of rock around its edge was barely visible through the pre-dawn mist that clung to the summit. Were those shadows moving against the snow? Shadows that might be the other half of our forces? The cold had numbed my snout, making it almost impossible to smell anything, and I could barely detect the scent of those around me, let alone confirm that the vague figures were Taral's troops.

Still, I pointed across to where I thought I'd seen the movement, and turned my head so that Dru would be able to hear me above the roar of the wind. "Taral," I barked. "Over there – I think!"

Dru's fur was rimed with snow, his ears flicking constantly to keep them clear of flakes. Only his eyes and nose were unfrosted as he acknowledged my call with a brief ear-dip, and a quick glance around told me that I must look much the same.

"The snow is blowing too hard," I called, "and the mist is getting thicker. We can't see the dawn!"

"It doesn't matter," Dru called back, the wind whipping his words away so that I strained to hear though I turned both ears his way. "It's light enough now to see without night vision. We'll attack now. Taral will see us and follow our lead." He patted my shoulder. "Extend your wings, Zarda – give the signal to attack. And then follow me."

With that, he stood up, waved to the waiting wingless to do likewise, and plunged over the lip of the ridge, spear raised ready to throw. In leaps and bounds, he hurtled down the first few spans of precipitous rock, legs pumping as he reached the gentler slope below, his howl faint but unmistakable even above the roar of the wind. A beat later, wings extended as he had ordered, I followed him, losing what little breath I had as I hit the icy rocks below, fighting for air as I forced my legs to a stumbling run. Behind me and around me, Drax poured over the ridge, howling and roaring as they bounded from rock to rock, from snow patch to boulder, from ice-rimed moss to scrubby fern to scrawny vinegrove.

We left the worst of the howling wind and blowing snow the moment we leapt from the rim. Down in the bowl, though it was still cold, the wind abated, and the scrub grew thicker as we rushed toward the settlement. Leaping, bounding wingless pounded past me, barking and roaring. My knees brushed ferns, my feet trampled frozen moss beneath the snow, and my numb nose caught hints of something that smelled like kerzh.

Ahead of me, Dru was jumping about like a kervhel, his howls echoed by those pelting after him. I strained to listen for answering calls from Taral and his troops, but if there were any, they were lost in the distance. All I heard were the attack-howls of Dru's wingless, the rumbling beat of nineties of feet – and my own labouring breath.

From above, the Koth dwellings had looked to be no more than ninety or so spans away. If I had been able to fly in that thin air, I would doubtless have reached them in less than nine wingbeats. But as I followed Dru through that endless snow and vegetation, I realised once again that covering any distance on the ground always takes longer and seems further than it does from the air.

I saw a Koth emerge from a dwelling, then another. Against the backdrop of their own dwellings, they looked for a moment to be no bigger than the average Drax, but as Dru and his vanguard closed on them, I realised the enemy were almost twice the size of our biggest males. Their jaws were heavier than ours; their teeth, as they roared defiance, showed two rows of razor-sharp points; and their wings…

Their wings were magnificent, unfolding into arcs of serrated black that were each bigger than four Drax wings put together. Their deep-throated roars of defiance were horrific, and I doubt I was the only one who almost stopped in her tracks.

Koth were pouring out of dwellings now, tying tunic straps, brandishing spears, roaring and howling. Three of them took off, their wings beating hard as they began to rise into the air, and I may have whimpered and faltered in my rush toward them as their war-howls carried to my flattened ears. A moment later, a shower of arrows from beyond their eyrie brought them crashing down, and I realised that Taral and his troops had survived their own climb and were rushing to join us. A Koth spear arced out of the sky, and I jinked and dodged, feeling the rush of wind as it brushed past my right wing. Belatedly, I realised that my wings had served their purpose for now, and folded them tight against potential battle-damage. Seeing a line of Koth rushing toward us, I grasped my own spear tighter, and laboured on.

Despite my experiences in the battle on the *Spirax* plateau, I was a Fate-seer, not a fighter. I kept my spear raised, ready to throw, but there were wingless and guardflight all around me, matching my pace, and I guessed there had been some quiet agreement to protect me. A few paces ahead, Dru's spear found a new home in the right shoulder of a large male Koth, who roared with pain and swerved away. I stumbled over the arrow-pierced body of another Koth, buried my spear-point in the ground, and wasted precious beats pulling it free, while all around the eyrie, Drax and Koth alike fell to arrows, spears, and bites.

My protectors joined the melée, leaping onto the Koth in threes, and wrestling them to the ground in snarling knots of fur and teeth, while I slowed to a shambling walk, clutching my spear in both paws as I waved it ineffectually from side to side. I'd have been easy prey for a Drax nestling, let alone an angry Koth, but fortunately the fighting had moved away from me. I had to take a moment, catch my breath, and rest my trembling legs. A span or so from the Koth dwellings, exhausted and spent, I turned my spear upright and leaned on it, sucking long, painful breaths and pressing a paw to my chest, where my heart throbbed fast and vigorous. As I stood there, floundering and gasping, the sickening smell of blood and waste assailed my nostrils, and I flattened my ears as howls of pain and anguish joined the battle-roars.

Flattened ears or no, I couldn't miss the high-pitched squeal, quickly silenced, that came from the nearest dwelling. Alert now, I moved cautiously to the moss-covered structure and gave it a tentative sniff. There was bubblestone beneath the moss, and a nose-withering waste-pit nearby that I almost trod in, but the doorway – a thickly-woven mat of kerzh-grass, plastered with mud – was closed. Was this the trap I feared? Were there more armed Koth waiting inside the dwellings, waiting to leap out at us?

"Some help over here?" I called, and young Ravar left Yaver and Bolby to stand over the Koth they had captured and bounded across, a bloodied spear clutched in his right paw. His left ear had been bitten and his ochre tunic was ripped, but his ears signalled satisfaction at a task well done, and he reeked of conquest and relief. "I heard a noise from inside," I said. "It may be nothing, but…"

His ears twitched and he bared his teeth as he glared at the door. "Let's find out."

The door was less than half our height, but it opened outwards, and Ravar had some difficulty pulling it open against the gusting wind. I'd like to say I lent a paw, but I did little more than lean tiredly against the edge of the door while the half-grown heaved and strained. I heard Taral's bark, and saw Veret hurrying over to help us, but before he could reach us the door gave up the fight and sagged open. Ravar staggered a little at the sudden movement, and the squeal from inside was accompanied this time by a series of fur-curling snarls.

But no-one emerged from the structure and as I sniffed cautiously, the overwhelming odours were of fear and surprise, the smell reinforced by more high-pitched squealing that issued from the darkness within.

Ravar gripped my arm as I peered inside. "Be careful, Zarda. Let me go first."

I sniffed again, put down my spear, and blinked to night-vision as I peered into the gloom. "It's alright, Ravar. I don't think there is any danger." I had to duck my head to move inside. Any grown Koth would surely have had to bend double to get into the dwelling, and I couldn't help but admire the twofold defence against the elements – the door that pushed tighter into its hole as the wind blew stronger, and the small space it occupied.

Inside, the smell was stronger: nestling-waste, stale food – and terror. As I peered through the smoke that issued from a pit in the middle of the dwelling, I found the source of the squealing: a nestling, cradled against the fur of its dam. The female's eyes were fearful, and terror poured from her bristling coat, but her growl was menacing and her teeth snapped a vicious warning that I should go no closer.

I raised both paws to show I held no weapon. "I am not going to hurt you," I said, hoping she would understand the tone if not the words. I took a quick glance around, to make sure there were no other Koth lurking in the gloom.

No. There were two nests – one huge, one tiny – a pot over the fire, woven baskets, and a flat stone shelf where cooking pots of horn and bone were stacked. Save that everything was a half-size bigger than anything I would use, it all looked achingly familiar. I thought of the Koth ruins we had found in the Forest, the way they had been built in spirals – just like the settlement here. The Koth had grown avalox once; now, they coaxed zenox and kerzh to take root in hostile ground, and kept beasts for fur and fodder. They had raided our crops, attacked our people, burned what they couldn't carry – but as I backed out of the dwelling and stood up, I realised that perhaps these creatures were not so very different from ourselves.

I turned round and ducked out of the doorway, to discover a phalanx of guardflight, bows drawn, standing ready to loose their arrows at whatever was inside. "It's just a dam protecting her nestling – just as any Drax female would do." I gestured in the general direction of the cluster. "There are probably more in the other dwellings. Don't hurt them, please."

At a nod from Veret, the bow-strings were relaxed, the arrows un-nocked. "The battle's over," he said. "No need for anyone else to get hurt."

"Over?" I took a breath, heaved another, needing time to process what he was saying. We'd won? We had truly defeated the Koth, as Vizan had foreseen? It didn't seem possible – yet when I raised my head to look past Veret's shoulder, all the Koth I could see were on the ground. A few were clearly dead, nines more were wounded, whimpering with pain or snarling what I assumed were obscenities, but most lay at the feet of triumphant Drax, their quiescence doubtless encouraged by the spears that threatened their throats.

I spotted Dru, Taral, Shaya, and Jotto, all of them standing, none with so much as a scratch so far as I could see. There was Nixel, Oztin, Chiva – and there, in the midst of the fallen Koth, his mane awry and his tunic splashed with mud and blood, was Dru.

I spiralled a paw across my tunic and breathed a prayer of relief and thanks as I watched him pick his way through the battle's aftermath, murmuring to a wounded guardflyer here, congratulating a whooping half-grown there. Already, many were howling our triumph. Already, nines of guardflight and hunters with green 'healers' belts were moving among the wounded, treating whimpering drax.

There were so few Koth, so few! Where were the rest? Had they seen us climbing, and gone to lie in wait till we were off-guard, or sleeping? Their dead, their wounded, and their defeated were outnumbered by a ninety of younglings, ninety-nine guardflight, and a few nines of eager hunters. I sniffed for any scent of hidden Koth, smelled the anger and despair of those we'd wounded or captured, and barked across the trampled vegetation, "Is that all of them?"

"Yes." It was Taral who replied. Leaving Jisco and Nixel to keep watch over a massive brown-furred Koth, he strode over to stand alongside me, and beckoned for Dru to join us. "All that dread and anxiety, all those patrols – all those cycles when we waited for them to come down on our necks. All for these few."

Dru joined us, a bloodied spear held low, his left paw clutching a few straws of the kerzh-like grass. "Have you seen what they've been eating? What they've been trying to survive on?" He shook his head, ears drooping in sympathy. "No wonder they started raiding our farms! Their own stuff is pitiful. I don't know—"

"Zarda!" Shaya picked her way through the bodies and debris. "You have to proclaim the victory, or it is no victory." A carry-pouch dangled from her left paw, and from it she pulled a folded cloth and handed it to Dru. "The banner you requested, Lord, with Varel's compliments."

As Dru took the white cloth and tucked it into his tunic belt, the clouds that had misted the scene parted briefly, and I glimpsed Vizan's Light, the light that the Spiral had sent for us just before our previous battle. It was fading now even by night, but it was still bright enough to be visible in the lightening sky. It was a good sign, a blessing – a confirmation that the Vision was true, that the Koth were lying at our feet, not lying in wait.

We had won, thanks to the Spiral and the wingless it had sent. All that was needed now was the ritual chant.

"The larger dwelling in the centre of the settlement, Dru," I said. "Their leader's dwelling, perhaps, or the place where they planned their raids. It seems a fit place to stand for our proclamation."

With Dru beside me, I stepped across the icy ground, the path between the dwellings winding in a familiar spiral, though it was wider than the paths through any Drax cluster. I hadn't given any thought to how we might climb onto the edifice, which was at least three times my height, but fortunately the Koth kept hollowed vinelogs beside their dwellings to catch rain and snow, and I tipped over a near-empty one to use as a first step up. I was breathing hard, and now that I had to clamber onto the roof I rather regretted my choice of vantage-point, but fortunately Dru was more agile that I when it came to climbing – and jumping. Flexing his knees, he leaped past me onto the moss-lined roof, reached down a paw, and hauled me up.

One last ascent, moss ripping under scrabbling claws as we took the few paces to the apex of the dwelling, then Dru and I stood facing the victorious and the vanquished. Below us, a few spans from the vinelog I had overturned, lay a dead Koth. All along the spiralling pathway, the guardflight who had followed us provided a ribbon of colour against the bleak landscape. Red tunics, just as foreseen so many moons ago. Beyond the eyrie was more red, mingled with hunters' ochre and the various coloured tunics of the wingless, as all those still standing turned to face us. The icy breeze clawed through my fur and tugged at my own tunic, slapping it against my knees, and I dug my claws into the moss beneath me to make sure I wouldn't sway – or worse – in the gusts. A wheezing breath filled my nostrils with the scent of Dru's excitement and triumph; another, and I smelled the moss under my feet, and the smoke from the fires that still burned in the dwellings around me.

It was time.

I spread my wings, and raised Dru's paw as I began the ritual chant. I had scratched it on a scroll-leaf and kept it in my tunic pocket, terrified that I might forget the words and gestures when it came to the moment. But I needed no notes, no scratchings. The words were as clear in my mind as when Vizan had recited them to me, and I barked and howled without a pause as I thanked the Great Spiral for granting us victory over our enemies. As I reached the final victory-roar, and Dru joined his voice to mine, he raised the banner over his head, and that long-awaited Vision was come at last.

Thirty

"**Y**ou know, Fate-seer, there were times when I doubted every word you said," Shaya said as we waited inside the central Koth dwelling for Dru and Taral to arrive. Manel sat next to Jotto, huffing in distress because Tonil had been badly bitten and had sent her dam to the meeting in her place. Young Yaver had an ear twisted their way as they muttered and growled, but was clearly more interested in looking around at the spartan interior, which contained little more than a carved bubblestone table and a few stones to sit on. Even the torches had to be set in the ground, as there were no sconces to hang them in. With no see-shell, and a low door that closed itself against the wind, it made a gloomy chamber. "I even doubted the Great Spiral at times." The hunter dipped an apologetic ear and lowered her head in a small bow. "I apologise. I should never have doubted you – and I certainly should not have doubted the Spiral's purpose in sending the wingless."

"You weren't the only one to have doubts, Shaya," I said. "I know my abilities are slight, especially compared to Vizan – or even to Dru. Right up until we herded the Koth back into their dwellings, I kept expecting more of them to come out of hiding and counterattack."

With their low doorways easily guarded by three Drax armed with bows and spears, allowing the uninjured and walking-wounded Koth to return to their own homes had seemed the easiest way to keep them both scattered and secure. Their more severely wounded were being tended by our own healer-trained hunters and guardflight; their dead had been separated from ours and laid out with respect.

Now we just had to decide what to do with the survivors.

Taral ducked into the dwelling, and overheard my last remark. "I've sent a couple of nines of guardflight and wingless to check right across the bowl for any possible ambush," he said. "Nixel and Oztin have gone to check around the rim – they said they want to see what's beyond the mountain, over to the west. Everyone else is taking turns watching the Koth."

I sighed, recalling the sight of one of the younger males howling over the body of a shaggy giant which was, presumably, his sire. "I'd not expected to pity them."

"Nor had I." Dru had followed Taral into the dwelling, and everyone acknowledged his presence with an ear-dip and a bow. As the young Prime circled the table to sit on one of the larger boulders, we each found our place and settled onto a rock. The dwelling smelled of bubblestone and moss, along with the distinctive slightly sour smell of Koth. Furs had been spread on the ground, the hairs on some of them worn away where the Koth had stood, shifted and scratched over the cycles. I wrinkled my snout, wondering whether the furs were ever changed, and checked to see whether anything moved amid the long, greasy hairs.

"Too cold for fur-ticks," said Taral, as he noticed the direction of my gaze.

"Too cold for much of anything to survive," I said, "including the Koth. If we leave them here, they'll not be a threat to us for long, I think."

"We can't leave them here, Zarda." Dru leaned toward me as he spoke, then looked around to make sure we were all seated. There were a couple of growls and murmurs, and I recognised Manel's voice as she muttered that the only good Koth was a dead Koth, but she subsided when Dru held up a paw for silence. When he spoke again, it was to address everyone, and to pose the question I'd been wondering about for some time: "We've won our battle. We've defeated the Koth, just as the Vision predicted we would. What do we do with them now?"

No-one spoke, and for several beats the silence was broken only by the sound of our laboured breathing, and the muffled howls of distressed Koth. I looked at the intricate carvings on the bubblestone table, followed the pattern of swirls and knots and spirals, wondering at the time and patience and skill that had gone into turning a functional object into something beautiful.

It was Yaver who broke the reverie. "I'd never seen a Koth," he said, paws clasped in front of a copper tunic spattered with what I assumed was Koth blood, since he showed no sign of injury himself. "Out there on Kalon's Lake, all I heard were the fables of dreadful creatures with sharp fangs and vicious claws, and when we came to the Expanse, all I saw was the smoke and the slashing they left behind after a raid. But…they're not actually that different from us, are they? Just bigger."

"And smellier," Shaya put in, waving a paw in front of a wrinkled snout.

Manel sat with arms folded, reeking of hostility, and I remembered her outburst in Kalon's dwelling moons ago, her understandable bitterness over the death of her dam and sire. "Let's not forget what they've done," she said, her tone sharp. "Raided, wounded, burned, killed. My Tonil is out there now having her bites tended to. We can't just tell them not to do it again, and leave them to lick their wounds!"

"Then what do we do?" Shaya extended an arm and swept it around to indicate the dwellings beyond the walls. "They have females with nestlings. Younglings. Half-growns. Some are howling for nest-mates and sires who are lying dead in the snow. I saw a couple of them trying to mend slashed wings with little more than mud and spit, till our own healers offered their own herbs and poultices. As Yaver says, they're like us. We've even been able to communicate with them, after a fashion."

Manel snorted. "Just because they understand a spiralled paw or an offer of a healing herb doesn't mean they're anything like us," she snapped. "They're killers. *Killers.* And I say we put the lot of them out of our misery."

"Have those nestlings killed anyone?" Jotto retorted, earning a snap near his snout from his nest-mate. "I'm sorry, Manel, but I can't rip out the throat of a hatchling that's barely left the egg."

It was my turn to flick an ear and nod agreement. "Some of the words I've heard the Koth use are similar to ours," I said. "And it's clear from their carvings, and the way they've built their cluster, that they worship the Great Spiral as we do." I scratched my snout, looked from Shaya to Jotto to Dru. "We cannot kill them. They are as much the Spiral's creatures as we are."

And as I spoke, the Vision came, a Vision similar to one I had Seen before, back on Kalon's Lake, but now returned with a clarity and understanding that I had previously missed: *Forest, lake, crops. A serpent roasting on a spit. Koth flying over the lake, flying from island to river to Falls camp. Drax wielding knives with Koth-carved handles. Koth wearing drax-woven tunics.*

"Zarda?" Taral stood over me, a paw on my arm, concern in his tone, and I realised I'd fallen off my rock seat and now lay in an undignified heap on the fur-lined earthen floor. "What did you See?"

I waited till Taral had helped me to my feet and resumed his seat, dusted myself off, and raised my eyes to the curving walls of bubblestone that closed over our heads. In the roof-stones, glinting in the torchlight, small white stones had been set in a spiral. "I Saw their future," I said. "And ours."

"I suppose it makes sense," said Shaya, her tone grudging. The debate in the Koth meeting place had grown heated since I'd outlined my Vision; even the chill interior seemed warmer, though perhaps that was just my reaction to being growled at. Several sets of ears, Shaya's included, indicated discontent with the solution I'd Seen, but at least the hunter sounded and smelled conciliatory: "If we leave them here, they'll still be a threat to us."

"What if we cut their wings?" Yaver suggested, tugging at his beard. "They can't raid us if they can't fly."

Jotto pointed out the flaw in that idea. "And what happens in a couple of cycles when they've hatched younglings with perfectly good wings?"

"Why are we even debating this?" Taral got to his feet, placed his paws on the stone table, and looked around at those gathered around it. "Zarda has given us the answer. We don't need Kalon's Lake or its islands any more – let the Koth have them. They'll be able to grow their own crops, hunt for fish and meat, feed themselves. They'll not want our food, and in any case they'll be too far away to raid even if they wanted to."

"It just seems…" Manel's ears twisted in disappointment and resignation as she shrugged. "They've raided and killed and maimed for generations. Who knows how many Drax they've slaughtered over the cycles? And we're rewarding them with a better place to live?"

"We've killed and maimed them too," Jotto pointed out, turning an ear in the direction of the Koth death-howls which still continued in the other dwellings. "They've not gone unpunished, Manel."

Taral pulled a Koth knife from his belt and held it so that the light from the torches illuminated the exquisitely-carved handle. "As for trading with them, as Zarda Saw," he said, "well – have you seen the workmanship on these knife handles? Quite extraordinary. I've already had three guardflyers and a hunter offer me goods they haven't got in exchange for this one – but I'll not be trading it."

The wail of a Koth nestling carried through the bubblestone walls, and I thought of the knots of defeated Koth I'd seen herded into their dwellings. Dwellings that had become guarded prisons from which they could not escape. Their ears and wings had drooped with despair as they'd bent to duck in through the low doorways. Their fur was dirty and matted, and most of the ones I saw had teeth missing. "I expect it's hungry," I said, as the wailing continued. I glanced across the table at Shaya. "Sounds a bit like our Drax younglings did, when we had to ration the food on our journey, doesn't it?"

An ear-dip, a slight nod. When I had spoken with her back in my own dwelling she had voiced reservations about showing the Koth any mercy, but it was clear now she would no more be able to kill them all than I could. She turned to Manel and put a sympathetic paw on her shoulder. "We know now why they raided us, Manel. Why they took our crops, stole our animals. They must have been desperate."

Jotto grunted agreement, turning his ears away from the direction of the wailing that continued to sound from the next dwelling. "They must have been struggling for food for a long time."

Taral nodded, the scent of alarm and disgust leaking from his fur as he went on: "When we were rounding up the wounded, we found bones," he said. He swept an arm toward the doorway, to indicate the area outside. "They're lying in heaps out beyond the dwellings. Those great horned things mainly, but some..." He wrinkled his snout, flattened his ears. "I think some of them were Koth. One or two were recent enough to still have flesh on them – enough to show that they hadn't just eaten the heart."

"They eat everything," said Jotto, his own snout wrinkling with disgust. "Everything except the face and the wings. Savages!"

"We don't know that they always do that," I said. I looked up at the stones set in the roof to remind myself that these creatures also worshipped the Spiral. That they also deserved its protection. "Maybe it was forced on them by the freeze these last few cycles. The Spiral knows it's bad enough here now, in the growing season – what must it be like when the ice is thick on our rivers, and the gales pile snow over our dwellings?"

Dru, who had sat silently listening to all the arguments, cleared his throat and stood up, looking around to make sure he had everyone's attention. "Zarda's Vision has shown us the way," he said. "In any case, the Koth are to be pitied, not hated. Did you see the nestling that Zarda found? Its dam could barely regurgitate enough to chew on, let alone fill its stomach. Scarce wonder it's wailing." Ears up, tail rigid with resolve, he directed a steady gaze at each of us in turn before he added, "Remember the legend of Tomax the Bold?"

I nodded, and flicked an ear to acknowledge Dru's choice of fable. "Tomax won the Spiral's approval by showing mercy to the moon-monster. We should follow his example." I pointed upward. "Especially as it's clear the Spiral holds a special significance for the Koth too."

"But the Spiral doesn't watch over the Koth as it watches over us," said Jotto. "We wouldn't be the victors if the Spiral had not blessed us."

Dru tilted his head to one side, as he always did when he was considering something important. "If we guide the Koth to the lake in the north, as Zarda's Vision has suggested," he said, "then surely their defeat will have led to a blessing for them too?"

"I agree," said Taral. "I've watched Koth lick each other's wounds, seen how they care about each other. For all that they eat their own dead, they're not animals to be slaughtered, Manel, and I'll not order my guardflight to kill them in cold blood. But they can't stay here, either. That leaves us with only one option."

Manel sighed, and pulled her spear across her lap to caress its shaft with a paw. For a moment, I wondered whether she would continue to disagree, perhaps even carry her fight to the next Koth she saw, but after a moment she stuck the spear into the ground and looked across the table at Dru. "You're wiser than I am, Lord," she said. "For myself, I'd have cut their wings and left them here to starve. But...you're right, all of you. The wingless were thought to be a curse, and they've proved to be a blessing. Maybe the Koth will prove to be a blessing too, if we give them a chance to hunt and plant and gather."

"They'll certainly have no reason to raid," said Taral, reinforcing his earlier point.

"Then we're agreed?" said Dru, looking around at us one more time.

"We're agreed."

"Aye, Lord."

"Yes."

"Then all we have to do now," said Dru, getting to his feet, "is find a way to explain it all to the Koth."

Epilogue

Cycles have passed since that day and, as I write these final pages, I can hear the gruff barks of Koth traders as they fly in from the north. They'll have spoons, knives, bowls, and spears, all intricately carved and decorated as only the Koth can. They'll be wanting fresh zenox, loxcakes, woven tunics and sea-caught fish, among other things – and we'll be able to provide them, thank the Spiral.

The colder seasons remain harsh, but have not grown any worse since the Great Freeze that saw the Manybend ice over and Kalis banish the wingless. As for the growing seasons, they have been kind, and our clusters no longer have empty dwellings or hungry drax.

They do have wingless drax – full-growns, half-growns, younglings, nestlings. They are part of the weave of our lives now, welcomed and respected for their different abilities, admired for their part in vanquishing the Koth. The guardflight, too, are esteemed everywhere, though their defensive role has been curtailed in these more peaceful times. They still patrol the *Spirax* plateau and the borders of the Expanse, but those flightpaths are more for the tradition and the ceremony than for any expectation of trouble.

The door opens as I scratch 'guardflight', and Taral enters my Fate-seer's dwelling, bending his head to rub snouts in greeting. He picks up a couple of the scroll-leaves I've finished, glances at them, places them back on the table. A shaft of sunlight through the see-shell illuminates the dust and detritus I've neglected while I complete my story, and I brush a paw at a crumb of loxcake as Taral says: "You're almost done, then? Are you going to mention the reaction on the Expanse when we brought the Koth down the mountain with us?"

"No." I've filled another leaf, and pick up a fresh one. "Compared with everything that went before, it was a minor incident, easily dealt with."

"That's not the way I remember it," he says, flicking an ear. "Tea?" He plucks a jar of avalox from the shelf behind me, sniffs it, and takes a pawful across to the pot on the hearth. "I seem to recall a certain Fate-seer having to spread her wings and roar from the *Spirax* balcony before some of the crowd would listen."

"And I seem to remember that the guardflight helped." It had been a difficult moment, certainly, but once Dru reminded everyone that my Visions had been ignored before, by Kalis and Fazak, the smell of outrage and dissent had subsided. '*The Koth will no longer be on the mountain,*' he'd roared. '*They'll have no need to raid or kill. Zarda has Seen this, and we will accept it.*'

They had. Of course there was grumbling and growling, but many drax were still recovering from the depredations of Kalis's rule and no-one openly challenged the decision. Any anger and disappointment was channelled into new planting, new hatchlings, new skills, and when those Koth-carved items began to appear, even the most sceptical put aside their hostility and wondered what they might trade in order to possess such beautiful objects.

"What about that enormous float that Nixel is building at the mouth of the Manybend? You ought to say something about that, don't you think? Koth and Drax working together to make something..." Sitting back on his stool, Taral spins a paw, searching for the right word. "Something astonishing."

"It'll be astonishing if it stays afloat once it gets into the ocean," I retort. Still, it is a remarkable endeavour, and he's right, I should mention it if only because of the partnership that Nixel has forged over the past cycle. The ambition he once spoke of, to discover what lies 'beyond the Forest', beyond the ocean, beyond anything we know, has discovered kindred spirits in three of the Koth he traded with for tanglevine timber and blades. The float they're constructing has high sides, a central pole for a wind-catcher, and a carved, pointed prow which Nixel hopes will carry them over rough seas. On Cloudsend, after our defeat of the Koth, he and Oztin stood on the mountain's highest point and looked west. The scratching on the map – 'more mountains' – had been right, for that is what they saw, stretching away into the distance. *"We know now what lies that way,"* Nixel said, when I queried his sea-going plans. *"But I still want to know where the ocean goes."* Oztin is going with him, as are several nines of other wingless, and some eager, winged half-growns. I've not yet Seen whether they will succeed, and perhaps I never will, but if they do manage to stay afloat, the Spiral alone knows where they might go, what they might find. The edge of the world perhaps?

How I would have liked to talk about it all with Doran, or even Shaya – but my old friend is gone these many cycles, and the hunter went to her last nest a moon ago, immaculate to the last. It was an honour to share her heart, and satisfying to see Ravar approved as Chief Hunter in her place. He and his wingless nest-mate fly far and hunt well on the vlydhs that Cavel and Ellet tend in the orenvine plantation.

Taral is bent over the pot, stirring the tea. He's a little stooped now, even when he stands straight, and there's grey round his muzzle, but I'd still back him in a fight, should he ever need to finish one. I'm still not sure what I did to deserve such a drax as my nest-mate, but I thank the Spiral each day that he overlooked my failings and chose me. I doubt even Zalat, our hatchling, is yet able to match him for strength, or accuracy with a bow...

Hatchling. Zalat would howl at me for scratching that. He's a full-grown drax now with a youngling of his own, but I can't help but think of him as he first hatched, all wet fur and drying wings.

He's shown no aptitude for the Sight at all, but fortunately I'm not short of an apprentice. Cavel and Ellet hatched a wingless pup with a gift that surpasses even Dru's, and I know that, once the Spiral takes me to my last nest, Doret will make a much better Fate-seer than I ever was. Just now, she's taken a vlydh to the Hollow Crag, to finalise the arrangements for submitting my story to the archives. I don't know why Hynka thought it was so important that I scratched it all down – I'm sure a fable-spinner would have done a much better job of telling it – but she persuaded Dru that it would be a good idea, and he persuaded me.

As for Dru, he's become an exemplary Prime, adored by the *Spirax* heralds, revered by Drax and Koth alike for his courage and wisdom. Outside his Council, few know he is gifted with the Sight, for he often credits me with Visions he's had himself. He Saw Nixel's float before the first logs were lashed together – though even he doesn't know what might await it out on the ocean. He Saw that clever, inventive Chiva would become his nest-mate after she'd hatched her Proving Egg with Oztin. And he has Seen that his own wingless hatchling, Gavan, will be accepted as Prime in his turn.

Despite his now-advancing years, Dru continues to fly by vlydh to three clusters in each moon. With Gavan at his side, he listens to every grumble, every difficulty, and resolves disputes with wisdom and fairness. I worry that he takes too much on himself, and there have been occasions where he's made decisions that might have been better discussed at Council, but not for nothing is he known as Dru the Peacebringer.

Long may the fable-spinners tell his tale.

And so it is that I reach the end of my story. As I commit these leaves to the archives, I hope that the wisdom of Vizan, the loyalty and courage of Taral, and the bravery and acumen of Dru the Peacebringer shine through my words, and that all those we lost are remembered.

Written by the grace of the Spiral,
Zarda the Fate-seer.

.

THE END

Acknowledgements

Sincere thanks to everyone at Mirror World for their unflagging enthusiasm and engagement with this entire trilogy from 'Unreachable Skies' through 'Exile' and on to 'Ascent'. Robert Dowsett has carried out his usual amazing job with the line edits, while Justine Alley Dowsett has provided another brilliant cover design. Thanks both.

To my beta-readers, Annie Smith and Alec McCreedy, thanks so much for the feedback and constructive suggestions. It's easy to lose track of minor plot points, so I really appreciate the help in making sure I got everything tucked away.

Thanks once again to James Swallow for the writerly chats and encouragement; to all those who have posted or tweeted or blogged about my books on social media; and much love to my family for all the help and support over the years.

About the Author

Brought up in Staffordshire, England, Karen now lives in West Sussex where she is enjoying her retirement. When not writing she enjoys reading, watching films, local WI and U3A activities, volunteering with the South Downs National Park Volunteer Rangers, and spending time with friends and family. She has also flown in a Spitfire!

Karen has written articles on films and British history for a number of British magazines including 'Yours', 'Classic Television', and 'Best of British'. In 2009, her essay on *'British Propaganda Films of the Second World War'* was published in *'Under Fire: A Century of War Movies'* (Ian Allen Publishing). She also wrote a number of online articles and reviews for The Geek Girl Project (www.geekgirlproject.com), as their British correspondent.

Karen's short stories have appeared in anthologies by Fiction Brigade (2012, e-book), Zharmae Publishing *('RealLies'*, 2013), Audio Arcadia (*'On Another Plane'*, 2015), Luna Station Publishing (*'Luna Station Quarterly'* December 2015), Horrified Press *('Killer Tracks'* and *'Waiting'*, both 2015; and *'Crossroads'*, 2016), and Reflex Fiction (*'Voicemail'*, published online 2017). She also won second prize in Writers' News magazine's 'Comeuppance' competition in 2014 with her short story *'Hero'*.

'Ascent' is the third and final book in the *'Unreachable Skies'* trilogy and Karen is now working on her next science-fiction novel.

You can follow Karen on Twitter @McKaren_Writer, or check out her website at www.karenmccreedy.com

To learn more about our authors and their current projects visit: www.mirrorworldpublishing.com or follow @MirrorWorldPub or like us at www.facebook.com/mirrorworldpublishing

Why 'Mirror World'?

We publish escapism fiction for all ages. Our novels are imaginative and character-driven and our goal is to give our readers a glimpse into other worlds, times, and versions of reality that parallel our own, giving them an experience they can't get anywhere else!

We offer free delivery within Windsor-Essex, Ontario and you can find our novels as paperbacks or ebooks in our online store, or from your favorite major book retailer.

To learn more about our authors and our current projects visit: www.mirrorworldpublishing.com, follow @MirrorWorldPub on Twitter or like us at www.facebook.com/mirrorworldpublishing